The Axalan Revelation

BOOK TWO OF

THE STARGUARDS
Of Humans, Heroes, and Demigods

Raymond Burke

THE STARGUARDS

Raymond Burke is a British-born author - The Axalan Revelation the second in The Starguards series. His background includes an early life in Canada and the US, employment in the British Army as an aircraft technician, an MSc degree in Archaeology from University College London, and short-article writing. He is also a member of The Mars Society. Raymond cunningly lives without a fridge, satellite TV, iPods, and he also can't drive. He's a self-confessed 21st century caveman . . . and loves it! Through all, he has been a keen and aspiring writer. He currently lives in London.

To

The most badass friend in the galaxy

Acknowledgements

A grateful thanks to my many supporters and friends who have encouraged my writing ventures: John Mcmillan, Nigel Livingstone, Mark Emsley, Chris Bellay, Mark Veal, Dave Baseley, Neena Katwa, Lori Buttermark, Anke Marsh, Leigh Mack, and Carl Bialik. To my fellow writers Nick Cirkovic, David P. Perlmutter, Jon-Jon Jones, Stephen Marriott, Anne John-Ligali, Helena Halme, Soulla Christodoulou, Nilam A. McGrath, Andi Lutz, and Benjamin Smith. And to the members of the LOTNA sci-fi group for their continued inspiration and friendship. You are all very much appreciated.

To my family for engendering and enduring my creative passions.

Cover design by Blondie's Custom Book Covers and Jody Smyers Photography. Special thanks to KJ Waters. And additional thanks to Janet Dado for her spaceship designs.

Lastly, many thanks to Glen Pearson for formatting.

Any leftover errors are mine alone to claim.

I can spell; I just like to make words up!

BOOK TWO

THE EARTH AXALAN WAR
Of Pasts and Futures

Prologue

The Planet Chryria, the Fourth Cycle after the Expulsion

>*Escape! Escape! Escape!*< The word flitted around the disembodied consciences of the thousands of survivors.

They babbled and squabbled, scurrying about the last of the Great Psionic Temples which had not yet been destroyed by the invaders. There was no one left to fight for them, too few of themselves to restore order, and they had no allies, having subjugated everyone into slavery.

It was over.

Their Second Great Age had now ended and escape was their only option. They agreed to fling themselves upon the mercy of the universe and seek forgiveness. After advancing through their galaxy conquering and enslaving with their formidable psi powers, establishing an order that had lasted millions of years, they had finally come to their own end.

Their most feared weapons had been their slaves, the Surge. These space-borne, nomadic creatures could survive in the cruel vacuum of the void, their metallic bodies absorbing all forms of energy for sustenance, allowing for various energy discharges, or to change shape at their extremities, especially in flight. They were sentient, telepathic, and travelled in hordes of up to five thousand; there being in excess of one million such hordes. To the Chryrians' regret, the Surge had been deceptively-looking gentle creatures, but their ingrained sense of justice and order would be turned against the psi-beings. The Chryrians had taken advantage of the metal beings' telepathic nature and enslaved them, ruthlessly using them to wage war.

The end of the Chryrians had come by way of invasion and rebellion. A virulent race of energy beings had emerged from the depths of eternity—the Lore. But the Chryrians had had the perfect counter-weapon in the form of the Surge who could absorb and repel the Lore's energy. After an eternity, the Lore had weakened, as had the Chryrians—perfect timing for the Surge who revolted, instigating a three-way battle, which destroyed the Chryrian's world. Homeless and defenceless, their great civilisation in ruins, the remaining Chryrians had taken to the void, floating on the universal currents.

The journey had been very long, many dying along the way, many lost or left behind in the void or on other worlds. But others had persevered, surviving the perils of space for aeons, until they had detected the faint presence of life on a small, blue world, still in its primacy.

The desperate Chryrians had arrived in clusters, in a wide arc across three great landmasses, and in time they had encountered some of the indigenous life forms, isolated tribes who had worshipped them as Gods. The Chryrians, now benign and repentant for their previous imperious actions had befriended the inhabitants, but the exhaustive journey had robbed them of some of their lifespirit and they were dying. Their hope of being remembered in this universe and their renewed commitment to preserving life was now in jeopardy.

But a grand solution had been hit upon. Their worshippers had minds like their own, though on an order much more primitive. If agreed upon, a merger of minds could be formed, the hosts also bestowed with the memories of the Chryrians and their incredible psi-powers. The Chryrians wished to share their wondrous powers in an effort to help these primitives understand their world and ensure a secure future, without making the mistakes that they had. These powers would also enable them to live for millennia.

But the Chryrians had also left their new flesh-bodied hosts with powerful enemies—the Lore and the Surge—who they knew would come searching for them. The future of this world and the Chryrian-minded beings would now be fraught with unimaginable danger.

However, not all of the empowered corporeal-beings could cope with their powers and madness ensued, causing the near annihilation of some tribes, the survivors scattering themselves around the world. But on the plains of a hot, dusty continent, one dying member of a tribe held on tenuously to life.

CHAPTER ONE

The Sahara, 2403 BC

Perversely, it was the shouting he missed. Not the loud, hateful shouting in his ears, but the soul-shrieking of the mind—the dissonance of accord. It had made him feel alive, his body singing in mindsong; pain and ecstasy in union. Now it was gone, ripped away, silent both in the real surrounding wasteland and in the desert of his mind. Silent and dying.

Aranu of the D'anaa people lay among the desert rocks for days, his life slowly ebbing away in the unrelenting heat of the day and the deadening cold of the night.

Only those few days ago, he and his older brother had clashed over the leadership of the tribe, Aranu wanting to live by the peaceful ways taught by the repentant Chryrians. The aliens wanted this world to benefit from their mistakes and sacrifice. But his brother had resisted, wanting to conquer their rival tribes and then beyond. Their young sister, who could have ended such quarrels, had embarked upon another of her explorations she revelled in so, and had not been there to pacify either of them.

A tremendous psychic battle had ensued between the brothers and their allies; psychic bolts hurled among the naked men and their wooden clubs, clattering sticks and stone weapons. The fighting raged in the physical and psychic worlds, dissonance unleashed, combatants on both sides killed, until only the brothers alone fought for their lives. In one vicious assault, Aranu had been felled by stones and sticks driven by telekinetic rage, which left him more dead than alive. His treacherous brother, standing over him face shadowed by the broiling sun behind him, had disappeared, leaving him for carrion.

His lips were dry, his blistered tongue unable to move, the pain in his body hampering his already laboured breathing, his psionic energy draining away so much so that he couldn't heal himself. Aranu imagined his dissonance aloft, free of him in flight. There was not much time left. In a last effort, he gathered together all his remaining energy and hurled out a desperate psychic scream for help. The light was fading fast, or were his eyes closing for the last time?

Aranu did not know.

As his eyes were closing in a final sleep, he hallucinated: the air beside him sparkled and shimmered and then split open in a bright swirling cirlce. A young boy, paler than the sand with black hair, had emerged from the ripped sky. He looked down and smiled at Aranu, who tried to smile back at his vision, but passed out instead.

Consention Military Base, Earth Frontier, AD 2216

Aristedes stared down at the young African. If he had been any later, he might have died, but then again, being an Astral he could have gone back to an earlier time. But he had also been lucky upon his return to the future.

"Emergency medical personnel to the dock, I repeat, emergency medical personnel to the dock.." Aristedes heard upon alighting from his portal on the dock.

The supply freighter, *Gantsford*, had been attacked with multiple casualties reported. It had limped back to Consention Base. Aristedes casually infiltrated the frenzied activity, the injured ferried on gurneys to the med section. Sticking by his casualty, Aristedes followed the medics through the gun-metal grey corridors as they rushed the half-dead man to the medical bays. Among the late-shift med-staff, Commander Lynn Kellis awaited him for a report.

"What the hell did you call me for? It's just a frieghter attack!" She was not amused.

Tension on his face, Aristedes waited as a nurse trollied the rescued patient away for treatment.

"Because of him," he answered tersely, pointing at the retreating patient. "He's not exactly from around here!"

"What'dya mean? What're the stats on him?" she asked, her British accent cutting through the surrounding staff's medical techno-babble. She had just rushed in herself, sweeping her brown hair back into a ponytail. "I don't see any markings on him. Hell, he hardly has any clothes on!" she said, staring after the mystery man.

To Aristedes, Kellis was an enigma herself. At a young age, well thirty-five-ish, she was the over-all commander of the research departments on all Earth bases. But she kept her own life as secret as her work and experiments in her own secret facility at Zero Star, where she was something of an expert on aliens and extrasensory powers. Though how she came to be so, Aristedes did not know.

Kellis, Aristedes and his sister Zane, her two aides, had been visiting the twenty-two forward deep-space bases all the way from Bleakstar Base, Starfalls Command Base, and Fort Barnard, toward the January Satellites in such a way as to firmly make Consention Base the last stop before heading back to Zero Star.

On the previous bases, Kellis' team had been officially collecting data for Earth Command, but unofficially they had been conducting an unauthorised mission for another group—outside of the Earth Council's knowledge. Their actions were under need-to-know orders, and the commanders of these bases did not need to know. On Consention, however, they were also visiting the base's commander, Commander Xaul Relentus, an old friend of Kellis', who knew something of her covert enterprises. How these two knew each other and ended up involved in a secret group, Aristedes also didn't know. But he wanted to find out.

Kellis waited for Aristedes' answer. But before he could, one of the nurses approached them.

"Isolate that one," Kellis pointed at him.

The nurse hesitated, not recognising Kellis as a member of base staff, but upon seeing her uniform rank, obeyed.

Rank still does have its privileges, Kellis smiled.

The rescued man was placed in an isolated medbay as the doctor arrived. She turned her attention back to Aristedes. He sometimes found it difficult to fully express himself when alone with her. It must have been especially difficult now, having thrown everything into disarray by bringing onboard a severely injured stranger, Kellis certain to have to invent a cover story for her aide's discovery.

Aristedes and Zane had only been with her for a couple of years and would probably stay for at least the duration of the war, but then he and Zane did have their own personal mission to accomplish. At twenty-one, his mature bearing belied his age, people mistaking his attitude for haughtiness, but Kellis knew better, Aristedes had been bred for leadership. And he was still learning.

For Aristedes, this was another of those awkward moments. His whole life so far was one chaotic moment after another, even for a time traveller. The aftermath of the Magna Aura battle had been as mysterious as The End on Galatia. Lord Aeon, the Astral leader, Aristedes and Zane's father, had disappeared during the battle though he had not been directly involved. Blame had fallen on his cousins, Netherlord and Archron, and even his own sister, Timechantress, but they had pleaded innocence. It seemed that some other dark powers lurked in the void.

The war-weary and wary Astrals had then been dispatched by the Celestian Knight, Phasia, to find Lord Aeon, but the brothers Archron and Netherlord had rebelled, Celestra, the latter's daughter by Timechantress, following suit.

The Astrals were split. Helexius had taken over, and with too few to search, efforts to find Lord Aeon had been hit hard. Frustrated, Aristedes and Zane had fled the Chronopolis to mount their own search, declaring that they would never return until their father had been found. The two had been strangely attracted back to their home world of Earth, only to find it at war with the Axalan Empire. They had elected to stay, whilst searching for a possible time-displacement theory to their father's whereabouts, all the while trying not to influence the outcome of the war. But now Aristedes had rescued this refugee from time, whose mental scream he had somehow heard in the temporal void. And he had to explain this to Commander Kellis.

"Er, Commander, I think we should talk in private," Aristedes said sotto voce.

Kellis rolled her eyes and indicating an empty examination room, shoved him in. Normally, in delicate situations like this, Kellis would have activated a sensor inhibitor, scrambling any listening devices that may have been concealed. One could not be too careful, nowadays. But Aristedes and Zane emanated a natural force which functioned the same way.

"Speak!" Kellis barked.

With no sign of his usual nervousness when around Kellis, Aristedes said, "That man has no uniform markings on him, because. . . he isn't in the military. And. . . umm. . . he isn't from. . . this time." He winced, waiting for her reaction, which he knew would not be slow in coming or nice to watch.

There was a momentary shocked silence, then "Go on. . . " she said, folding her arms, surprising Aristedes with a calm response.

Aristedes told her about hearing the mental plea and saving a man from over four thousand years ago—the near-impossibility of it all.

Kellis smiled, ever fascinated by Aristedes' tales of time travel, talking as if he had just walked across a room and picked the man up.

That's what was so charming and innocent about him and his sister, though she liked Zane for other reasons.

"So, the upshot of the story is that this man is strongly, hell, extremely telepathic, eh?"

"Yeah, my head is still aching from his scream!" He rubbed it.

Kellis looked at him, Aristedes did seem a bit dazed.

"You should get yourself checked out as well," she said, slightly concerned.

"No, I'm fine, really," Aristedes replied. "Besides, what would I tell the doc?"

"Fair enough," Kellis smiled.

She rubbed her chin in thought, Aristedes watching her thought processes, her dark brown eyes seeming to follow the visuals of her mind. She was so different from the women of ancient Greece, yet with her beauty and grace, she would have fit into the old-world society perfectly. He would have to take her there, someday, after the war.

A smile, as always, ended her brainwave. "It's a bit late, but we'd better go see the main man. We'll need a cover story for him."

They exited the room. Kellis, knowing Doctor Brosus would be busy with the patient, asked a familiar nurse about the casualty's prospects.

"Fifty-fifty at the moment," the nurse reported, hurrying off to the room.

"Thanks, Rannie. Keep him isolated. We'll be 'at top'. Call us if we're needed," she waved on her way out of the med section. They proceeded into a lift, "Command deck," Kellis ordered it.

They rose swiftly in silence.

This could work, Kellis told herself. If this person survived, was as powerful as she thought he was, and could also be trusted with her other assets at Zero Star, they could go on the offensive, but it would take a lot of selling to the Earth Council. If all else failed, she could play her trump card.

They owe me. Those bastards on Earth owe me, big time! And she would not let them forget that. She also had Aristedes and Zane.

Only she and Xaul Relentus knew about them, not even the Special Council members knew about their special heritage. Two years ago, Kellis had been investigating a mysterious computer failure on her base at Zero Star when she had found them rifling through the computer data base, apparently searching for traces of information about their father, who had disappeared in a war—one of many lost and tragic casualties she had mistakenly thought at the time. How they had evaded security had baffled her. Though they had been dressed in Earth military uniforms, Kellis thought them spies working for the Axalans and would have had them shot. However, upon seeing Zane, she had instantly rescinded the order and had them imprisoned instead.

Kellis remembered that day, so vividly. She had visited the two in their cell, Zane looking so young and innocent. Kellis knew even then they could have escaped if they had wanted to, but to them, this was just another adventure. She suspected they were up to something, even if looking for their father, but as long as it coincided with her goals, then they could stay, if they wanted to.

Kellis had then surprised the two youngsters by revealing to them that she knew who and what they were. The Astral siblings had looked at her in astonishment, but not given anything away. Why woud they trust Kellis? She said it had been a gift of hers to know a superbeing when she saw one. A bit of a lie, but it had stuck ever since. And she had offered the two a place in her facility, which they had accepted, becoming her indispensible aides. They could use her facility to search for their father and she would use their powers and expertise on certain matters, though they could not assist wholly in the war effort; Aristedes had insisted upon this: This was a human matter; Kellis agreed.

Lord knew there'd been enough temporal disruptions already, she had thought to herself.

The Astral's powers had been her secret, but she had eventually revealed them to Xaul Relentus. He was an experienced officer, and like her, a member of a secret organisation unknown to any of the Earth Council members. His help could be needed in the future. Over time, Kellis had become like a big sister to Zane, almost as over-protective as Aristedes was. The young Astral had always asked Kellis why she smiled so whenever she saw her, to which Kellis had always answered, "Because you remind me of someone I knew, long ago." *And wasn't that the truth,* Kellis reminded herself.

Kellis sighed: *She was getting too old for this*. She had not signed up for this, but been literally dumped in the middle of it. But hopefully, this mysterious interloper from the past would be able to help them.

The lift stopped, the two exiting to walk down the corridor toward Commander Relentus' office.

"I'll do the talking, Aristedes. He gets nervous around you, for some reason," she smiled, to which Aristedes feigned a frown.

She chimed the door. The door opened, sliding back.

"After you." Aristedes doffed an invisible hat, allowing an amused Kellis to enter the office first.

Aristedes smiled to himself. *He'll be more nervous when he realises there's a mindreader on his base.*

The dissonance was harsh. So many unfiltered thoughts and emotions; stress, anger, sorrow and confusion.

Where am I?

He wasn't dead. There was too much pain.

Aranu sensed his surroundings, fading in and out within spasms of churning pain drawn from the depths of bottomless pits. The last thing he remembered was the boy stepping out onto the desert from the rip in the sky. Now he was here, wherever here was. He was lying on a bed, in a room with shiny, bright walls and noisy boxes with flashing lights he did not comprehend. People garbed in strange clothing walked about him, talking in an incomprehensible language, and his body, attached to strange translucent reeds, ached. Aranu concentrated on his inner self. His body was now knitting itself back together, helped it seemed by whatever these people were feeding into him. The healing process was bringing back his strength, both physically and mentally. Pain and anxiety relented as he relaxed.

Testing his abilities, he touched the mind of a nearby woman, a healer, a nurse called Sara Rankin, who had been looking after him. He learned her language, English, probed a bit more, and what he saw amazed him.

His kingdom, in what was now North Africa, was long gone, buried beneath the deserts of time. His people and others like him were unknown. There had been upheavals, both natural and man-made, over the millennia: hundreds of wars, famine, plagues, and millions of sufferers and deaths. Weapons of epic magnitude, moments of infamy, great leaps for mankind, giant steps in learning, lost explorations, and countless discoveries. And now man had reached the stars. But others had wanted them for themselves: the Axalans.

Aranu reached his mind out further and gleaned more information from the others around the nurse. In 2145, Earth spaceships had been attacked by unknown adversaries. The attacks had continued unabated, with an ultimatum to surrender, or Earth would be destroyed. The various Earth Governments had naturally refused and in 2148, the war had begun. Little was known about the beings who called themselves Axalans, except for a few extracted facts gained from spies, on both sides of the war. They had originated from a region of space they called the Red Cluster. They had escaped detection by Earth or by anyone else by deciding centuries ago to deliberately mask their electromagnetic signals. They were humanoid, with males and females; tall, blue-skinned and blue-haired.

As Columbus was sailing the Atlantic, the Axalans had already embarked on explorations through their neighbouring stellar systems, in the name of their Emperor. For hundreds of years they had expanded and colonised, not encountering any intelligent life, until they had encountered human explorers. Now Earth was in their way.

By the twenty-second century, Earth had a competent space-fleet. The Axalans, at first, had assessed the humans' effectiveness before committing to a full attack. However, a few scouts had been captured around Mars and Earth forewarned of the attack. For years, Earth had its back up against an interstellar wall, though the war had never actually reached Earth itself, except for the mysterious terrorist event of 2210 in New York, which had been attributed to the Axalans. But somehow, Earth had turned the tide at Proxima Centauri, the Axalans suffering defeat after defeat. The war had simmered down, the tacticians giving way to the strategists. The year was now 2216 and Aranu was in a formidable deep-space military base, right on the frontier of the war.

Aranu assimilated all this information.

All of this could have been avoided, he thought. *If we had stayed together and followed the Chryrians' ways, Earth would have been much different. I couldn't make a difference back then, but maybe now . . .*

But he had to get stronger first. Aranu rested, settling into a deep meditative state, letting his body heal. It was a new world he was in, a new time, but human nature was always the same.

"He's a what? From where? And when?" Commander Relentus bolted up from his chair, his muscular frame attesting to his years as a marine. "And you brought him here?" he shouted, waving his arms to indicate his base. "Suppose he doesn't cooperate? Ah hell, I might as well not talk, he knows what we're thinking anyway! I need him off this base, Lynn. Take him back to your Zero Star. He'll be at home there."

He paced around his antique oak desk, hands on hips. His office was a bit too dark, as if space was leaking in from the large square portal behind him.

"He's a bit weak at the moment, sir," said Aristedes, stopping short earning a hard stare from Relentus and a sharp let-me-do-the-talking look from Kellis.

But Kellis backed up Aristedes. "He will need at least a couple days before we can move him, Xaul. And I'll personally deal with this myself. We'll handle the cover story. If he's a superbeing, then none of your boys go in there, he's mine."

Relentus nodded agreement, calming down enough to sit down. He didn't want his men anywhere near 'it'.

"Anyway," Kellis continued, "I wanted to talk to you about that project I wanted to initiate."

Aristedes' head shot over to Kellis. *What project?* He hadn't heard of anything, but had suspected she was up to something.

"You're dismissed, Aristedes," Relentus ordered, his hard face brooking no smart quip or dissent.

Aristedes snapped his head back in surprise. Before he could even form a 'what' on his lips, Kellis nodded agreement. He reluctantly acquiesced.

"Yes, sir," he mumbled, still in shock, as he turned and headed for the door. Once outside he waited in the corridor. *How could she be keeping secrets from me?* he thought. *I'm her aide.* He sulked as he waited for Kellis to come out.

Back in the office, Relentus shook his head. "He's a good kid, Lynn, impetuous, loyal, but he should know his place. You spoil him and his sister. Aides? They're only kids! And they shouldn't be out here."

"You know they're not just kids. And sooner or later I'll have to tell them what we're doing. We'll need their help, speaking of which, the project?"

Relentus leaned across the desk. "I'm not in a position yet to offer you any kind of help or guarantees. While Zero Star is known to Commander Earth Forces as Earth's insurance, the United Earth Council knows nothing about it, and if C.E.F. wanted to authorise your plans, then he would do so and for good reason: the end of the Earth would be close. But it isn't. So sit tight."

His desk lamp illuminated his face, which showed strong angled features protecting deep blue eyes and greying, almost blue, hair at the temples.

Remembering why Kellis had come in the first place, Relentus asked, "So how was the 'data research' you conducted? Do you think you'll need it?" he said with a slight quirky smile, fishing for information.

Kellis returned his smile with one of her own. The data research she had conducted had really been to insert a secret computer program into each of the bases' systems. It only scanned for certain beings and only Kellis had access to the information.

"You never know. Maybe." She shrugged and smiled enigmatically.

14

"Being secretive, again, aren't you?" countered Relentus.

"We both may be a part of ExA, but there are some things I can't and won't tell you. You know, personal stuff."

If Relentus was hurt by the remark, he tried not to show it.

"Personal stuff, well you should have said. I understand, we both serve the Commander Earth Forces, anyway."

Kellis laughed. "Hah, rumour has it that you're next in line for promotion to the 'big post'. You've turned down promotions to be out here in space, but one day, you'll have to accept the Generalship, so when you do, don't forget us little guys, right?" Kellis tried to sound cheerful, but inside she was disappointed.

"I've turned down those promotions, because I want to be where the action is," Relentus' deep voice replied. "And besides, I'm only forty, loads more time to go yet."

Kellis accepted his answer, for now. "Well," she said, standing to leave. "Don't keep them waiting too long." She stood up. "Gotta go, Xaul. Pleasure as always and I'll keep you informed as to our guest."

They shook hands.

Relentus made a noise under his breath. "Just keep an eye out, Lynn. In the meantime, I'll post a couple of security outside your guy's medbay. I don't need any more surprises."

"Yeah, I know, thanks." Her face brightened up. "Oh, by the way, do you think you could keep your men away from Zane. She can take care of herself, but there're a few over-zealous types."

Relentus shrugged his shoulders, looking a little tired. "Hey, what can I say, they're marines," he said.

Kellis shook her head and laughed. Marines had been the same in her day as well.

"Get some rest, Xaul." Kellis could see he had probably been up for three straight shifts.

He winked at her. "Will do when you do!"

Sharing a laugh, Kellis left the office.

Outside, Aristedes looked at her forlornly. Kellis clapped him supportingly on the shoulder.

"Let's go get Zane. We have some talking to do."

Aristedes perked up. *Now we're getting somewhere!*

Zane propped herself up on the table managing to topple her bottle onto the floor, which spun on its unbreakable side, to the raucous laughter of the assembled troops in the rec hall. Pretending to be drunk was hard for Zane, a slip of a girl, whose Astral metabolism prevented intoxicating potions and poisons from damaging her innards. But Lieutenant Paolo had insisted in this silly drinking contest, as always, and against a seventeen year old at that. Now he was somewhere under the table and Zane proclaimed the winner by his unit surrounding them—another fifty credits in her pocket.

She staggered to her feet, remembering at least to sway from side to side flashing a smile, more dimples than lips. Waving a big goodbye to her admirers, many of whom she had turned down offers of a gentlemanly escort back to her quarters, Zane had gone through the sliding doors, the noise and merciless teasing of Paolo instantly cut off from the outside as the doors had slid behind her. She breathed a huge sigh of relief, stood up straight and wandered off to her quarters.

"Zane!"

She looked behind her to see Kellis and her brother approaching. She grinned at them.

"Whooof! What . . . is that smell?" Kellis recoiled, wafting the air around her, "Have you been drinking again, kid?"

Zane tried to look ashamed. "That's the third time this week, Zane," Kellis continued with a smile. "Maybe I should tell them your little con game, eh? How much did you win this time?"

Zane showed her the gold credits. "And all for the war cause of course," she grinned.

"Cheeky!" Kellis replied, ruffling Zane's black bob of hair, which she hated. "C'mon, the three of us have some talking to do."

At Zane's baffled look, Kellis and Aristedes walked off toward a lift, ascended several decks and walked to Kellis' quarters, where she enlightened Zane to Aristedes' rescued guest.

"So what use will this guy be to us, once he's well again?" asked Zane. The three sat in Kellis' small quarters, which was regal by Consention's functionalistic standards. "Are we taking him back to

Zero Star with us?" she asked, curious as ever. "We don't even know him." She swung aimlessly around on the swivel chair.

"I was going to tell you this when we returned to Zero Star, but now seems as good a time as any" Kellis said, sitting on the bed. "Intel out of the January Bases recently reported covert activity by the Axalans, but it's no conventional force. They were clocked as superbeings. Very powerful and within striking distance of the Forward Bases. Word has it that Earth Forces has no defence against them, but we know better don't we? This is exactly what ExA and Zero Star were set up for, advanced technology, weapons, and other such assets." She emphasised 'other such assets' and leaned conspiratorially toward the siblings, raising an eyebrow.

"Who, us?" said Aristedes, warily, rubbing his chin. "And that man in sick bay? I don't know, Kellis. We could alter the course of the war." He sounded hesitant. "His call came from nowhere. It's almost impossible what happened."

"Well it did and you brought him here. Maybe it's for a purpose, to help us." Kellis leaned back on the bed, thinking.

Aristedes made a non-committal sound.

"Can't you look ahead and see what happens, then?" quipped Kellis, even as Aristedes shook his head, a wily grin on his face. She knew better than to ask. "Hey, a girl can try, can't she?"

Aristedes regarded her once again. She was so casual and cool about things, that it seemed nothing could bother her, because she had seen it and done it all before. He reckoned she'd be comfortable in any time period.

"So, what's the plan?" Zane was eager to get the topic going again.

"Okay, impatient aren't you," Kellis grinned at Zane. "There's you two, me, this guy, if he lives, plus another on Zero Star."

The two Astrals looked startled at her revelation. Kellis smiled.

"I haven't been keeping things from you on purpose. She's been on Zero Star since before you arrived, though not in a state fit enough to receive visitors, something I hope to remedy when we get back. I'm hoping we can form a counter force to the Axalan's secret group and push forward Earth's boundaries at the same time. The only thing I need is Commander Earth Forces' approval. It would give us additional protection and resources. So, until I hear from him, this conversation is just that: talk." Kellis sighed, checking her watch. It was pretty late. "Right, I'm hitting the sack. Us mortals need sleep, you know." Winking at them, she saw them to the door, "See you bright and early. And we'll check out this mystery man then, if he lives."

"G'night, Lynn," Zane said, sounding slightly disappointed. She was a dedicated night owl and wanted to hear more about the stranger.

"Goodnight, Commander." Aristedes gave a sideways glance to his sister. He'd make sure she would stay out of trouble during the night.

With the door closed, Kellis walked across the room, loosening her pony-tail, finishing off in front of the mirror. She always stared at herself, a quick evaluation just to make sure she was still herself. But she was the same; a thirty-five year old, few facial lines, athletic, but with a weight of life which hung on to her like a weary two-hundred year old. She dropped onto her bed. She was pretty tired and as usual in times like these, her thoughts wandered back, back to her old days.

"God, how things have changed," she said aloud. "You guys would have loved it here."

She got ready for bed and upon hitting the pillow, dreamed of days gone by and old friends.

Morning couldn't come quick enough for the two Astrals, so Aristedes had taken himself and Zane a few hours forward in time. Kellis found them waiting for her at the med section. She looked them up and down.

"You could have at least changed, you know, give the appearance you actually slept like us normal people," she sighed. "Failing that, be polite enough to bring me along next time."

"Next time," promised Zane. "Can we . . . ?" She gestured toward the doors, anxiously bobbing up and down, waiting to go into the sick bay, her blue eyes alight with eagerness.

"Let's go then." Kellis led the way through the med center, encountering doctors and nurses who nodded greetings their way, until she saw the nurse she wanted, who by the looks of it was just about to end her shift.

"Rannie! Morning, how's he doing?" Kellis caught up to her.

Rubbing her neck, Nurse Rankin grimaced as the three entered, lowering her cup of steaming ration-soup. Having run out of coffee and tea, ages ago, and with supplies not expected for a while, it was soup morning, noon and night, which coffee-addict Rankin seemed to be tiring of.

"I hate mushrooms!" Rankin complained, "especially in soup!" She stuck out her tongue. "Three days in a row, now. Three days! Oh, sorry, moaning again. Morning to you, Zanie," ruffling Zane's hair in the process, which Zane hated a little less than being called Zanie.

"Rannie?" Kellis reminded her. "The patient?"

"Oh, yeah. Doc Brosus is still in shock I think. You'd better go look for yourself. He's been waiting for you."

"Who, the Doc?"

"No, the patient. Go see . . ."

Kellis and Aristedes could only look at each other in confusion.

"He . . . he's been waiting, huh?" Raising her eyebrows in surprise, Kellis looked over to the room, where Rankin had indicated the patient to be, two beefy security officers outside.

"He said that he'll only talk to you."

"He did, eh? This should be interesting." Nodding to Aristedes and Zane, they walked over the room.

The lights suddenly flickered, everyone looking up at the overhead fixtures, but they seemed to be in perfect working order.

"Oh, I forgot," said Aristedes suddenly turning back to Rankin and presenting her with a little jar. "Here, to my favourite nurse." He gave her the jar.

Rankin's eyes almost exploded out of her head.

"Aristedes! This is coffee! Real coffee! My God, where'd you get this from?" She gripped the jar smelling it deeply like she could inhale the whole thing.

"Now, that would be telling. Wouldn't it?"

He left her standing there, incredulous, still clutching the miracle jar to her chest in amazement, as other nurses gathered around in the presence of the holy relic.

Kellis shook her head in wonder. Aristedes was getting better at slipping away, right in the company of others, with only a slight, flickering effect to mark his journey.

Love to know what it's like, she thought, but the reality scared her.

"Any more miracles?" she asked quietly.

"Nope. Only one per day," he replied, smiling ear to ear.

"Well, the one from yesterday is right through that door," said Zane, rolling her eyes, clearly wanting to get on with things.

"Pushy!" Kellis laughed, activating a hidden recorder on her collar, as they authoritively stepped by the guards and into the room.

Kellis and Aristedes stopped short as they entered the single med room, Zane bumping into Arsitedes. Kellis turned to the Aristedes, the thought this couldn't be the same man zipping through both their minds.

On the bed, lay a strong-bodied, healthy man, a far cry from the half-dead, bedraggled one that had been brought in a scant nine hours ago. Short-cropped, black curly hair and a hint of a beard framed his dark features, with confident eyes scanning his visitors.

Kellis couldn't help but notice that he was quite handsome as well, in a time-weary sort of way. Before she realised what she had done, she blushed as the man in the bed looked over at her and smiled.

Damn! Don't you ever read my mind again, or I'll kill you! The poison thought struck its target.

"I am sorry for invading your privacy, Commander Kellis. But you were transmitting rather loudly," he said, humour in his voice. He sat up a little. "I'm Aranu of the D'anaa Tribe or if you prefer the more modernised name of Aaron Danor. I don't know how precisely I came to be here, but I thank you . . ."

"Aristedes," the Astral introduced himself.

"I thank you, Aristedes, for saving my life. I was very close to death and thought I was dreaming when you appeared out of nowhere like a mirage." He looked at the ceiling, his eyes drifting, as if remembering past times. "There was no one else alive?" he asked, in a slightly melodious accent.

"No, you were by yourself," answered Aristedes, wary and curious, yet more amazed at Aaron's recovery.

"What happened to you? How'd you heal so quick? And how does an ancient African come by telepathic powers?" Kellis asked. She realised she was reeling off questions without reply.

Aaron laughed; a husky sort of sound, the kind of sound when the voice hasn't been used for a time. But Kellis suspected it came more from the fact that he didn't have much in life to laugh about. He turned onto his side and gazed at her again, their eyes meeting.

"You're transmitting, again, Commander," he said.

"Turn it off, Mister," Kellis warned, "Now!"

"I can't. But I'll turn it down a bit, if you like?" He smiled disarmingly. "And who's that there, hiding like a little bird?" he asked, spotting Zane half-hidden behind her brother.

Zane, standing very close to her brother, shyly introduced herself, "I'm Zane, his sister," she said nodding at Aristedes.

"Well, it's nice to meet you, too. And if it's any consolation to you two, I can't read your minds," he revealed, his face knotted in concentration. "It's like you're everywhere and nowhere at the same time." He sounded intrigued at that.

"A little trick we learned from our guardian, a long time ago," Aristedes said, thanking Spheron's spirit.

"Could you answer my questions first, Mr Danor?" inquired Kellis.

"Aaron, please."

"The questions, Aaron, please," Kellis relented, exasperation tinging her voice.

"You wouldn't believe me if I told you," Aaron said.

"Try us!" Aristedes challanged boldly. "We've seen a few things in our time, been a few places."

Smiling, Aaron replied, "I don't doubt it, young Master." He paused slightly. "The plight of my people begins millions of years ago on a world called Chryria, where the Psi beings there were destroyed by their slaves and invaded by the darkest of creatures called the Lore . . ."

A sharp inhale of breath broke short his story, the pale faces of the two youngsters, catching Aaron's and Kellis' attention.

"You know the Lore?" Aaron asked, his face full of fascination.

"They are the ancient enemy of my people," stated Aristedes gravely. "But we destroyed them, though I'm not sure how that war's time period corresponds to Earth's timeline," he confessed.

21

"So, that can still be in the future. For our sakes, I hope it was the past. They are a mindless brood, but they will hunt their enemies to the end of time and back," Aaron whispered the last few words.

Aristedes and Zane looked at each other: mindless wasn't the way they would have described the Lore they knew. This had to be another brood of Lore. The fear in Zane's eyes was evident, Aristedes holding her hand. Their father could still be out there fighting the Lore.

"Go on with your story, please, Aaron," Aristedes said as calmly as he could.

"Well, some Chryrians escaped, eventually found Earth, my tribe, and before they died, merged with us, giving us their powers, hoping we would use them peacefully. But malcontents, like my brother, wanted to rule. We fought. I lost. And then here I was," he said, looking at the three. He seemed truly grieved.

"I can take you back, you know," said Aristedes, gaining a compassionate look from Zane, but a mild shock of resistance from Kellis.

But Aaron smiled, shaking his head, "I wouldn't want to go back. I thought about it, but changing the Earth would seem like the wrong thing to do. And I'm sure that the Chryrians would not have approved. I think you know what I mean," he said, casting a knowing look at the two youngsters.

"You've learned a lot in an awfully short time, Aaron," said Kellis, who'd been listening with some interest, also learning new things from Aristedes and Zane.

"Well, the medical staff's minds were available, so quite naturally, for my own protection and for the necessity of communication, I acquired some information. I'm also what you call psychokinetic, not only telepathic, but I'm too tired to move anything for you at the moment. And I must say that this century is most remarkable. I'm going to like it here," he said, lying prone again.

Kellis said, "You'll need a place to stay, Aaron. You can't stay on this military base, you know."

"Are you recruiting me?" Aaron replied in mock surprise.

Kellis smiled, not knowing if he read her mind again, but not bothering to warn him against it.

"I could have use for your . . . talents, let's say."

"You intrigue me, Commander."

"Kellis, please!"

"Kellis? Not your given name?" he probed.

"I'm used to it. Take it or leave it," Kellis snapped in neutral mode.

"Kellis, it is." He smiled back. "And I would be pleased to join you, the young Master and the Lady. You all seem to be exceptional company and I won't be so . . . lonely." His smile turned sad. He let out a sigh, a tiredness overcoming him. "I think I'd better get back to healing myself."

"Of course," Kellis agreed. "You really were half dead when you came." She got up to leave.

"Um, sorry, why did you call me 'young Master'?" asked a curious Aristedes.

A grin widened on Aaron's face, tiredness falling away.

"You may be able to hide it from others, but I can tell you are a prince or something like that, a leader awaiting the right to his kingdom. And Zane there is just as important and so unafraid for one so young."

Zane beamed at the compliment.

"The two of you protecting each other, until the day you can return. I have seen it many a time in my travels around the desert tribes' royalty. Times change, but people remain the same."

Aristedes looked stunned. Zane was captivated by Aaron, Kellis could see. She would have to keep an eye on the impressionable girl.

Aristedes spoke without his usual caution.

"We were born on Earth, but only relatively recently discovered our heritage and abilities as time travellers."

Aristedes still remembered that day and the shock when his father, Xathanius, had introduced them to Phasia, a stranger made of purple energy. They had thought her to be a Goddess from Olympus. But she was much more than that. She had told them of the Celestian Knights, their ancient kin, and then trained them for war.

"We used our powers to save our cousins, the Starguards, on another world in a system called Magna Aura."

He could still vividly visualise, watching from the Chronopolis, the blue glow throughout the Magna Aura system as the Starguard Azure had used her half-Lore heritage to destroy all the Lore commanded by her father, the Traitor Synther.

"We succeeded, but our father, and our people's leader, was lost in a war with the Lore."

Worryingly, Aristedes reflected, along with his father's disappearance there was also the nagging fact that the Traitor Synther's body had never been found. Nobody knew for sure if he was dead. Aristedes wondered if the two events were connected.

"My uncle commands where we live, which is fine, but not everything is . . . peaceful," he explained glossing over the troubles with the other Astrals. "So Zane and I ran away to find father ourselves. I'm sure our people could find us if they wanted to, but as long as nothing reckless is done, they'll leave us alone to search." He shrugged to end his tale.

Kellis was surprised. They had never told her this much of the story before when they had first met. It looked like they had found a new friend.

"We'll find him someday," said Aaron, laying back down looking at the ceiling lights again, wistfulness soaking his voice. "I lost my parents when I was quite young, but now I've lost the rest of my family, my beloved sister, even my brother . . ." his voice caught.

Kellis thought she saw a tear well up in his eyes as he turned his head away, but she convinced herself that it was a trick of the light.

Awkward silence briefly pinched the air.

"Er, well, thank you for your time, Aaron," Kellis said. "Now get some rest and I'll be back later."

But Aaron was already sound asleep.

The three visitors looked at each other and departed quietly, leaving Aaron dreaming of a life long ago.

Duties kept the three apart in the morning. But at lunch, Kellis got around to asking Aristedes about his world, the mess offering a bit of privacy for them to talk.

"Do you want to tell me more about what you told Aaron?" she casually asked. She spooned into some potatoes and meat supplement, which surprisingly did taste of potatoes and beef.

Aristedes looked up at her from across the table they shared, his fork lingering in gravy-drowned mashed potatoes and soya-crafted peas.

"Not really," he answered. "What I told Aaron was basically the entire story." He took a mouthful, chewing thoughtfully.

"Well, I was reading between the lines and I'd say that there was trouble in paradise, or wherever it is you come from. Aaron's right, you know, if you need help, we're here to give it to you. Just because I'm a plain-old human being doesn't mean that I can't help," she stated.

Aristedes laughed aloud, startling Kellis.

"Kellis, you are no more a 'plain-old human being' than I am. There's more to you than meets the eye. So, until you tell me your life story, I'll keep mine to myself, okay."

He had tried to keep his voice down, but several people had looked over, Aristedes and Kellis giving them their everything-is-okay smile.

"You could always take one of your trips and find out," Kellis teased. "I'd be none the wiser."

"Ha, no, no, no," Aristedes wagged a finger at her. "Don't think that I haven't been tempted, but it's not allowed," he replied.

"I don't understand," said Kellis, genuinely confused. "You went back and saved Aaron, you got coffee from somewhere, so what's the matter?"

"I can't really explain *all* the laws of time, but here's my version: All my people are attuned to the complexities of temporal motion, its causes and effects. The universe isn't just an open road to be travelled haphazardly; it has its own codes and rules. Break them and the whole fabric of the universal highway crashes. Sure, little harmless trips to pick up some coffee and the like are okay, but on a larger scale, the universe takes notice. In those cases, exchanges may take place, say, you change the past then the future is compensated for in some way and vice versa.

"In a way I don't fully understand, I was meant to hear and save Aaron and bring him to the future. He has a role to fulfil; what that is I don't know. And as for you, you also have a role to fulfil and if I start searching your past, it could compromise our efforts now or cause unsettling ripples to surface in the future. So I hope you understand that though I may be flippant about my travels, it's only because I stay in the calm, shallow waters of time and not the raging currents."

He looked at her sincerely, Kellis seeing emotion in his eyes she hadn't seen before.

So you're a little human after all, eh? she thought. *There's hope yet!*

Aristedes tucked back into his meal, pulling a sour face. "Hmm, I'm just going to reheat this," he said heading over to one of the many wall-mounted micro-heaters.

Kellis watched him. Aaron had been right: Aristedes held himself regally, even when he tried to hide it. She thought of Aaron, a refugee from another time, stranded and alone. She knew just how he felt. But there was more to it as well. Was she attracted to him? Kellis winced. The first thing she would do upon returning to Zero Star would be to get her hands on a strong telepathic limiter. Having thoughts like these was just too embarrassing and compromised her mission. She was still in thought when Aristedes had sat back down to the table, delightedly savouring his re-heated meal.

Kellis looked at the mish-mash of food, at her own meal and back at his mess. "How can you eat that stuff? It looks disgusting!"

Aristedes looked at her mocking innocence then back to his food. "Are you kidding? I love this stuff. It's just like mamma used to make," he joked.

Kellis shook her head in wonder. *No wonder your life's screwed up!* She took another look at his plate.

"Can't wait 'til we get back to Zero Star and real food." She finished off her meal. "Okay, gotta go. I'll leave you and your gourmet dish together. See you at twenty hundred to see Aaron again," she said, excusing herself from the table.

Mumbling with mouth full, Aristedes waved goodbye with his fork.

***

Zane was in the rec hall again, lounging on a generously comfy couch which inhabited the lower rear end of the room. This time she was abstaining from the usual after-hour activities.

Security officer Lieutenant Paolo, a happy-go-lucky sort, was trying his luck with her again. And Zane was resisting, but just enough to spur on the young officer. Every time she, Kellis and Aristedes had come to Consention, 'Lucky' Paolo—few knew his first name and no one dared look it up or at least kept it to themselves—had always been their escort, part of the liaison team. And as nurse Rankin was Aristedes' favourite, Paolo was Zane's.

Aristedes frowned on any budding relationship, considering Zane to be too young. In real time, she was only seventeen. Zane knew her brother's relationship with Rankin was only a game of flirtation, considering she was almost twice his age, but Kellis had urged Zane to live a little, just a little, and no more. Besides, Zane felt safer with Paolo, some other troops lacking that certain emotive and cognitive quality she preferred. He also made her laugh, which she rarely did nowadays, all the more so because she was ashamed of not being a true Astral.

Out of all the Astrals, Zane was the only one who could not travel time independently. That had been discovered soon after Phasia had taught them the rudiments of time travel, but Zane had been able to only flit around in real time, making her seem to move incredibly fast. In polite company she was a late bloomer, but to others, especially her boisterous cousin, Celestra, she was a cripple. The effect had made for an insecure life until she and Aristedes had left the Chronopolis. Now Zane found herself among real people again, enjoying life and what it had to offer. If she could, she would stay, but soon she would have to return to Zero Star, her erstwhile home.

"A credit for your thoughts, Squirt," Paolo joshed lightly. He leaned over to rest a nose length away from Zane, who instinctively smiled, staring into his eyes.

"Guess!" she said, flashing her eyes at him, to which he grinned back.

"Ooh, let's see." He squinted in thought. "Could it be about the war?"

"Um? No! Try again."

"Hmm, this is tough. Could it be about that stranger from the freighter your brother had isolated in the med bay? Is he more handsome than me?"

Zane stared into his dark eyes. Paolo was handsome with a claimed Chinese-Hispanic heritage. He had held her hand once, his copper-coloured skin making her's tingle. They could talk to each other about almost anything for hours. But she chided herself, almost feeling sorry for Paolo, not knowing about their past.

She put on a happy smile for him. "That's classified, and no! Or is that no and that's classified?" she teased.

"Well then, it must have been about me," he whispered, their faces drawing closer together, their lips about to touch.

"Zane!"

She jumped at the sound of her brother's voice, who had just entered the room and approached their table.

"Hello, Aristedes," Paolo greeted him cautiously, getting a frosty stare in return. He looked at his watch, "A few hours to go yet, but I'd better start filing duty reports. I'll catch you later," he waved to Zane, a tight smile directed at Aristedes, as he vacated his chair and left.

"How could you?" she hissed at her brother, embarrassed, trying not to draw the attention of other small groups in the room, as Aristedes sat in the vacant chair. "It was only a kiss!" She slouched back into the couch.

Aristedes twisted his mouth in brief regret. Nobody knew how free she felt here better than him, but they had other things to take care of first and he reminded her of that.

"Sorry, Zane, but you know forming attachments now is not the best thing to do. And besides, if something permanent did happen between you and Paolo, how are you going to explain to him in fifty years, why you hardly look any older, eh?"

"Good genes?" quipped Zane, looking away. "He's not a bad guy you know. He reminds me of an Athenian boy, Araxthenes. Do you remember those days, Aristedes?" she asked, her eyes glistening. "I wish I could go back. I wish I could see mother again. I wish . . . I wish none of this had ever happened to us."

28

Tears started to well up in her eyes, Aristedes hesitantly reaching across to console her. This was the first time he had seen Zane cry since their father's disappearance. And it was his fault.

"Shh, shh, come on Zane. It's not that bad." He wiped her tears away. "I know how you feel. I feel the same way, but bury it behind work. I forget you're not as strong as me," he goaded with a light jab of an elbow.

"Am, too!" she replied with a reluctant smile.

"Not!"

"Am!" she giggled, trying to look serious, tears forgotten. "I hate you. Making me laugh when I don't want to."

"Well savour that, 'cos someday, I might not be around to make you laugh when you want to," he said seriously.

"What's that supposed to mean?" a fully attentive Zane shot back.

"It just means you never know what will happen, so take life as it comes and don't rush it."

She laughed, "As spoken by a true, roving time-traveller. Good advice, brother," she said sarcastically. "I wouldn't buy a used spaceship off you!"

"Why would you want to?" He titled his head quizzically.

"Never mind," she sighed.

Then she went quiet, Aristedes knowing what she was thinking.

"Do you think father is dead?" Her voice was quiet. "Are we wasting our time here?" Zane's blue eyes glistened brightly imploring an honest answer.

Arsitedes shook his head. "No, I don't think so for either question. We were drawn to this time period for a reason. Either he is here or was here and we just have to find that link, that hidden trail which will lead us to him." He frowned, verbalising a stray thought. "Perhaps that's why I found Aaron, I don't know."

Zane nodded thoughtfully. "And Synther?"

It was a question they both didn't want to think about, since Aaron had mentioned the Lore.

"I hope he is dead. Netherlord and Archron claimed they destroyed him. But you never know with them two. But father would know. And that's why we need to, and will find him!"

29

Zane smiled in appreciation, Aristedes hugging his sister around the shoulders until she felt better.

"Anyway, back to the reason I was looking for you. Kellis is seeing Aaron again in a couple hours. Want to come?"

"Of course. I think he's quite lovely. How old do you think he is?"

"Looks thirties, but probably older. Too old for you anyway," he teased.

"No, not for me, dummy!" Zane protested, stabbing a finger at her brother. "Did you see the way he and Kellis looked at each other? Talk about smouldering!" She blew air from her lips. They looked at each other, conspiratorial smiles on their faces. "On second thoughts, think I'll give this one a miss," she said. "At least love is blossoming somewhere!" She regarded Aristedes with a look that made him feel guilty.

"Yeah, I suppose I can find something else to do then. They're showing a vintage film tonight and I mean with real film. This I've got to see!"

"Well, have fun," she said.

"And what are you going to do?" he asked, knowing her answer.

"Oh, this and that," she said coyly. "And I'll stay out of trouble. Promise."

"Make sure trouble stays out of you," he said, instantly cringing at his own words.

"Hey, that's not fair! I don't believe you said that. Apologise!" an offended Zane playfully slapped Aristedes on the shoulder.

Aristedes laughed, "Okay, I'm sorry. That was a bit below the belt wasn't it?" He laughed again, dodging another slap. "Alright, alright, I'm going," he said.

He backed away from the couch, hands held up in mock surrender, Zane's glare following him all the way to the door. Before he left, he pointed a not-too-stern reminder at Zane, whose tight-lipped glare softened into a smile and a poked-out tongue.

"Brothers," she sighed.

***

Kellis stood impatiently outside Aaron's med room door for a couple minutes longer.

"Where are those two?" she asked herself, checking her watch again, which showed a few minutes after twenty hundred.

The guards were still there, but only now to keep others out, rather than the patient in, and nurse Brannigan had taken over for Rankin.

"Mary Ann, if my aides show up, tell them to come straight on in, okay?" she said to the freckled-face blonde, who nodded.

Kellis knocked on the door and upon Aaron's 'enter,' walked in, remembering to thumb her sensor inhibitor, just in case.

Kellis saw a difference straight away. Aaron looked fully healed, Kellis not failing to see how much more handsome he looked than before.

"Wow! You heal fast," she said. "Looks like we can move you out tomorrow then!"

"Hello, Kellis. Yes, almost fully healed. The med-staff have also been helpful. Where will we be going, if I may ask?" He propped himself up against his pillows.

"My facility. A place called Zero Star," she said, sitting down next to his bed.

"And what goes on there?"

"You'll just have to wait and see. Unless you already know."

He held up his hands, "No! I promised I wouldn't do it again, and I haven't. I can control it more, now that I'm feeling better. You're not going to hold that against me all the time?" he asked plaintively.

"Sorry, but trusting people isn't one of my stronger traits. Too much has happened to me and I don't want to be caught out like that again." She mentally chastised herself for sounding so bitter.

"Well, any man who doesn't appreciate you, I'd say good riddance to him."

"A man?" said a surprised Kellis. "If you're talking about a personal life that I may have once had, then you're wrong. I haven't seen any one for ages. And probably never will," she said, looking directly into Aaron's eyes, challenging him to state otherwise.

"That's too bad," Aaron replied, staring right back. "Seems like you could do with someone you can trust."

31

"I trust Aristedes and Zane, Xaul, this base's commander, maybe a few others," she said, mentally ticking off the others on the fingers on one hand.

"You can trust me as well," Aaron assured her.

"We'll see."

"Speaking of Aristedes and Zane, where are they?" he asked.

"I don't know. They were supposed to meet me here, but they didn't show up! I'm surprised they didn't tell me beforehand."

Aaron laughed. "I think they wanted us to be alone."

Kellis stopped, open-mouthed. "Why?" she pretended not to know.

"I thought that would be obvious," Aaron said.

"You're presumptuous!" she haughtily spoke as her cheeks flushed.

Aaron smiled, "Perhaps! But you know it. Here I am in a strange time and place, met a woman like no other, yet after only a couple of days, I know . . ." He paused, not knowing what else to say. "Don't ask me how, but I know, like I've known you for a lifetime. Trust me."

Kellis returned his radiant smile with an increasingly frosty one of her own. She rose from her chair.

"Well I've never met you before, mister. You've got to earn that trust, starting tomorrow, bright and early. I'll see you then. Get some rest." Her feigned indignation almost faltered when Aaron gave her a departing flashing smile.

Outside his room, Kellis made her way immediately to the lower levels and the botanic bay, where she could relax. She also finally allowed herself a smile.

The damned audacity of the man! she thought.

Handsome, charming and bold, especially for a man who hadn't seen a woman for four-thousand years. But was she ready? Then she remembered how the subject had come up in the first place:

"Those cunning little brats," she muttered under her breath amongst the greenery. "What do they know about Cupid, anyway?"

There were a few sheepish smiles in the morning as Kellis met Aristedes and Zane on Consention's hanger flight deck.

Commander Relentus, his aide Simon Exmoor, and Paolo with his security squad had come down to see them off. Aristedes and Exmoor were deep in conversation a little way off from the group when Kellis had arrived. Earlier, during the night shift, Aristedes had transferred Aaron to Kellis' personal ship, the *Esprit De Corps*, by teleportation—or a lateral temporal shift, as Aristedes described it—to avoid undue attention. Paolo and his men maintained a discreet circle about them as the visitors prepared to leave.

Relentus clasped Kellis's upper arm. "Drop by anytime, Lynn," he said. "And next time, let it be for pleasure and not business." He raised his eyebrows to emphasise his point. "God knows you don't get away from work often enough!"

Kellis threw her head back in humour. "Do you think I came all the way out here just for business, when I could have coded you? It's always good to see you, too, though I'm afraid business has cut it short," she tilted her head to indicate her ship and the passenger inside. "I'll let you know how it goes. And you keep me informed also," her veiled reference to their project getting a grunt of approval from Relentus.

"Will do, Commander," he said.

"Commander," Kellis nodded in reply. "Mr Exmoor," she addressed Relentus' civilian aide. She did not know him too well, but she was sure she had heard the name before, somewhere in her past. It did not help he avoided Kellis on her vists and the furtive gaze he gave her added to her suspicions. But the fact Aristedes seemed to know him well bothered her.

Exmoor raised a hand in greeting without getting too close as Aristedes and Zane approached Kellis. She shuffled the siblings along, Zane having a final look at Paolo, who nodded a farewell.

Kellis turned back at the threshhold of the *Esprit* and saluted the officers. She had thought by now that the practice of saluting would have gone away, but it was still customary and being a dutiful member of the Earth's military, such things, especially now, were hard to throw away.

Consention's flight deck was cleared and the *Esprit* whistled out into the silence of space.

"Safe journey home, *Esprit*," intoned Consention's controller.

***

Aaron had found it quiet comfortable in the *Esprit*'s crew compartment while on Consention, the technology on display intriguing him, but nothing had prepared him for the view offered of his surroundings as *Esprit* rocketed from the base. There was nothing but deep space and a few points of light. The exhilarating sense of freedom and wonderment almost brought tears to his eyes.

"She's a good little ship; a converted Earth Forces Starship combat shuttle prototype. One of a kind," Aristedes boasted. "Enough room for crew of ten, weapons, very fast and dependable." He went on describing systems, but Aaron wasn't paying attention.

Aristedes stopped talking, noticing Aaron's eyes glued to the view beyond the portal.

"Beautiful, isn't it?" commented Aristedes. He stood beside Aaron, sharing the view of the black expanse speckled by distant stars.

"It is like looking into the sky where I lived, but you travel through it as easily as one walks upon the ground. Amazing!" Aaron was enthralled.

"I'll have you know that this is the fastest ship in the entire Earth fleet, as well," said Kellis, entering from the pilot's cabin, followed by Zane.

Aaron looked at her shocked, Kellis understanding his fear.

"Computers control many things, even my girl here," she patted a bulkhead. "Anything threatening that arises, she'll warn me." She smiled at Aaron's nervous disposition. "You'll get used to it, believe me."

She fixed him with a stare reminding him of their conversation the previous night. They hadn't spoken since about it. And they weren't going to.

"I see," he replied, understanding the implied message. "So, this ship of space is fast then?" He twisted his lips to smile.

"Yep, and not just because of its thanium engines, either. Aristedes?" she instructed the Astral, gesturing to Aaron to look out a view port.

Everything looked normal, until the stars had swirled together, racing mesmerisingly by for an instant, before returning to normal.

But Aaron saw that they were different—the alignment was different. They were in a different place.

He was stunned. "How . . . ?" he managed to whisper.

"The 'how', you know. Aristedes just used his powers to teleport us. But I don't think you mean that. How far?" she guessed.

Aaron nodded slowly.

Kellis answered, "Fifty light-years."

With all his information gathering and learning, Aaron's eyebrows shot up in shock.

"We've just turned days into seconds. It's needed sometimes when mission time is at a premium or to avoid a tedious journey. I get bored easily." She shrugged. "Aristedes has kindly dropped us about an hour away from our destination, right Aristedes?"

The Astral nodded confirmation.

"I'm impressed, Aristedes. Someday, I'd like to meet the rest of your people."

"Someday," Aristedes half-promised.

Aaron just smiled again and returned to seeking out the galactic views.

The something that had bothered Kellis about Aristedes and Exmoor got the better of her. She walked over to Aristedes.

"You and Exmoor seemed to be getting along rather well," probed Kellis.

Aristedes smiled. "Believe it or not, his family are old friends of my family," he said, almost inviting Kellis to ask more. But he said "You may ask, but that's all you'll get."

Kellis shrugged nonchalantly. "It's just that I thought I'd heard his name before. Probably a relative," she said aloud, but the coincidence was too much.

Aristedes feigned a frown, sauntering off to the pilot's cabin. Zane joined him to give the grown-ups more privacy.

Kellis was glad for the company and happily pointed out cosmic facts to Aaron as they passed various stars. After a while, Aaron's brow had furrowed, Kellis ready for his next question, or so she thought.

"What is thanium?"

"That's a strange question," Kellis said, her eyes narrowing in suspicion.

"I'm curious, because on reviewing my information gained from Consention's medical staff, I noticed thanium was discovered in mysterious circumstances. And for some reason, that point sticks out in my mind."

Kellis thought well and hard before answering. "Well, all the history books state that after an explosion in New York, around the turn of twenty-first century, this new element, thanium, was discovered. It came in handy after the Superhero war and the nullification of all nuclear weapons on Earth. That's it! End of story. No other real details, except it's a bloody great energy source. But..." she leaned in conspiritorially, "what nobody knows is that Zero Star has ninety percent of the original remaining stock. The rest is used to make synthetic thanium to power Earth and the warships. That enough info for you?" Kellis finished her little history lesson.

"Except the part the Starguards played in that explosion in New York, but thank you, yes," Aaron admitted. "What happened after that?"

Kellis looked around cautiously to where the young Astrals sat in the pilot's cabin.

"Well, it was a mysterious event. No one really knows what happened after, except the Starguards died, and our lives on Earth changed forever." Kellis seemed to look back into her own past. "It's almost forgotten history though, Aaron, so we may as well leave it at that, yes?"

Aaron nodded his acquiescence, though still seemed to have a few more questions. But instead he watched as the shadows on Kellis' attractive face disappeared, a new light shining its way into the crew compartment. Aaron looked up and out of the portal for the source of the light, his eyes widening in shock.

A giant, yellow star lay directly ahead, flares flickering out as if to engulf the ship at any moment.

"Kellis! The star! We're too close!" But as he turned to warn her, he saw no fear on her face. "What? Don't you see it? What's wrong?" he shouted, pointing at impending doom.

"Nothing's wrong," said Kellis, bemused in the face of burning death, "That's home. Welcome to Zero Star."

The *Esprit De Corps* pierced the star's corona and plunged into its heart.

CHAPTER TWO

Long, long ago, before the recordings of history, the Gods, after fighting a terrible war against the forces of darkness, sought refuge. They ventured countless centuries far across the universe away from the fields of war through torturous space and generational strife before discovering worthy worlds to call their own. The King God, Xaal, took a world for himself and gave each of his favourite seconds a world to command. Thus were founded the five red worlds. Their peoples became known as the People of Xaal. And Xaal handed out the First Laws and they were simple:

Revere thy God above all else.
Proliferate thy selves, lest evil take thy place in the world.
And fear not thy brother; be loyal, for he is not your enemy.

The People of Xaal had lived by those laws, generation after generation. Eventually, the People of Xaal became the Axalans, breeding themselves, so that not only their hair was naturally blue, like their forefathers, but their whole bodies as well. In time, all would know the true colour of God.

It had also been prophesied that the Son of God would return one day and unite them with their lost brethren. They would know him by his mark and his name.

For millennia they had lived peacefully among themselves, until they had encountered their first stellar neighbours. And their law concerning them had been simple: conquer, lest they conquer you; thus had begun the war between the Axalans and the weak-coloured humans. The Axalan's name had become feared, the word 'axalic' coming to mean domineering, cruel and tyrannical in more congenial circles, but in others, the word had more profane connotations, such was the feeling of contempt for the Axalans.

And it was going to get worse.

His Most Sacred Highness, Emperor Xalarius the Exalted, lounged across his divan, a lazy smile spread across his face.

Dull red light shone through the lofty coloured glass panels of the royal chambers surrounding the public quarters of the Imperial personnage. (The Axalans preferred darkened interiors). The angular-cut ten-meter horizontal mosaics depicted the building of the five red worlds while the vaulted ceiling, resplendent in blues and golds, historied the deeds of Xaal, his sons, and their allies of the ancient past. Only one section remained blank, behind the Emperor; the future and the return of Xaal's son. Xalarius would have loved nothing more than to fill in those blank mosaics himself. It would have been an honour. But for now, he was attending to duties of the state.

Zzpp, zzpp – the noise whispered toward the Emperor, almost in symphonic harmony.

The artist across from him busily sculpted the Emperor's likeness from a rectangular block of holographic light. His light-sculpting tools eradicated unnecessary shards and waves of light, changing the colour and texture where necessary, the tone of the tools guiding the holo-sculpturist's steady hand and expert eye. With a final flourish of quick fluid touches, the completed work left behind a remarkable life-sized 3D likeness of the Soul of the Axalans, the considered son of Xaal. The sculpture shone in gold within the chamber.

"Your Most Highest!" the artist enthused, bowing and inviting his Emperor to view his work.

Xalarius inspected with enthusiasm, his multi-layered and coloured diaphanous robes flowed around his well-built, fragrantly-oiled body. His dark blue hair was a back-combed arched mane. A silken veil covered his lower face, his dark eye darting around his likeness.

"Excellent, Jallaar, your work exceeds itself every time. Expect a boon of one thousand dynastic rods come-the morning," he announced airily through his veil.

Jallaar was overwhelmed with emotion. "Your Most Highest, you are most gracious. Most gracious!" he bowed, grey-flecked hair of the veteran artist caught in his artwork. He started walking backward over the red stone-block floor, his arms outstretched, showing submission to the Emperor's will.

The giant, rust-coloured metal doors amid the glass dome opened of their own accord, Jallaar exiting the commodious hall, tears in his eyes.

One thousand dynastic rods were worth ten times more than the ordinary axalan rods and a hundred times more than a layman's rod. He was rich. With each precious bar, pure imperial currency, he would be able to afford ten comfortable abodes or immerse himself in the intrigues of power. Jallaar thought about it, but decided against displaying his new-found wealth. Avarice had never been his style, being a humble artist of advancing age. He would do better to invest his wealth wisely, which also meant doling the funds out slowly to his cojoineds and youngkin.

Jallar had negotiated the darkened maze-like, guard-lined corridors of the majestic palace, entering the many-pillared front public reception hall, when a familiar voice had called his name.

"Hello, Jallaar."

The voice dripped cold authority, even with its strange accent.

Jallaar stopped cold, fear gripping his heart. He forced a smile onto his face, before turning around to the sight of the Superions.

Jallaar's voice failed him. *Raxt!* he cursed to himself. He nervously smiled again.

"Is the Emperor alone now, Jallaar?" asked Mode, the Superion's leader; his voice deep and slightly melodious.

Jallaar just nodded yes.

Impatiently, Mode motioned to the four others with him and they followed him on down the hallways, leaving Jallaar shivering in dread from the brief encounter.

"Raxtra'vraken!" he swore aloud, hoping to ward off the demons.

How the Superions had come to be here, he did not know. They were the colour of Axalans, but did not talk or act like Axalans. There was something wrong about them and it worried him they had the complete confidence of the Emperor. It could have been because of Mode, a cold-spirited person, whose cruelty even by Axalan standards was formidable and because no one knew his face, hidden beneath a mask never removed in public. Of the others, all were as mean-spirited, dangerous and willing to obey Mode's every order. They executed the Emperor's will, but with such chilling tenacity and deadly zeal that even the entire Axalan warriory were afraid of them.

Jallar thought about the whispered fears from palace courtiers, but he had long ago given up contemplating the consequences if the Superions were to turn against them. It would be the end of the Axalan Empire.

Who cares about those cruk-eating ghuvuks anyway? his morose thoughts cheering him up.

Jallaar decided that come the morning, when he received his boon, he would spend it giving parties and celebrating until the end came. That way, he would be doubly happy: if the end did come, he would have been right in the first place and secondly, he would not have wasted his time worrying about it.

Jallaar stepped out into the red light, an orange sun glaring off the red rock surrounding the Imperial palace, which stood behind him like a massive rock-hewn sculpture, which it was, Jallaar's direct ancestors having helped to carve it. He walked as jauntily as he could through the surrounding rock garden and the outer liveries by the main gates.

Without looking back, he mounted his *veem*, the one-wheeled vehicle speeding out of the royal grounds across the red desert, a swirling storm about to form in the far north. Jallar looked up. He had forgotten it was high tide. Arega and Srorn rose in the distance above Axala, their red craggy features almost visible. And although it was day, Ela, the distant blue companion to orange Xal, shone beyond the moons. There was nothing auspicious in their positions, but Jallaar could sense changes were coming.

Jallaar raced faster, downward, until he was beyond the high desert and into the yellow-grassed suburbs of Axala's capital, Migr Lantris. He stopped on a slope overlooking the sprawling spired city. He loved it dearly and all it stood for, but if this splendour was to end at the hands of outsiders then now was the time to celebrate.

"Welcome, my friends," the Emperor proudly pronounced to the bowed five Superions before him, his translated voice purred over their comms. "Come tell me, what deeds and adventures have you embarked upon."

He rose from his throne and sauntered gracefully along the darker red circle surrounding his throne, which no one, but his personal guards and granted guests, were allowed within.

"Your Most . . ." began Mode.

"Ah, I almost forgot!" interrupted Emperor Xalarius. "Look at this!" He pointed in glee to the light-generated effigy just outside the circle. "My sculpture, most magnificent is it not?" He stared approvingly at the image of himself. "Jallaar is a most gifted artist. If only all Axalans had such talent," he mused, caught up in the glow of the light.

"Yes, quite," agreed an annoyed Mode.

He waited a moment, discreetly clearing his throat, to attract the Emperor's attention away from his light-monument. And then again. He glanced to one of his companions and made a quick frustrated sideways motion with his head.

It took a while for the Emperor to turn his gaze away from himself. And when he did, there was a curious self-satisfied lilt in his voice and look in his eyes above his veil.

"Tut-tut-tut," he said to air in general, lolling his head in their direction. "Psyren, are you trying to enter my mind?" He tapped his head, walking toward the blue and green clad Superion. "I can feel you trying to feel your way into my mind, but you fail. Do you know why?" He stood in front of her, a calm expression on his face.

Psyren's emotions were hidden, as usual, behind a mask of sereness.

"Because of this!" The Emperor shouted dramatically, flinging aside blue locks on the side of his head revealing the external nub of a neuro-implant. "Axalan technology. It protects my mind from being read or forced and alerts me to any attempt. I've already warned you once, Weak-colour, do not defy me again." He stared down upon Psyren, a whole three heads lower than his; Axalans typically being at least two meters in height.

"As you command, Your Most Highest," Psyren bowed, sereneness gracing her blue-tinged features.

Mode smiled beneath his mask. The Emperor was learning fast: a Superion was not to be trusted.

"I will reprimand her upon our dismissal," he said.

"No need, Mode," the Emperor casually waved his hand to dispel any such notions, "I have need of all of you," he said cryptically. "But first, I'd like to congratulate you on your latest raids into human territory."

"Thank you, Sire. It only means victory for you," said Mode, wondering if the translator in his mask was working properly and where the Emperor's saccharine talk was leading.

The Emperor continued: "My spies have no knowledge of these bases you harass, for they would have informed me, long ago, if such places existed."

"Your spies are not misinformed nor stupid, but ignorant, because their information is gained from ignorant sources. Ignorance begets ignorance, Your Most Highest," stated Mode.

The Emperor was thoughtful. "And your sources?"

"We could tell you. If you want," Mode trod carefully with his words, the path of the conversation taking a decidedly worrying turn.

"No, don't." The Emperor raised a blue hand to halt any of Mode's further revelations. "When I want to know, I will know, but at a time and place of my own choosing. And in return for these deeds of victory, the Earth shall be yours," said the Emperor.

"Ours to rule," Mode reiterated to himself and the Superions.

"Consider it done," commanded the Emperor. "But," he said holding up his hand again before the Superions could think of being dismissed. "There is something I require of you, beforehand. A task." He paused, seeming almost embarrassed to talk. "There is . . . trouble in the Far Regions. Disturbances, which have reached my ears from the few ships which have returned intact from the area. They report a creature, with powers to match a star, is behind these disturbances. I require you to investigate, just to quell the peoples' fears," he stated in his calm tone, though Mode could hear the tinges of disquiet in his voice.

Mode looked to the other Superions: Zone, Warper, and Invadress ready for action, Psyren's cold exterior belying the tempest that lay within her. They had heard rumours, too, and were quite eager for more action.

"As you command, Your Most Highest." Mode backed up followed by his team and bowed, the doors opening for their exit and closing silently.

The Far Regions were a wild place; starstorms and unconventional phenomena persisting in the area. Only the most hardiest and foolhardy ventured that far into the dire backwaters of Axalan space. It was a natural defence, but if someone or something had penetrated the space and the Emperor was worried enough to send them, then there was real trouble ahead.

But that's what we Superions revel in, Mode sneered.

"Did you record all of that, Marrathanor?" the Emperor enquired aloud, once alone.

"Yes, Sire." A calm voice spoke in the Emperor's ear.

"Keep an eye on them."

"Yes, Sire."

The Far Regions were dead, but far from inactive. It was a wide void of half-a-light-year's worth of nothing but rock, space, and more rock like some past cataclysm had created a cosmic sandbox. Nothing lived there, not for long anyway. And it was dark. Broken worlds lay scattered giving off eerie sensor reflections from other crushed planetoids, creating dense zones of unnavigatable blackness. Add to that magnetic dust storms, electromagnetic anomolies, and other cosmically-unkind phenomena emanating from the rocks and the Far Regions was also a deadly region.

"Damn hell!" Mode cursed, holding on to a bridge console as the ship rocked violetly again.

The first storm had thrown them off course a quarter parsec. The second had blown out two engines. Even using Invadress' electromagnetic powers and engineering skills, they did nothing to counter the sheer ferocity of the magno-gravimetric pulses bombarding the *Dragon Charger.* So they had drifted, into the next storm, currently alternating between spews of magnetic eddies and onrushing gauntlets of meteroid strikes caused by plasma surges, which according to ship's sensors and recent stellar records shouldn't have existed .

"Engines online!" called out a relieved Invadress. "Start her up," she instructed Warper, their main pilot. "Let's get the hell out of here!" Her sentiments were echoed by everyone.

"Good job, 'Vay," Mode congratulated her.

Mode was not best pleased with their investigations. Their spacecraft, the *Dragon Charger*, a stolen Earth Forces combat shuttle, had been particulaly battered and they had only searched small areas for days on end with no sign of an intruder.

"Can we settle on that small planetoid to regroup?" Invadress turned to Mode, to which he grunted approval.

"This area is one big Choix!" Mode lamented. It reminded him of the time he had demonstrated his matter transforming powers to the Emperor. Killing the small forested area of Choix on a neighbouring system's moon, by turning the air into a suffocating mass of black liquid had convinced the Emperor the Superions should be allied to him. Now as Mode studied the screens, there was nothing out there, save for more dead worlds.

They sat for hours, bored, resting, making minor repairs while Invadress poured over what data they had collected.

"Found something!" she shouted triumphantly from her scanning station. "Some kind of residual energy readings."

Mode strode over, boredom raking his soul. He looked over her shoulder.

An unknown energy signature flashed on the screen. The others crowded around.

"This energy is what is causing the storms. Anyone recognise it?" asked Invadress, swivelling in her chair.

Everyone shook their heads. If Invadress, who could harness and discharge electromagnetic energy from herself and who knew other forms of energy readings, didn't know what it was, then how could anyone else?

"Any guesses?" Mode asked.

Invadress, her blue nose wrinkling in thought, answered, "Well, if I really had to guess, and this is wild mind you, I'd say it was some kind of temporal energy signature. Do you see here and here?" she said, pointing to some squiggly lines, which meant nothing to Mode and the others, "Someone or something is playing with time and space, I'd say." Invadress flexed her shoulders, stretching out the tension.

She was at a loss, but Mode had always trusted her instincts, even before she had taken up the name Invadress. Her hunches had never been wrong.

"Anything Psyren?" he asked the psychokinetic, who had been telepathically monitoring the area.

Quietly reposed in the corner, seemingly meditating, Psyren opened her eyes and sighed, exasperated.

"No. Nothing," she snapped. "Unless the intruder is wearing an anti-telepath implant like that bastard Emperor. He makes me sick!" she uttered through gritted teeth. "When are we going to take over the Empire? He's already getting suspicious!" She paced around the cramped bridge, arms folded.

Zone and Invadress grinned at each other. They had been wondering when Psyren would complain about the Emperor.

"Soon, Psyren, soon, but first comes the Earth Bases and our present agenda. We have the Emperor's favour for now, but in our second phase we'll take over Axala. Don't worry, all is in hand. Earth will pay for what it did to us," Mode promised.

Zone, Invadress, and Psyren nodded in assent, but Warper looked distracted, staring into nothingness.

"What's wrong, Warper?" noticed Mode of the flyer.

"Nothing," said Warper. "I just thought I remembered something. Something from my past."

He stood apart, his blue and black close-fitting armour's cowl was down, revealing dark-blue skin with curly black hair.

Mode looked over to Psyren, who discreetly went to work. After a nod from her, Mode asked, "What did you remember?"

"Slightly confused, Warper said, "Uh, I can't remember now. Can't remember. It's just gone. Probably another one of those meaningless flashes of nothing, just like the other times," he said forlornly.

"Don't worry, Warper, your memory will come back to you in time," said Psyren.

Quite honest sounding, thought Mode. She was a bitch of an actress at times.

"If you want, we can have another session to try and regain your memories, but as I've said before, those parts of your brain were quite damaged from before," she said in lightened tones.

"Yeah, I know, but thanks anyway Psy'; appreciate it," Warper said.

Mode almost felt sorry for Warper. He'd never regain his memories, not with Psyren manipulating them on his orders. It would jeopardise everything. They needed Warper, his tremendous aerial prowess and piloting skills were an asset they couldn't afford to be without. He was a good man, not the type Mode wanted, but as long as he didn't know the truth about himself, the better things would be for all of them. Afterwards, when Mode had his victory, Warper could then be terminated. The deepest of memories were the hardest to eradicate, though Psyren had assured Mode that she had purged the lot in their last session. And Psyren was one Mode could trust completely.

More so than the others, he thought.

But Mode wondered what would happen upon deeper incursions into Earth territory. They would surely be fated to meet up with their long-held enemy, who aided Earth as he aided Axala. Many a time, he'd wished she could be dead, but he knew that wasn't the case. He could see her hand in the war, playing vital pieces, rolling the dice, as it were. It wasn't Earth Forces he was more concerned about, but the secret power behind them, waiting in the shadows: Lynn Kellis, and any others who had survived with her. As he held the key to Axalan supremacy, she held the key to Earth's victory. Eliminate her and the war was Axala's. But first she had to be found and the raids on the Earth's forward bases were a way to draw her out.

"Right!" Mode clapped his hands together, having cleared his thoughts, "Power the *Dragon* up, Warper, we're going back. This region's deader than dead and nobody's home."

"What about the readings?" asked Invadress.

"What readings?" Mode turned to her, his voice darkly mischievous.

Invadress screwed her lips, a slight smile crossing her lips as her finger pressed a key on her console, the readings disappearing.

"Never mind," she said.

No need to worry the Emperor any further, thought Mode. And it was another advantage they held over him.

The Superions took off, vacating the mysterious area in haste, but not without a few more stormy passages and ship damage, back toward the heart of the empire.

There was something happening in the Far Regions and Mode's senses told him it wasn't good, the timing even worse. He just hoped with Axala and Earth already to contend with, there wasn't a third front threatening.

"Nothing?" The Emperor was incredulous. A purple tinge clouded his angry face as red blood rushed through his veins.

I forget they are almost like us, mused Mode.

The Emperor stomped around his red-circled throne angrily, a youthful male courtesian rushing forth with a pillow for His Divineness to punch, the Emperor narrowly missing the youth's head repeatedly in his efforts.

Outwardly, he had to accept it; after all, the Superions were here to serve him. Of course, he didn't trust them. But they both, in their own way, had the welfare of the Empire uppermost in their thoughts and the Superions wouldn't want it conquered, not by anyone else but themselves of course.

Yes! the Emperor grinned to himself, *the Superions are on my side for now*. But deep in his thoughts were doubts. If something was out there, could the Superions defeat it? And if not, then who?

"Very well," he said, calming himself down. He returned more regally to his throne. The pillow boy backed away to his niche in the wall.

"We could go again, stay longer. . ." Mode offered, hoping the Emperor wouldn't call his bluff. The *Dragon Charger* would take another beating. So would their nerves.

The Emperor raised his hand dismissively."No, I heard of the damage to your ship. Other mightier ships in my fleet were not so lucky. You are skilled indeed." He indicated Invadress and Warper.

"Thank you, Your Most Highest." Invadresss bowed beside Warper, surprised at the praise.

Sniffing vacantly, the Emperor stated, "We will monitor the Far Regions remotely." He had made his decision.

"As you wish, Your Most Highest," Mode sounded conciliatory.

The Emperor smiled graciously. His thoughts turned to another matter.

"Now we will discuss your other mission; the one you promised me *spirons* ago."

Mode smiled beneath his mask. *Finally!*

"Ah, yes," he said, thinking back a couple of months ago. "We are ready once the ship is fully repaired. But for it to work we humbly request that your fleet step up its forays against the Earth Forces' forward bases. Nothing too bold, just acts of aggressive probing to test their response times and hidden defence perimeters."

The Emperor's head tilted slightly as if he was distracted.

"Acceptable. One *spiron* from now. Act!"

"As you wish, Your Most Highest," Mode bowed.

Dismissed by a wave of the Emperor's hand, the Superions backed out of the throne room.

"Marrathanor?"

"Yes, Sire?" came the voice in his ear.

The Emperor sighed. "Do I have to ask?"

There was a slight pause. "I believe they discovered something in the Far Regions and are keeping it to themselves for an advantage over you!"

"My thoughts exactly," the Emperor huffed. "Your insights into their plan for the forward bases were also correct. Keep watching them. The Far Regions and their plans for the Earth bases may be connected."

"Yes, Sire." The voice in the Emperor's ear terminated.

The Emperor's thoughts turned dark at the thought of him losing the Empire. He glanced over at his light monument, the embodied essence of the Empire, and wondered if the light of the Empire could be going out for good.

CHAPTER THREE

Zero Star, or at least the blazing inferno surrounding it, was an illusion. Thanium-driven generators maintained a vast array of holographic images and scanner disrupters to fool any investigating ship's sensors. Once *Esprit* had passed through the projections, Aaron had seen a small, revolving silver globe—a space station.

A myriad of lit view ports, blinking lights, domes, bays, modules, struts, and panels greeted Aaron's senses.

"That's my baby!" Kellis cooed. "Home, sweet, home."

Aaron was impressed by the small planetoid, like nothing he had ever seen. He sensed Kellis watching him and his reactions.

"Zero Star is a total secret, in plain view. Cool, huh?"

Aaron nodded absently. All of that had been within Aaron's grasp. What he had not been prepared for, upon the ship being guided into an internal hanger bay by the dulcet tones of a dock supervisor and landing lightly on the deck, was the sight of Zero Star's crew.

They were Bions. And the fact the grey beings had once been human was even more astounding.

The existence of the Bions was still quite unknown to the population of Earth, except for a few select individuals and agencies who had zealously guarded the secret of their inception. The truth of the matter was that the existence and nature of the Bions was still one of the greatest cover-ups ever perpetrated upon the people of Earth, and was still in operation.

UFOs—Unidentified Flying Objects—had always been an interesting mystery to some people. Many of them still believed the Earth's first contact with aliens had come with the encounter and war with the Axalans, but that had not been the case. And even in this case, many people believed alien contact only stretched back as far as the mid-twentieth century when the United States had not only captured crashed UFOs, but had been in contact with the alien race that had sent them.

This had caused quite a dilemma for the aliens to have their technologically superior craft crash upon a primitive planet. Their own world, located in the Cepheus Surround, was coming to an end, their resources, both for war and survival, were diminished and the little grey humanoids were desperate to find a new home. Earth had been a distraction, but their scout craft had crashed and were seemingly irretrievable. So the Cepheusians had started secret negotiations with the U.S. government in order to regain their craft and any alive, or unfortunately dead, crew.

With their own space programme under way and the space race heating up, the U.S. was eager for any advantage they could obtain. The whole Cepheus Project was classified and handed to the U.S.'s newest secret agency, ELF—the Earth Liaison Force—a small committee formed by members from the combined services with a political overseer.

At first, not content with the situation on Earth, the Cepheusians had sent more craft and though most of them had escaped the hostilities of Earth's weather and other natural forces, some had been lost to man-made hazards, such as missiles. Not only did the U.S. have downed spacecraft, but now so did the other atomic nations Britain, France, China, and the U.S.S.R. All countries, though some opposed to each other, agreed that the Cepheus problem could cause a serious threat to their own and the world's security, so ELF had been expanded to become CEARA—the Combined Earth-Alien Reaction Agency—a group of scientists, politicians and military experts who worked independently from all government control and who effectively dictated Earth-Alien policy.

So it had been to them that the Cepheusians had made an astounding offer:

\\humans of earth/
perpetuate understanding cepheus surround and earth world/
alliance proposed//
cephs among humans as guides advisors technicians//
humans among cephs/ selection exchange//
cepheus surround dying no world no future/ have humans//
survive us honour us succeed us//
reply await/
firstcircle/ cepheus surround//

To say the members of CEARA were ecstatic was a mild understatement. Here was the chance of a lifetime presented to them on a silver platter, with no bloodshed and political hassles. CEARA had complete control over the matter and soon policies and agendas had been established to allow select humans to travel to Cepheus. With no outside interference or knowledge, and the Cepheusian's technology, the first humans—twelve from each CEARA member nation—travelled beyond the solar system. They were followed by two more such voyages, under cover of umanned payloads lost in space.

In due course, the human Cepheusians had to be genetically altered to survive the environs of space and their new home. While on Earth, the Cepheusians had carried out their terms of the alliance passing on their knowledge, until they had all died out of natural causes.

However, on the Cepheusian home-world, the transplanted humans began to gradually feel more distant from their Earthly counterparts—alien even. There were now over two-hundred modified humans on Cepheus, each one now professing complete loyalty to each other and their new world. It hadn't been their fault, just the natural effects of having a whole new world to themselves with which to begin a new civilization. To complete their transition from normal humans, they began to call themselves Bions.

This sudden change to the agenda did not go down too well with CEARA members when they found out. They had no official headquarters or group meetings to avoid detection and thus member cells often took longer to disseminate information also preferring off-line communications. |But a plot had been devised to take back control over what they considered to be their property. From their ranks, they recruited an operative to go to Cepheus with a team to negotiate a deal. Unbeknownst to the agent, he had been infected with a deadly virus which would wipe out the remaining Cepheusians and the Bions. CEARA would begin again, repopulating the planet with more loyal subjects.

The agent had been sent and within weeks had infected the whole planet. The agent had been discovered, but too late, for during his unwilling quest toward genocide, he had died of the same disease—insurance from CEARA discovery. The Bions however, proved more resistant to the disease and were able to save their own population. The original Cepheusians were not so lucky, dying out completely.

The Bions directly accused CEARA of genocide and attempted genocide, CEARA denying all charges. Cutting all ties to Earth, the Bions declared themselves an independent world. To enforce their point, they set up an orbital defence perimeter, stating if any Earth ship ventured into their territory they would be immediately destroyed. CEARA had lost.

The year on Earth was Nineteen Eighty-Six; Year One on the new Bion calendar.

The Bions consolidated their world by advancing beyond expectations of the Cepheusians. With a smaller population and differing needs than the dead Cepheusians, the Bions had managed to save their world from the brink of death. Within a couple of generations utilising cloning, age prevention techniques, further advanced genetic mods, and other technological innovations, there were now more than five thousand Bions in the year 35AE (After Earth).

Meanwhile, back on Earth, a ruthless policy of denial and disposal existed. CEARA members quietly disappeared and files were destroyed. Though a small covert group remained on sentry should they be contacted again, CEARA otherwise never existed, the Bions never created.

It wasn't until the outbreak of hostilities with the Axalans that the Bions broke their silence and contacted Earth, realising if Earth lost, they would be next. Bion self-preservation was behind Earth's continued survival.

Zero Star itself had then been built in the deep backwaters of Bion-Earth space twenty years into the war. After the first hostile encounter between Earth and the Axalans, the Bions had sent an emissary to Earth, who had managed to contact the surviving version of CEARA. A secret alliance had been drafted, the plans for secret forward bases, initiated and the CEARA files and committee re-instated and updated to become the Extrasolar Agency—ExA.

After two hundred and thirty years, selected humans once again voyaged to the Bion home world, in peace. A new era of cooperation beginning amid the terror of war.

"That is quite a history!" Aaron was impressed.

"Thank you," the young Bion, called Jo-Faen S'jx, replied. "We're very proud of our history and glad we have the opportunity for peaceful coexistence with Earth."

Like most other Bions, Jo-Faen was around 5'2", wiry thin with long limbs and torso. They were hairless but wore ornamental and functional covers over their bodies. Kellis would have described them as Dark Greys, if they had been fictional characters.

"And you're a member of ExA?" Aaron asked Kellis, having heard the whole story.

Kellis had her own special research and development division— of what, Aaron didn't know, yet.

"Yes, there are others like the C.E.F. Hawkhurst, Relentus, plus one hundred and fourteen others, scattered around Zero Star and Earth space. Now you swell the total by one."

Aaron smiled. He had quickly got his first induction into Zero Star. Escorted by Kellis, the young Astrals, and Jo-Faen S'jx, he had toured command and engineering sections, various spacious labs which threatened to overwhelm even his mind and grasp of science, and crew facilities.

Each of the sixty levels of Zero Star and segmented sections had specialized objectives and out of the seven thousand or so scientists and crew (not counting the myriad of robotic workers), less than a hundred were human. Any more and curious people on Earth would start to wonder where the brightest and talented minds were going.

The core of the station consisted of a huge cylindrical one-hundred meter diameter, forty-storey tall arbouretum filled with real plants and fauna, providing an air and water circulation and purificaton system; the foodstuffs providing the humans with nourishment, the Bions having developed different culinary habits and elimination processes. Off the vast garden was a purpose-built four-hundred meter square training area, which Kellis called the 'rough area' able to be converted into wooded areas, jungles, sea- and snowscapes, urban and rural, vacuum and gravity based; every scenario Kellis could think of had been included in her training area. She could also work out her frustrations in them.

"One of my favourite rooms," Kellis had confessed.

Throughout his first few days, Aaron had met virtually every single person on Zero Star. At first, the Bions had all seemed the same to him, but upon being aquainted closely with them, he could see beyond the ashen-grey rubbery skin, hairless bodies, and large multi-coloured glistening eyes, to recognise their individuality. The Bions could see extra colours and wavelengths humans could not. They had superior hearing, but their taste for food was seriously lacking, preferring a diet of red potato-like and purple mushroom-type substances. Even their favourite fruit, an apprel, their variation on an apple-apricot cross tasted like juicy glue. And chocolate made them seriously ill.

"Seriously," Kellis had warned, "don't eat their food."

Aaron had also been surprised how they had retained a lot of humanness in them, like their humanoid form, language (alongside a lingua-Bion), height, and genders, though they could not now reproduce sexually.

"We are true hybrids, with the best of both human and Cepheusian attributes," Jo-Faen explained, her gold, green, and blue-flecked eyes smiling. "Which is why we have a combination of Human and Bion forenames with a Cepheusian surname. We preserve our hertiage and honour our ancestors!"

In time, Aaron thought, humans would be proud to call the Bions brothers, whenever the truth would be revealed to Earth.

For now Deck 22, section 6, room 7 was his new home. Gazing out into the vast darkness beyond his porthole reminded him of just how far man, especially himself, had come. And for the first time, Aaron had experienced a pang of homesickness.

Leaving Aaron to rest and acclimatise to Zero Star, Kellis met up with Aristedes and Zane for dinner. A thought had been spinning around in her head for a while over something Aaron had said.

In the officers' mess, they were afforded more privacy and Kellis wanted to talk about a sensitive issue, though she knew interrupting Aristedes while eating was a hazardous mission in itself.

"So, something Aaron said got me thinking," Kellis started.

"Oh?" Aristedes chopped into his steak. "What's that

Zane watched on as her brother sawed through his meal like a mad surgeon; munching from her own delicate plate of salad drizzled with olive oil.

"The Starguards—"

Aristedes and Zane stopped eating and regarded Kellis diligently.

"If they died a couple of hundred years ago protecting Earth, because the Astrals placed them there and as they were your kin, why didn't the Astrals save them?"

A small smile of intrigue crossed Aristedes' face.

"Ah, Kellis, we've had many a talk on the subject of time. But now I'll tell you its biggest secret: Time travel is the universe's biggest joke!" He put his knife and fork down and steepled his hands in front of him, his fingers on his chin.

"To us Astrals living in the Chronopolis, we've only just taken the Starguards to Earth, so their deaths are still in the future, your past. Time is in flux to us. We may know what's happened to them, but in our timeline, the Starguards are neither dead or alive, until the event happens, which gives us time to act. The fact we haven't done anything yet shows time hasn't yet caught up to us. Another possibility is that in our future, beyond the current Chronopolis timeline the fate of the Starguards has been determined and they died for a reason or maybe even lived—we don't know what happened to them in that explosion. So that's why the universe laughs at us—all this power over time and we don't know the punchline yet!"

He grinned at Kellis, ripping into his steak, while she and Zane chewed over his words.

Food for thought, indeed, Kellis told herself. However, it left her with more questions. But to ask Aristedes more was to invite more questions about herself, which was best to be avoided.

They finished their dinner in silence.

***

"Ready, Aaron?"

Aaron nodded, standing by to undertake psi-tests with a Bion.

"How's that?" Kellis fitted a thin band of silver to her head.

"Scrambled. I can't sense you at all. Do you feel alright, Kellis?" he asked.

"Yes, so far. Just a bit dizzy, so the sooner you shut up the sooner I can take it off. Are you ready, Jo-Faen?"

The Bion nodded.

"Okay, then let's begin."

Aaron, Kellis, and young Jo-Faen were in an isolation room, Kellis wearing a telepathic-limiter to eliminate her mental emanations from the test. She'd never worn such a strong type before and the psionic interference-emitters were playing havoc with her head—like a psychic version of blocked sinuses. But it was necessary to monitor the test and reactions.

First, Kellis had to figure out who and what Aaron's powers were effective against. He couldn't read Astrals, humans were like open books, Bions were a little harder, but hopefully, if the chance presented itself, the Axalans would be easy to read. Kellis had also been putting Aaron through his telekinetic paces. He could move objects up to a ton in weight, as ably demonstrated in the Rough Area, but confidence in the air cut short his first self-powered flight. Psi-shields around his mind protected him from mind-probes as tested by Bion tech and when formed around himself and others could impressively hold out in the vacuum of space, the power/distance ratio being negligible. The sheer intensity of his powers were unquestionable, but Kellis wanted to know how sensitive it could be. Hence the test to penetrate Jo-Faen's Bion/human mind which had psionic properties of its own.

Jo-Faen had helpfully explained.

"Sometime in the distant past, millennia it has been said, the Cepheusians had developed a hive-mind, but had been forced to abandon it due to their planet's enigmatic collapse. The effort to revert to multi-mindedness and individualism had saved them for a few more millennia, but their world was still dying rejecting their existence, the biosphere altering radically. Their only discourse had been to find another world. So they had become space-farers, exploring the galaxy eventually coming across the Sol system. Mars had been their ideal planet, but the Earth and its inhabitants had intrigued them enough to send probes and scouts, which as you know led to disastrous consequences. But fortunately, the two sides begun a dialogue, which had ultimately led to Mars being abandoned, the hybridisation of humans and Cepheusians, and the saving of our home world through us Bions.

"We Bions still retain a part of the Cepheusian propensity for hive-mindedness like an aura floating in and out of our consciences, like a tangible sixth-sense. In fact, it had been this sense—a foreboding sense of doom—that had alerted us to the danger on Earth from the Axalans."

Kellis interjected, "Your test, Aaron, is to detect this ephemeral force in Jo-Faen's mind and ascertain any information."

"Okay, sure," he replied. *A normal day in my life exploring an alien mind!*

The two were semi-reclined in med couches, instruments monitoring their vitals and brain waves. Aaron prepared himself letting his mind go blank; letting it roam free and comb through the eerie dissonance of Jo-Faen's mind, alien images and thoughts breezing easily by. Jo-Faen had no secrets to hide and even if she did, Aaron wasn't interested in them.

In fact, Jo-Faen seemed to be enjoying the experience. She was of the younger, progressive generation who wanted Earth to know of their presence, but the elders were too cautious, willing to wait and see what the war did for them. Earth's response in defeat or victory would be their lone consideration. Meanwhile, Jo-Faen and others like her associated with the human contingent as much as they could, in order to learn. They would be the first ambassadors to Earth.

Right now, Jo-Faen's usually expressive black eyes were closed, as if she were sleeping, her slight chest rising to the beat of an enlarged heart, a tri-lung system regulating her breath.

Aaron could feel himself pulsing with her bodily functions, so unlike anything he'd ever experienced before, black blood coursing through veins of steel-like quality. The skin, though rubbery, was as durable as spaceship alloy and it was a fact that no Bion had ever cut themselves. Aaron drifted past bundles of nerves that would make even the top-most human neurosurgeon either mad with delight or just plain mad. The Bions had senses and feelings available to them that would take humans another couple of evolutionary steps to discover—

>*Young One!*<

Aaron stopped moving in the mindscape. His own heart thumped within his own ears.

Had he really heard that?

He had entered the Bion's brain, a mass of tightly wound blue-black matter. His mind's eye filtered out all of Jo-Faen's images until it was dark in the psi-scape, except for a blurry aura in the middle of the mindfield.

>*Do not be afraid!*< It pulsed in an indeterminate voice.

>*I'm not*< answered Aaron, not quite truthfully >*Merely surprised*<

>*We did not think we would see another of our kind again. Waiting for you*< the blur flashed.

Aaron's heart froze. >*Another? You are—?*<

>*Chryrian. Yes. Yes, I am. We are!*< It beamed with pride.

Aaron couldn't contain his emotions or words. The togetherness he felt with these others, yes, he could sense more of them now—hundreds of them—was enough for them to answer his questions.

>*We left Chryria before the end of the war. Our defeat was obvious. We drifted, before coming upon the world of the Cepheusians. We tried to merge minds with them, but they were not wholly accessible. It led to an unbalanced group-consciousness that eventually incited wide-spread madness, ruining their world beyond repair.*

>*We managed to separate ourselves from them, hovering in the psi-scape, but without the Cepheusians and their world, we would not survive, so we coaxed them into space to find a new home, whereupon they came across Earth and its inhabitants. We were delighted, for in the humans were suitable hosts, but we could not forget the Cepheusians. They would die because of our interventions.*

*So we compromised, making the humans and Cepheusians agree to
an exchange and eventual hybridisation. That way, both us and the
Cepheusians would survive in the offspring. The original
Cepheusians have died out, but we carry their thoughts with us.<*

>*Why have you done all this?*< asked Aaron.

>*For the protection of the Bions. We have foreseen that Earth,
Bion and Axala will unite to become more than allies and protectors
of the galaxy, but bretheren. Great things will come of them. Long
will they endure. Never will greater deeds be surpassed, or more
triumphant words be spoken. Such is their future. But only if the
Humans and Bions survive.<*

Aaron tried to take all of this in. This mostly made sense to him.
He'd been taken from Earth in the past, only to end up protector of
its future. Had his destiny been written all those years ago, or was it
now beginning?

>*Have you seen any others like me?*< he desperately asked them.

>*Yes, but this other is not compliant, but wild and filled with
anger. They will find you. And try to kill you!*<

Aaron was really confused now, but before he could say anything,
his thoughts were answered in a last prophecy:

>*Daana Aranu, for wont of revenge; for need of love, sacrificed,
this day, his life for the greater glory!*<

And then they were gone.

Aaron floated alone in the psi-scape, horrified at that last
proclamation.

*Haven't I sacrificed anything, yet? What had they meant? Who
was this enemy?* A sudden chill went down Aaron's spine. *It couldn't
be! Not after all this time.* He slumped to the bottom of the dark
mindfield and lay on its murky dreaminess, fighting back the
memories of four thousand years ago.

>*No! Not Now! No! No!*<

"—No!" Aaron's eyes shot opened.

A worried Kellis and Jo-Faen knelt beside him, concern on their
faces.

"What happened?" he asked feebly.

"You tell me," said Kellis, "You were there!"

"I don't know," he said, tentatively.

"Did you find anything?" asked an anxious Jo-Faen.

"No, at least not what I expected," he lied a bit.

"It was like a semi-dormant residual hive-consciousness. I must have gotten too deep and lost in the alien psi-scape and panicked." He smiled ruefully, more at his half-truths than any embarrassment. "You've got quite a mind though, Jo-Faen," he added.

"So I'm always told," said a smiling Jo-Faen, removing monitor cables from her head. She looked at Kellis who was still tending to Aaron, sighed, and quietly left the small, sterile room.

Kellis and Aaron were silent for a few minutes, Kellis gathering data from her computers. Aaron mentally reviewing all he had heard.

"Your heart stopped, you know, for a few moments. Twice!" Kellis stated in clinical tones.

"Really? I hadn't noticed," quipped Aaron, the mere thought making him feel weak again.

Kellis glared at him, looked at her readings, then back at him again   "Yeah, right. This relationship is based on trust you know. If you're going to keep secrets from me already, then we're finished."

"Relationship? I didn't think we had a relationship."

"I meant a working relationship," Kellis stressed with a wry smile.

"Yeah, right."

Kellis glared at him again.

"You know, your lips may be saying 'no', but your mind is saying 'yes'."

"Never mind what my mind says. Read my lips. And besides you're psi-blind." she said, pointing to the telepathic-limiter still attached to her temple.

"It doesn't take a mind reader to know what's on your mind," Aaron said. "Now if we're through, I'm going back to my quarters to rest. It's been a long day. If that's okay with you?"

"No. It's not," replied Kellis sharply. "I've got something I want you to see first." And she threw off her lab jacket.

Protected in the womb of Zero Star was sub-deck zero. It was quite hard to find, next to impossible really, as it wasn't on any of the station's blueprints. It didn't exist. It was Kellis' secret domain. Here were her personal pet projects and black works. Here she could escape and be herself, protected from prying eyes and ears surrounded by heavy shielding with entry denied to all, save herself.

Inside one of the deck's wing labs lay a large transparent bath-like tank, filled with blue liquid which if touched would have frozen the offending intruder's appendage instantly. And in that tank, through the swirling mists, a being of beauty floated, precious white skin in ice-cold blue. Cold wisps of air spiralled into the air, ice particles bobbing gently on the surface. Low, steady beeps of machinery were the only noises in the room, metallic cables and various other connections supplying, monitoring, and extracting vital materials.

She slept serenely in the breathable liquid, unaware of the world outside, oblivious to the changes that time had wrought since last she was awake, heedless to what awaited upon re-awakening.

It wasn't long now.

"What's this all about then?" grumbled Aristedes, upon meeting Zane in the main lab on deck one.

"Dunno. I'm as much in the dark as you are," replied Zane, sounding miffed. She had been torn away from catching up on journal reports. "Kellis said to meet her and Aaron here, so that's what I've done, same as you."

"Okay, okay, don't get your temporal knickers in a twist. I was only asking." Aristedes sighed. "I can't see that it has anything to do with anything in here," he said casting a glance through the lab. "These experiments are mostly complete." They seemed unnecessary to him as if for show only.

"That's because it doesn't," said Kellis, with a sardonic smile on her face, as she entered the lab with Aaron in tow.

Aristedes and Zane looked at her in bewilderment, for Kellis was garbed in an environmental suit, a thin, one-piece, silver-fibred uniform, which with an accompanying personal forcefield could be worn for light duties in the vacuum of space. Kellis regarded them with humour in her eyes; she loved pulling surprises on the young Astrals. Without saying another word, she gave a follow-me nod of the head and walked off toward a darkened wing of the lab.

Aristedes shrugged, annoyed, glancing at Zane and Aaron, before following Kellis. Zane followed, noting that Aaron also looked a bit confused. As for Aaron, when Kellis had told him she wanted to show him something and had then thrown off her jacket, the implied actions—only in his mind, it now seemed—had not happened. Instead, she had simply donned the silver environmental suit, called Aristedes and Zane with some instructions, and then led him down to her main lab on deck one. At least the siblings were as confused as he was. He was gratified to see that they could be surprised and he noted that Kellis still wore her telepathic-limiter. Either she didn't want him to know what was going on, or there were others she was protecting her mind from. Aaron thought about that for a while, almost too absorbed in his thoughts that he almost missed when Kellis, not ten paces away in front of him, walked through a wall and disappeared.

"Why am I not surprised!" remarked Aristedes sarcastically, throwing up his arms. He followed and stepped out from the holographic wall. "This whole place is a holographic warren."

Kellis waited for the other two to appear. Zane arrived, cautiously peering around in amazement and gave a low whistle.

"Geez, Kellis, you sure like spooky places don't you?"

Aaron was quieter, waiting for the next surprise.

Kellis grinned. This was her private world. The surrounding darkness only helped to convey a sense of transition from Zero Star main to her own level, where she controlled its environs. It had always been her little hideaway and now she had let in three others, people whom she trusted. Even Aaron. She felt she had made the right choice. She looked over at Aaron. Not two months ago, he been left dying in the deserts of Africa, four thousand years ago, and now here he was, adjusting to new times, places and people. Now he was sharing in a special moment. And they all knew it. A new bond had been formed, one beyond trust and friendship and to cement that bond, Kellis was about to let them into the core of her world.

The silence between the four spoke volumes, as Kellis activated her suit's forcefield and silently walked off into the dark interior, the others following. The portholeless deck curved around, Kellis knowing they were near the station's core. The curve surprisingly finished at an airlock, space immediately beyond, the unblinking stars in the blackness staring in.

Without hesitation and to the alarm of the others Kellis hauled open the heavy metal door—to reveal another room.

Zane's gasp of surprise was met with a blast of frigid air, her breath becoming misty. Aristedes and Aaron were also suitably stunned, their eyes fixated on the object in the center of the dark room: a regeneration tank. And something was inside.

Again Kellis stepped forth without a word into the frosty beyond.

To Aaron it felt like participating in part of some religious ceremony—a pilgrimage to a holy relic.

Light within the room came from intermittently flashing instrument lights. However, the main illumination emanated from the tank, or rather the fluid itself, which glowed an eerie bluish light, catching the object inside in full light.

Kellis approached the tank and reached out into the fluid, her suit's forcefield protecting her arm. She stroked the being's hair, sending ripples around the tank, surface ice particle jangling in the cold liquid.

Aristedes looked down upon the figure in repose. She was absolutely white.

Gorgeously white, he thought. He couldn't take his eyes off her.

"She's beautiful," was all he could say. He just stood there staring.

"Hello? Earth to Aristedes!" called Zane, catching on to his changed mood.

Aristedes felt hot. For all his Astral powers and aloofness from matters of the heart, this one being was reducing him to a wreck.

"Who . . . who is she, Kellis?" he asked.

Kellis seemed almost as distracted, still stroking the snow-white hair of the female in the tank.

"She's my friend," she answered after a time.

She then looked up, suddenly, as if just remembering she wasn't alone this time. A haunted look crossed her face and she smiled, closing her eyes to hide the faraway look. She seemed to be weighing up her decisions. When her eyes opened again, she was sure of her choice.

"Her name is Starshina. We served together some time ago, but an accident put an end to our past lives. I ended up here, more or less intact, but poor Starshina ended up all changed and comatose, only able to survive in this isolation tank." She looked at the others. "Until now," she whispered.

"You mean she's human?" asked Aristedes looking down at the alabastered-coloured exposed skin and hair.

"Of course she is!" snapped Kellis, more than offended.

"Oh, sorry," shrugged Aristedes, to Zanes tittering and eye roll.

All this time, Aaron had been watching and listening intently. He understood now why Kellis had brought them, him especially, here.

"Even with all this technology, you cannot save the life of your friend," he said.

Kellis sadly shook her head.

Aaron continued. "So you've placed her life in our, my hands. There's a psychological problem. You want me to bring her back for you." The silence returned, the beeps of machinery like heartbeats of decision.

"Yes," whispered Kellis, a glittering like ice in her eyes. "Physically she is fine, but mentally there is nothing whichcan penetrate and repair her consciousness." She looked at Aaron for guidance.

Now Aaron understood the real reason for his tests with the Bions.

"I'm honoured, Kellis, that you trust me that much, so soon," he said. "I'm ready when you are."

Aristedes approached the tank and placed his hand into it. Kellis started, even though she knew his powers were keeping him from being frozen, she'd never seen Aristedes act this way before, watching him caress the cheek of Starshina. She was almost jealous at the attention he was paying to Starshina.

"To hell with honour, Aaron," he said, as if in a dream, "I'm doing this for love." Realising what he had just said aloud, he blushed, small smiles touching the lips of everyone.

"Whatever I can do to help . . ." Zane broke the awkward silence, "to stop my brother from pining away, I'll do it."

Laughter broke out, lightening the mood, somewhat.

"What are we to do?" asked Aaron.

"Well, first off," a more relaxed Kellis said, reaching for a thin silver oval object in a nearby panel, "I place this on Starshina." Aaron recognised it as a telepathic-limiter, but different. "This is a modified limiter," Kellis elaborated. "It's coded to let only certain thoughts and memories to be read." The implications of her statement wasn't lost on the others. Some secrets were to be kept. But at the moment, that mattered to none of them.

With the limiter in place on Starshina's temple, Kellis instructed Aaron on the procedure.

"Make gentle probings as you did with Jo-Faen, explore for Starshina's consciousness, explain where she is, and then accompany her to full consciousness."

Aaron nodded he understood.

A moment's gaze at the serene face in the tank then Kellis looked to Aristedes.

"The critical point is where speed is of the essence. Aristedes, you will teleport her to the recovery room, where Zane and I will complete any medical tests as necessary."

She clapped her hands, muffled by the environmental suit's gloves.

"Right, all set on the plan?" Everyone nodded yes.

Aaron had a little time to prepare himself, sitting on a close-by stool. He closed his eyes and concentrated, entering the psi-scape, where the cosmos was but an extension of the mind. He trod a steep starlit path down into a cold star's heart, delving deeper into the unknown realm of Starshina's mind. There was a momentary brief buzz upon passing the limiter's network, then a veil of greyness appeared, which reminded Aaron of smoke—the cloudy memories of one so long asleep, he guessed. The smoke gradually thinned, getting lighter and lighter, Aaron feeling the warmth of the light. But he couldn't make sense of it all. The deeper he journeyed into Starshina's mind, the more he encountered nothing save for freezing mists. Then the smoky-lightness gave way to a blockage. Aaron saw it as a great door with an icy wall of tangled webs of thought, which dwarfed him. He pulled hard and opened it.

"Aargh!!" he screamed.

A blaze of fire leapt out at him from behind the door. Before he could duck it engulfed him.

"I'm burning! I'm on fire!" he yelled, screaming in pain. He threw up his arms to protect himself.

Outside, in the physical world, Kellis watched in horror as Aaron recoiled in pain from the fires of Starshina's mind. Within the tank, Starshina convulsed. Sub-zero-degree fluid lapped over the tank's edge, Kellis and Zane instinctively moving back.

But Aristedes stayed with Starshina, holding her hand, trying to instill some calm.

"Aaron! Aaron, do something! Control it!" he shouted, as Starshina's body started shaking violently again, ice-fluid surging up and soaking his arms and chest, unaffected against his natural temporal shielding.

Aaron, still caught up in the fire of the mind, immersed himself in concentration, dousing his fears, blanketing and absorbing Starshina's pain. He pushed out his psi-aura further, bolstering his dissonance. A calming stillness ensued. Warm rain washed over him. The fire subsided followed by sudden coldness which swept viciously down and whipped around him. Aaron was forced to the ground, never having experienced anything like it in his life before. Starshina had been holding back the pain, a pain caused by fire for so long that its release had almost cost hers and Aaron their lives. He wondered at the torture her mind must have endured and how it would affect her recovery.

Rapidly, the erratic snowscape around him melted and froze into a fluffy snow-blue field and was decidedly getting chillier. Aaron shielded his eyes against the brutal winds. A bundle in the snowy distance caught his attention.

Approaching slowly, crunching through the deep soft snow, he saw that it was the body of a young woman, pale-faced, long blonde hair and amazingly-dark brown eyes, but undoubtedly the same snow-white-skinned woman in the tank.

"Starshina?" Aaron said in a soft voice. "Hello?"

Head movement. A slow nod. She turned her head and peered up at him, fear in her dark eyes.

"Who are you?" she asked in a little girl's voice, as it began to snow softly.

"I'm Aaron." He put on a friendly smile. "I know a friend of yours who wants to see you. Do you want to see her?"

Starshina was hesitant. Her face seemed to grow paler. She nodded.

"Who?" she whispered.

"Lynn. Lynn Kellis. Do you want to see her?"

There was confusion on her face. "Lynn?"

"Yes, your friend. She wants you to come back. Will you come with me?"

There was hesitation. She appraised Aaron, looked back to the comfort of her cold solitude then back to Aaron. She nodded again, this time with a slight smile, her dark brown eyes and hair becoming paler every second.

Aaron held out his hand and helped Starshina to her feet. She was actually taller than he and to his embarrassment, totally naked. He led her softly through the paths of her once-tortured mind, winter having fully set, the woman behind him now the image of her physical self in the tank.

"Your friends will help you now," he said as they approached consciousness like breaking through the ice to see the welcoming sun. "Don't be afraid," he assured her. "See?"

Showing her through her eyes and beyond the watery reflections, they saw Kellis holding Starshina's hand on one side, Aristedes the other, with Zane at the foot of the tank, and Aaron's body still sat in the chair, motionless. It disconcerted him somewhat to see his own body from the outside, but he still had work to do.

"Follow me," he told her. She smiled understanding. "I will lead you out."

They walked together through the snow field, a nice winter walk, up hills toward the star-lit sky again. They neared the consciousness barrier.

Aaron shivered as he said: "I'm going, for now," he said. "But I will see you again," he promised. Releasing his telepathic link, he slipped back into his own mind.

A voice woke him from his voyage. He opened his eyes taking a deep breath.

"Are you okay, Aaron?" asked Kellis, once he had recovered.

"Did you know what would happen—the fire?" he asked in a sightly groggy voice, knowing the answer before he'd finished the question.

"Not fully, but I expected some . . . difficulties," Kellis confirmed, looking uncomfortable. "I'm sorry."

"Don't worry," Aaron replied, feeling slightly misled and annoyed, "Everything is fine now."

Kellis looked at him about to say something.

"Hey!" Aristedes' shout grabbed everyone's attention. "She's looking at me. She's aware of us," he blurted.

Pale blue eyes stared unwaveringly at Aristedes' dark blue eyes. He smiled down at her and to his astonishment, she smiled back. He looked up at the others, pride on his face, as if this achievement was his greatest accomplishment.

Kellis was beside him instantly. Aristedes could sense the excitement within her. She was close to tears, but her voice remained as steady and professional as ever.

"Okay, Aristedes, phase two. That's if you can disengage yourself from her for a moment."

Aristedes blushed again, Zane giving a bark of a laugh.

"Where to?" Aristedes asked.

"Through the bulkhead to your right is an isolation ward. Starshina should be able to breath and function on her own, now."

Aaron kept a physical and telepathic eye on Starshina as Aristedes prepared to teleport her. She looked peaceful now, a smile on her face. And then she shimmered out of existence along with Aristedes. Hearing activity in the other room, Aaron followed Kellis and Zane out of the cold room, through a seamless sliding door and into what was an isolation room, much like the one he'd been in on Consention Base, except it was cold in here, too. Starshina was radiating cold.

Kellis and Zane completed their checks, Aristedes having been made to give way. A special bed had been prepared for Starshina, around which various diagnostic instruments had been placed monitoring and analysing her internals and psycholoigcal profile, but they had been used sparingly, Starshina's system having held up well. Human twenty-third century and Bion technology, ageless Astral powers, and Chryrian wisdom had combined to save her life. All through this, Starshina had stared at Aristedes, a shy, innocent smile on her face, a sheepish grin on his.

Hera, it's enough to make one sick! thought Zane, though she happily watched her brother make a love fool of himself.

Aaron, however, was more concerned with Kellis. Even though she appeared okay, he could tell something was amiss and he guessed it had something to do with the fact that ever since regaining consciousness, Starshina hadn't once acknowledged Kellis. It was as if she didn't know her.

At that exact point, Kellis looked up at him. For a split second, he saw the disappointment in her eyes. Then it was gone, concealed by her busy activities.

"Where am I?"

Everybody froze.

Starshina's wispy, soft voice had taken them by surprise.

Kellis recovered first. "You're among friends, Starshina," Kellis said, tears welling up in her eyes. She gave Starshina a hug, Starshina's arms embracing Kellis reflexively.

Pale eyes turned to Kellis. "Who are you?" whispered Starshina.

Those words hit Kellis like a physical blow. But Kellis, lips pursed with determination, holding back the tears said:

"I'm Lynn, your friend. You've been . . . not well, for a long time. But you'll get better. I did."

"Lynn? Lynn." Starshina tested the name in her memory. "Yes, I remember. It's been so long, so long . . ." Her voice was a dreamy song as she drifted off to sleep.

Lynn watched over Starshina, stroking her hair.

"You're gonna be alright."

CHAPTER FOUR

Earth was already at war. It didn't need another one. The war against the implacable Axalans had dragged on for decades, yet was very popular on Earth. After all it was about humanity's own survival. More than any other war, including Twentieth and Twenty-first century wars, this one had been beamed into billions of homes in all its graphic 3D detail, via the ever-trusty, virtual war correspondent.

However, there were some battles fought which were never reported on and which Earth would never hear of. In fact, there were battles fought which officially never took place and some not fought which did. These 'never-battles' sanctioned only by Commander Earth Forces himself, were carried out in secret from Base 51, or the 'War Nest' as it was affectionately known by its crew. And it was they who had fought and won the biggest and last of the never-battles.

Two hours ago

"Status, Langley," requested Captain Lars Seton, leaning forward in the command chair of the hunter ship, *Falcon.*

Recalled from the Earth-Axalan Front, Seton and his three-ship force had been under way on their mission for three hours, way beyond the twin red giants of Chaykin's Stars, in search of their prey.

Or rather, we're hanging about as bait waiting to be nibbled at, thought a cynical Seton.

"Nominal, sir," replied the operations officer. "Still in approach pattern delta; two AU out from Easter Planet. All sensors clear," she coolly reported, as only she could.

Seton, somewhat dissatisfied, frowned, nodding a weary acknowledgement as he exchanged glances with his first officer, Riley. This was the sort of mission he had dreamed of. Yet, even though he craved this battle, he was finding his will to fight faltering. Back at the Front, where the *Falcon* had been on reconnaissance missions, the Axalans were bold adversaries, never absent. But here, their quarry had yet to reveal itself. Seton was both dreading and anticipating the encounter.

Do or die, he thought to himself.

The fact that the War Nest crews had given their sole enemy the moniker Starfighter Machine was of no consolation. Even now, the deceptively chilling tribute to it echoed in Seton's mind:

'What are little Starfighter Machines made of?
Venom and spite and all things not right.
That's what little Starfighter Machines are made of!'

It had been heartily sung openly during the first few encounters, but now its tune haunted them at every defeat. Starfighter Machine was like a dark dream, fast becoming a nightmare of mythical proportions. It was fearful, powerful, and of no known species. Hostile, non-communicative, and not part of Earth's war strategy, Starfighter Machine had to be destroyed.

Seven months ago. Deep space
"Holy Hosannah! Would you look at that!"
Or so the record books state the first words were upon discovering an amazing world.

Easter Day, and one Captain Stanz Roggeveen had ventured past the farthest point of human-explored space beyond Chaykin's Stars, scouting for any backwater Axalan activity. Instead, he had stumbled across a solitary, idyllic world. He had duly dubbed it Easter Planet. Some lower-deck historian in the crew had noted that a namesake, if not an ancestor, had pretty much done the same thing on Earth when Easter Island—or more appropriately Rapa Nui—had been discovered over five hundred years ago. Whether Stanz Roggeveen was conscious of that, he never acknowledged it in his logs.

Studied from long range, it also happened this world was rich; rich beyond reckoning with metals the ship's sensors could not identify. Enough metal to build a whole new fleet, enough for this world to become a vital base, a world from which to strike back at the Axalans. Earth needed this world. Easter Planet could win Earth the war.

But as Roggeveen's ship, the *Harrier*, had closed in on the planet to retrieve samples, they had been attacked by a creature. Some of

74

the crew had said it was some sort of spaced-out, maniac, robotic fighting-machine. Roggeveen had put up stiff resistance, but had been forced to retreat. That had made him even more determined to have this world.

So he had called in reinforcements, claiming—legitimately at the time—he had been attacked by superior forces, possibly an Axalan weapon. The War Nest had dispatched the space carrier, *Eyrie*, along with the destroyer, *Phoenix*; the other, *Thunderbird*, remaining at base. They were to hunt down the unknown menace and destroy it.

The small hunter-class ships were sleek, bird-like, rapiers of reinforced quadrasteel death with the latest lasers for talons. With a crew of seventy or so, the capability to go undetected, and strike anywhere, anytime, had distinguished the ten bird-named hunter ships at the Battle of Centauri Proxima, six years before. That daring assault against superior Axalan advance forces had bolstered Earth's forces and hopes, establishing an off-world beachhead. It had also earned one young Lieutenant Lars Seton, after taking command of his striken ship when his superiors had died, the coveted golden star medal and a promotion.

Roggeveen's hunter force had approached Easter. And out of nowhere had been attacked again and devastated by the same mysterious foe. All the shell-shocked crews had reported seeing was fleeting darkness dealing deadly, bright light. They had said it moved at the speed of thought anticipating their every move. Though the hunter force could have been totally destroyed, the remorseless marauder had withdrawn back into space, leaving mightily relieved crews to limp home in broken ships.

Roggeveen had not been so lucky. He had been the only one to die. Some had taken this to be just revenge, an omen to leave well enough alone.

However, Earth Forces Command had other ideas and within weeks the War Nest had re-fitted the hunters and re-assessed their strategy. They were not going to be defeated by this inhuman antagonist. It was definitely not Axalan—it was too subtle a weapon for them. It had also been ruled out as a potential ally: communicating with it, what little they had attempted, was impossible. There was no other choice. Earth needed Easter Planet.

The Starfighter Machine had to be destroyed. And Seton and the *Falcon* had been recalled from the Front for the vital task.

Even then, Seton had been drawn to Starfighter Machine; fascinated even. It reminded Seton of himself, an earlier self: wild, hungry and unafraid of death. He was passing through his late thirties now, grey flecks of hair starting to push out the brown; fiery blue eyes turning ice cold within a weathered face, the desire of battle wearing thin. This was his last chance at glory.

Seton had remembered his conversation with the Nest's Base Commander, Commodore Hoult on his return from the Front, concerning the new enemy: "

"How do we know how strong it is, or how many more there are?" Seton had asked.

"We won't know until we destroy it!" had come the Commodore's sharp retort.

Soon after, Earth Forces Command had again ordered a series of probing, unmanned attacks, to no avail. All ships lost to Starfighter Machine. That was when Earth Forces Command had lost patience and ordered an all-out attack. Seton's opposition to the plan was a lone voice in the void, even as he was appointed the mission leader.

Do or die, he recited the mantra himself. *Command's orders.*

So the hunters had advanced again and bombed the hell out of Easter. For hours on end, long range destruction unleashed living death, turning a lush world into a barren, broken wasteland. A job well done.

And still it had survived.

The thing, the Starfighter Machine, had stormed up from the bowels of oblivion and poured down upon the hunters, drenching the crews in unforgiving energy, melting skin from bone, eating bone from sinew, turning man into the primordial soup from which he had evolved.

Seton could almost smell the bloodied, broken, and imploded bodies drifting in the dead cold of space.

Hunters were blown to dust, spread to the solar winds, sunk to the depths of fathomless space, lost beyond hope.

Starfighter Machine returned to its dead world.

Only the *Falcon* had survived by, in Seton's words, a stroke of luck. Starfighter Machine had seemed to overlook them. But his crew had claimed they owed their survival to Seton's intuitive and incisive command. Praise like that rankled Seton. Sometimes life owed more to luck than skill. Starfighter Machine had let them off.

Hope was fading fast. Not only had the Axalans increased their activities along the Front, there was also growing concern that Starfighter Machine would encroach beyond its territory, a second war front to be avoided.

Something had to be done.

One week ago. The War Nest

Commander Earth Forces, General Augustus Hawkhurst, an ultra-hawk with retro-imperialism written into his genes by successive generations of military forefathers, had chaired a 'light' conference, the holographic images of himself and his war-committee convening with War Nest's command. Seton and Riley sat with Hoult and his staff at one end of the oval table across from the images.

A scientist briefed: "On study of the data gained from recovered probes ejected from the ships before destruction, it seems this creature consists of an unknown metallic alloy, whether it is robotic or otherwise in origin. It also somehow thrives on energy, enabling it to absorb and negate the ships' weapons and systems, and to redirect that energy back against our forces. However, analysing its tactics and trajectory it only attacked when anything entered within a quarter AU's distance around Easter."

"Thank you, professor MacMillan," Hawkhurst dismissed the scientist. "As we at Command see it we have two choices: a massive overload of Starfighter Machine or a complete energy drain. Command have opted for A, if such a thing was possible." His lips were a grim line of determination.

It would have to be, Seton had mused to himself, not entirely sure if anything would work against the Starfighter Machine, not sure why he had such thoughts. *I don't really want revenge upon the thing, do I?* He didn't know. His silent reticence had attracted the attention of Hawkhurst.

"You have concerns, Seton?" the frosty-browed general had asked tersely, his image wavering as he continued. "This thing damn-well near destroyed our fleet; knocked them from out of the skies; killed your friends, my men. Do you doubt this mission?" had asked his grave voice.

Seton didn't want to look away from C.E.F Hawkhurst's steely gaze He knew the General was not really talking about the deaths of other crews, but of one soldier in particular. Seton had bad memories about that, too.

"I just have a bad feeling about it all, sir," Seton answered the hologram in as even a voice as he could, willing his heart to beat slower.

"Well your orders are now tabled," he confirmed, even as Hoult and the other captains responded to beeping screens within the table. "You report to me how you feel after you kill that sonovabitch!" The General's voice echoed around the room, even as his image winked out.

The meeting over, the mission agreed, Seton, who had commanded and survived, intact, more missions than anyone else in the hunter-fleet, wondered if he would be returning.

Five hours ago

After days of mission training and briefings, the *Falcon*, the only serviceable hunter and the remaining destroyer, *Thunderbird*, equipped with the newly-devised, star-killer pulse-torpedoes, a lethal plasma concoction intended to overload Starfighter Machine, had ventured out on their quest. They were joined by the support carrier, *Griffin*, loaded with a thousand battle-hardened Foreign Legion Aero Commandos, the only unit to have fought hand-to-hand with the physically-superior Axalans on a frozen moon around Centauri Proxima driving the aliens back.

The FLAC, a notoriously merciless unit, could kill anything, it was said of them—even if it was already dead, others dared to joke. And Starfighter Machine was surely a ghost of death. The FLAC had never lost a battle. They were there just in case things got nasty.

Now they were hunting in the dark.

One hour ago. Deep space

On the *Falcon* bridge, Seton took a sip of his strong green tea—he looked down sharply into his cup—

Not tea, whatever it is! Hot, bitter and dark. He raked his tongue across his lips, disappointed, putting the cup down.

Consoling himself, he glanced around the bridge, admiring, not for the first time, his tenacious crew's efficiency. No raw recruits made it to the War Nest, it was strictly third-year veterans and above after a rigorous selection process.

Seton, with sixty-one percent of his original crew still intact (the rest were due to transfers and five deaths) had the best record and one of the best crews in the entire Earth fleet. They had put that down to Seton, who had been in some pretty dire scrapes throughout his career, but had always come through virtually unscathed.

He and General Hawkhurst's son, Plantagenet or 'Tad' to his friends, brothers in all but name, had been destined for the top. They had been deemed some kind of twenty-third century wonders, demigods, among the fleet, who had turned down promotion after promotion to Earth Command to remain in the thick of battle. However, young Hawkhurst's premature death at Centuari Proxima had ended Seton's meteoric rise, despite his promotion to captain.

No one really knew Seton, his drives; his secrets. But this time he felt others thought his time was up. And he did not welcome that. Starfighter Machine be damned.

I'm not dead just yet, Seton vowed to himself.

He was about to ask for another status report from his operations officer, Lieutenant. Langley, when the same blonde officer's head had snapped up in surprise.

"Sir! I'm getting some mighty funny readings from the vicinity of Easter!" she excitedly announced, her Martian accent even more pronounced.

Seton almost grinned, his smile twisting grimly.

"Define 'mighty funny' Lieutenant?" he asked, ignoring Langley's uncharacteristic flap.

Oblivious to any slip on her part, she reported, "Readings are erratic, but of an energy consistent with the Starfighter—Jesus Jupiter!" her blue eyes widened in disbelief; "The readings just went off the scale . . . and then died. It's gone! But . . ." She hesitated as she anxiously tapped away at her controls. ". . . But I've pinpointed its last position!" She looked back up at the captain, youthful, freckled features belaying vast experience both in space and on the Martian Plains.

Seton rose from his chair with his cup, careful not to rush and spill his drink. On reaching Ops station in front of him, he confirmed his subordinate's readings. Not that he didn't trust her, he just had to see for himself. But sure enough, something strange was happening around Easter.

One thing Seton had always relied upon was his gut feeling. And he was listening to it now.

"Alert *Thunderbird* and *Griffin*: we're going in."

Nervous glances were exchanged among the crew.

"Helmsman Bray, set course for Easter," he ordered. "This is the Captain. Stand to!" snapped over ship's comms.

The bridge lights dimmed to battle stations. Seton returned to his seat, but did not sit down. He found his standing up in times of adversity gave others confidence and kept them on their toes.

Falcon aimed purposely for Easter. They were being lured in, Seton knew. But it was his job to fly into the unknown. They would be the bait and if Starfighter Machine attacked, the *Thunderbird* and the FLAC would move in for the kill.

Maintaining wary caution in their velocity and approach as they neared Easter, Langley read out the distances.

"Passing one AU!"

Everyone's senses clicked into automatic alertness. Machinery bleeped away, counting down the eternal-like seconds.

"Point seven-five!"

The total concentration of the bridge crew focused as one—the *Falcon*'s eyes. Seton, in detached authority, stared straight at the main screen as if he could reach out and touch the blackness beyond.

"One half!" Langley called out.

The bridge seemed hotter, sweat clearly visible on some foreheads. Fists clenched in anticipation. Eyes narrowed. Hearts beat faster. Anxious prayers were invoked as the line of death approached.

Time passed in slow motion. Space lost all reality.

Langley gritted her teeth, "Point two-five AU!"

. . .Came . . .

. . .And went.

And no attack. Unbearably so. There were no signs of relief—everyone was still seemingly holding their breath.

Seton could feel the tension around him, everyone looked to him, but he liked that. He drew strength from it. He looked around the darkened, compact bridge.

Matt Riley, ever-dependable, strode the bridge hunching over various consoles trying to figure out what they were all thinking:

What the hell was happening?

Seton knew Riley from before the war and was known to be an outstanding officer, always following orders. With an uncanny ability to always land feet first, he'd been dubbed 'Resourceful' Riley, Seton not knowing Riley to be without an idea or plan for something. The crew loved him and Seton often wondered how long his own or the crew's morale would have survived without Riley. It sometimes even made Seton jealous. But he could be a bastard at times and reminded him so much of young Hawkhurst.

There were calls from *Thunderbird* and *Griffin*, as anxious and as mystified as they were.

Seton ignored them. He was about to take a gamble.

Time to do or die.

"Take us down, helm," he ordered, voice steady and calm.

The bridge became deadly silent. All eyes bore into him, astonished.

"Take us down," he firmly repeated, staring resolutely at the ship's forward screen.

Helmsman Bray, somewhat uncertainly, obeyed.

Seton had to find out what was happening on Easter. And meet his destiny.

He could feel Riley at his shoulder.

"That wasn't in our orders, sir," he discreetly pointed out to his captain. "We don't know what's down there!"

Seton gave his long-time friend a reassuring look. "Riley," he said in an almost faraway voice, as they stood together at the captain's chair, "Do you trust me?"

The question seemed to catch Riley by surprise.

"Yes, of course," he said, wondering if he'd hesitated too long.

"Then do so, now." He looked deep into Riley's eyes, "For all our sakes." It was all he could say. He smiled again.

How could Riley or anyone else know how he felt? How ever since as a young boy, he had just felt as if he didn't belong in the land of the living. So he had hurled himself into battle, to face death, a death that never came. And yet in this war others had followed him to that brink. Young Tad Hawkhurst had matched Seton's desire, but for Glory, out of duty to an expectant father. A father who had callously driven a wedge between the two during the Battle of Centauri Proxima, after years of watching Seton eclipse his son.

But it had been Seton, commanding the dying ship, who had issued the fateful battle orders from which young Hawkhurst had never returned. Only Seton had known the real motive for his action: Tad had his moment of glory. Only Seton carried that burden alone. Now Seton tired of death; wanted to give something back, to prove something to himself. But that damned thing out there, that Starfighter Machine, awaited him, taunted him with one last look into the face of death. He could feel it. He had to meet it; to face death once more. And live.

Seton looked at Riley to see if he understood, but there was nothing, save for a glimmer in his eyes that he couldn't quite place.

Riley was silent. He returned Seton's look, searching for answers. He had known Seton for ages, but had never understood him. He never would.

"Trust me," Seton repeated.

"I'll be with you," Riley replied, placing a comforting hand on Seton's shoulder.

Seton gave him a weary smile as Riley turned and walked back to his station.

"This is the Captain. Maintain battle stations, prep for descent," Seton confidently announced over the ship's intercom. He turned to Riley behind him, "Matt, ready a field unit."

Riley obeyed. If there was any surprise at that order, he didn't show it. He contacted the appropriate crew.

Busy action whirled around Seton as the crew readied for battle. The planet loomed larger on the *Falcon*'s main screen.

I'll just die if I don't come through this alive, thought a humourless Seton.

Minutes later, angry swirls of fiery red and yellow-brown gas marked *Falcon*'s thrust into Easter's turbulent atmosphere, silent, save for periodic readings from bridge crew.

Seton ordered the *Thunderbird* and *Griffin* to stay in covering orbit until they were needed. There were protests from the captains.

"I repeat Captains Neillo and Sand, you will stay in covering orbit, until I say otherwise."

"*Sacre bleu!*" Neillo, commandant of the FLAC cursed.

"We'll be bait!" *Thunderbird*'s captain Sand replied.

But both commanders remained in orbit to Seton's relief.

Cutting through the volatile atmosphere, every jolt upon the *Falcon* from buffeting winds, was like an attack upon the ship by invisible forces. It jarred everyone's nerves even more. But they persevered.

Helmsman Bray charted a course to near the last known position of the enigmatic energy readings. Seton felt strangely calm.

Falcon burst out from the menacing clouds, dead, black ground below, parts glistening as if scorched into multicoloured glass.

"There," pointed Seton at his comm screen, relayed to the main screen for Bray to see. An area of flat brown wasteland.

"Aye, sir," came the helmsman's reply, inputting the coordinates.

Falcon landed firmly, barely disturbing the hard plasma-blasted ground .

Almost immediately after, Seton made a choice.

"Landing party, Matt. Eight, including us. Full field-suits. Armed. Docking bay in ten," he tersely ordered.

Riley opened his mouth to contend the decison, but Seton's glare brooked no response.

"Yes, sir." He turned to commsman Marsh to call up the relevant landing crew.

Ten minutes later after a quick inspection and address, the suited landing party exited the *Falcon* into the poison air of Easter and fanned out over the still smouldering, ashen hills, devastated by their past bombardments. Black smoke blew everywhere, Seton's helmet visor also reading sub-zero temperatures.

Readings for the Starfighter Machine's last position was six kilometers to the north in a rugged area. They set off.

They had only been out for a scant ten minutes, when contact with the *Falcon* and the ships above had been unexpectedly lost, due to, Seton was told, atmospheric disturbances. He looked around to *Falcon*'s position hidden behind the hills. But only constant thick smoke blew across the land. He could see nothing.

"Keep trying to regain contact," Seton told Ramierez, the accompanying commsman.

"Aye, sir."

They trudged through the ash for a distance, up and around a system of ridges to where a huge deposit of metal had been indicated by their readings. As Seton topped the rise he stopped dead, a horrific scene spread achingly before him.

There were bodies. Metal bodies. Thousands of them. Tens of thousands. A sea of bodies as far as the eye could see, the glistening land, of every colour and more which they had seen from above as they landed.

Seton stood in silence, too choked to speak, his mind a jumble of thoughts.

"My God! What have we done?" Riley gasped, before the others could, his shaky voice crystal clear in Seton's field-suit intercom.

But Seton somehow knew the truth, knew what had happened.

"We didn't do this!"

The others turned, mouths agape, to question him.

The bodies, strewn everywhere, dead, but intact, had been dead long before Easter had been discovered, Seton knew.

"It's a graveyard," Seton simply said. "The last resting place of a metalloid race."

And Starfighter Machine had been its protector, the others started to realise, like an alien, metallic Anubis. They felt like graverobbers.

The silence rang through them like a death-knell. Seton said his own private prayers. Long minutes passed by, the wind blowing swirls of ashes into the air, until Seton broke the mesmerising spell.

"Ramierez, can you raise *Falcon*, yet? Report our situation?"

"Not yet, sir . . . too much interference. Sorry," he added softly.

Seton knowing his last word expressed more than just his inability to cut through the interference. He felt for him.

"Better yet," Charmers, the commanding security officer spoke up, "Call the *Griffin* and get the FLAC down here. Let them kill the last of 'em and get the hell out of here!"

Seton felt his anger rise, just staring at the burly man who shrugged his shoulders in defence. The officer was afraid, but no fool. Seton turned to Riley for support.

Riley also shrugged, as much as he could in the bulky field-suit, his tone defensive.

"With all due respect, Lars, we've already exceeded our orders. What else is there?"

Seton looked off into the distance, blinking as the metal sea glinted eerily from reflected sunlight that somehow filtered through the choking atmosphere.

His voice was barely a whisper. "I was hoping to make peace."

A splutter of surprise escaped Riley's lips, a look of amazement on his helmeted face. He marched up to his captain.

"Peace!" he practically spat. Seton never failed to surprise him. But it had not been unexpected.

Different eyes beheld his captain and friend as he reminded himself of his orders and duty to his ship. If Seton couldn't carry out his orders....then. Riley remained aware of the weight of the armament belted to his waist.

"Here is a world of a dead race," Seton continued, "There's only one survivor. Yes, this is a battle, Riley, but a battle for peace! And I can win it if you give me a chance." He looked at Riley earnestly.

Riley brought a gloved hand up to wipe dust from his faceplate, disguising his nervousness.

He shook his head. "Captain, I think you're forgetting, sir, that this one survivor can make us all extinct. Just like them out there!" Riley pointed to the metal sea. "It don't need saving, it needs to be killed! Those are our orders!"

There were murmurs of agreement. Riley stood helmet to helmet with the captain, waiting for a reply.

Discreetly, his right hand inched slowly toward his side-arm, a pulse-pistol.

Charmers saw the movement and mimicked Riley. He didn't understand Seton sometimes, but if Seton insisted on this course of action then something would have to be done. Sooner rather than later.

Riley stared Seton in the eyes, but before Seton could respond, Ramierez called out.

"Sir, I just got the *Falcon*! Garbled. Then dead on all frequencies. I think . . . I think they needed help, sir!" He sounded unsure and worried. The wind had picked up, threatening even to drown out Ramierez's words through the intercom, but Seton had still heard the fear in his voice. They were all scared.

"I think we should leave, sir. In fact, I strongly recommend we get the hell out of here, now!" Riley reiterated Charmer's words. "Damn the beast and let's get away alive! Let the *Thunderbird* and the FLAC deal with this!" He shouted.

Seton was again surrounded by murmurs of agreement.

Charmers unclipped his side-arm, ready.

Seton is mad, he thought. If Riley was to take action, Charmers knew which side he would be on.

Seton winced at Riley's idea. But they were on a hostile world and cut off from their ships. Seton looked up into the skies, but of course could see nothing untoward. Yet, if only he had the chance, he knew he could do it.

Just one chance, he grimaced.

He turned away from Riley and his men to look out once more over the sea of dead. He had to think, fast.

"You go!" he ordered. "I'll follow . . . soon," he lied.

His men looked about in confusion between Riley and their captain, not sure what to do.

Seton listened as the wind picked up, howling through his intercom. It was brisker now and a chill down Seton's back made him shiver. Instantly he remembered he was wearing a sealed field-suit, the wind couldn't possibly affect him. But he knew what he had just felt. It was the shiver of fear, that primal force which always alerted oneself to another's presence.

They were not alone. Seton spun.

And it was there: Starfighter Machine.

It stared down upon them from on top of an adjacent ridge, like black doom beneath the ruined sky. Seton's men whirled as one and saw it too.

Nobody moved. No one dared breathe.

Seton couldn't believe his eyes. The creature was incredible: an eight-foot-tall monolithic mass of solid, black metal, humanoid in shape with legs that ended in spikes and arms ending in three spike-like appendages. Its diamond-shaped head, though non-discernable of facial features, regarded them coldly from upon shoulders which curved up at the ends into vague winglets. There were no markings on its 'skin' despite the barrages it had taken during battle. It was pure menace, a terror to behold.

Slowly, ever so slowly, Seton edged past his men, ignoring Riley's harshly whispered protests and his now-drawn weapon. Spreading his arms out in a non-threatening gesture, Seton stopped roughly halfway up the ridge that Starfighter Machine stood upon, the unbowed enemy seemingly regarding them with indifference.

"Magnificent!" Seton whispered in awe.

"Captain!" Riley whispered into the field-suit's intercom, "Move away slowly. I'll try for a clear shot." His right hand held his weapon still pointed in Seton's general direction.

Charmers aimed his weapon, matched by his four security crew.

But Seton did not move or utter a word. He could only see Starfighter Machine.

"For God's sake, Lars, move it!" Riley repeated in harsh tones, his body shaking. Sweat, or was it tears, stung his eyes, and his breath was heavy in his ears.

Seton ignored Riley.

It all made sense to him now. This was the moment he had dreamed of as a boy—his last day—his day of judgment. Now it was upon him. And he knew somehow Starfighter Machine knew that. Whatever language Starfighter Machine used or however it thought, Seton knew there was a bond between them, something psychic he thought, both death-seekers in their own way. Starfighter Machine had fought for something beyond its own life, something Seton never had done.

It was then Seton's wish for death deserted him. Here in front of him was his reason to live. A redemption of sorts. But now it was too late. The nature of the beast could not be changed. Starfighter Machine knew no peace; not in the human sense. It had brought Seton here to show him death. Someone always had to die.

Riley had his orders. He remembered when he had first heard his secret orders, just before the 'light' conference at the War Nest, and how he had replied: "I've never understood the captain; but to betray him?"

He had questioned General Hawkhurst's orders, at first, but Starfighter Machine was to be destroyed at all costs. Earth's future could depend on it. Anything or anyone contrary to that was expendable. Riley would take control of the *Falcon* and bring the crew back if Seton deviated from the plan. Riley realised Hawkhurst had known all along what Seton would do. And had used it; used it to avenge his son. But worse, Riley agonised, was that Seton knew that Hawkhurst knew he would disobey orders.

Typical Seton.

Riley didn't know whether to admire Seton's courage or to damn the arrogant audacity of playing into Hawkhurst's hands.

Bastards.

And he was one himself. But he had his orders.

Do or die! Riley echoed Seton's oft-repeated creed.

Hawkhurst had ordered the same. Just as Seton had ordered young Hawkhurst to his death. Riley never knew if Seton had willingly sent Tad to his death for whatever reason and he doubted even Seton knew himself. But it was happening all over again. Seton had to be stopped.

For his part, Seton didn't care about anything else, save the Starfighter Machine.

How alien we are, Seton thought, *to ourselves and to others.*

Riley, aimed at Seton, about to press the trigger.

Sweet Jesus! he thought to himself. *Stop Seton!*

Mute and motionless, the Starfighter Machine stood there as Seton gingerly approached it. He figured he was dead anyway, no matter how far he tried to run away. He inched closer and closer and yet nothing happened. His men were deathly quiet, until . . .

Seton touched it, snatching back his finger.

Nothing happened.

He pressed his fingers a little longer. His heart raced around within his chest, making him feel sick from the blood rush.

Starfigher Machine's skin was metal, yet of a metal Seton had never touched before. There was no internal humming, nor was it hot or cold.

He turned to his men, a huge grin on his face.

"I think it's dead or dormant, or whatever. It isn't switched on."

The men weren't sure if to be overjoyed or scared witless.

Seton caught Riley pointing the gun at him.

Riley hesitated a beat then holstered it. If Starfighter Machine was dead, Seton didn't need to die.

"So, now what, sir?" Riley found his voice, asking as innocently as he could.

Seton was about to answer when there was movement over a nearby hill. It was Langley, her tall lanky Martian exo-skeleton-enhanced frame recognisable as she led a five-man team over to her Captain.

"Sorry, sir. We had to make sure you were . . ." She stopped short as she saw Starfighter Machine and then the metal bodies. She whistled in awe.

"Flinking Phobos!" she swore.

"We thought you were destroyed," Ramierez breathed a sigh of relief.

"We thought the same of you," Langley breathed out.

The two groups converged, exchanging stories, until Seton caught their attention.

"I want it!"

The babble of voices stopped.

"Sorry, sir?" Riley asked.

"I said 'I want it'. We're taking it with us." Seton's voice was firm.

Riley's eyes almost bulged out of his suit. "Uh, I . . . I don't recommend. . . . such action, sir," he stammered.

"It could be a trick, like the Trojan Horse!" Charmers joined in.

Without taking his eyes off the statue-like alien, Seton said, "This thing could have killed all of us, at any time. It still could. It won't matter if we leave it here or not. I think it's time to make peace, if we can, if it's not dead. So, I want it. Do you hear me? I want it! That's an order!"

Seton got his way.

A containo had been dispatched from the *Thunderbird*, once comms had been re-established. Starfighter Machine had been sealed in and returned to the orbiting destroyer.

They had left the dead world, never to return.

The reception back at the War Nest had been mixed to say the least. Seton, the war hero, had done the impossible again and actually captured the Starfighter Machine.

Head up, hands clasped on his desk back in his office on the War Nest, Seton had asked, "Do we need to talk about what happened planetside?" he asked Riley, sat across from him.

Eyes resolutely ahead, Riley shook his head. "No, sir." Nothing else needed to be said. He removed his hands from the metal desk leaving damp marks behind.

Seton handed Riley a comm padd. "Transfer accepted. Anywhere you want."

Riley nodded. He was done here. "Thank you, sir." He stood up, saluted, and left.

Seton sat alone in his office. "Do or die," he smiled.

Command had been furious at first, but as the months wore on and Starfighter Machine seemed dormant enough, it was decided to study the creature for any advantages it could give.

Easter Planet had been quarantined with no expeditions permitted under threat of death, lest it 'revive' the alien overseer. And the prospect of using the bodies of aliens, even for its metal, seemed inhuman. But while exobiologists had treated their new toy with respect, Starfighter Machine refused to yield its secrets.

One of the scientists knew they would gain nothing here, but if Earth-based scientists got their hands on it, then any relevant data would be lost, buried, misinterpreted, or hoarded. There was only one thing to do. Returning to her quarters, she sought out a long-hidden device. When she had found the communicator, emblazoned with a stylised sword-hearted hawk, she keyed in half-forgotten codes. After a while, the device beeped an acknowledgement, much to her relief.

And she sent her message to a far-off place called Zero Star.

Interlude

The Magna Aura System

"Hades, that hurt!" cursed a zapped Lightstream, rubbing her arms, as she floated dejectedly in space. "Celestra, that bitch!"

As with all Astrals and Starguards, Lightstream's natural temporal powers protected her from the harsh vacuum of space. She hung in space sweeping back her long blonde hair. Zane had once described her cousin's red and gold uniform as a cross between a Roman soldier and Supergirl. Lexa didn't totally understand, but as Lightstream, all she knew was fighting the Lore and keeping Magna Aura, the Chronopolis, and her birthplace of Earth safe.

But there was a problem with the Magna Aura system. Her father, Helexius, had asked Lightstream to investigate after communication and their surveillance of the system through their main crystalator orb had been lost. Lightstream had bounded in from the timestream and been promptly cast out of the temporal portal.

A forcefield? A confused Lightstream frowned.

But the forcefield was impenetrable even to her—indeed she had positively bounced off it with some force. The forcefield wasn't just temporal, it had an extra-dimensional lattice layered within the substrates—Celestra's work, Lightstream knew the patterns and frequencies she could see through the timestream and beyond as bright swirling strings and bubbles.

Lightstream couldn't use her stealthy portals to slice through from normal temporal space or even from phase space. It was an anti-Astral field. And it was sealing Magna Aura off not only from her, but also the entire realm of time and space.

But why? Lightstream thought to herself, staring through the invisible field (in normal space that was) toward the yellow sun of Magna Aura. She herself was stranded past the orbit of Aurana, the last of the Magna Auran worlds, and somewhere within were the twin planets of Halcyon and Placia, where most of the inhabitants lived.

The Astrals had already planned to transport the Starguards Sceptre, Altair, Urana and Azure, even if against their knowledge and will, to protect the Earth from any Lore attacks. That would have left Decion, Astara, Alpha Rion, and Cirrius to defend the Magna Aura system, along with the Astrals. And hopefully, Novan was still on his voyage to find his mother, the Goddess Elysius, after his vision. So why was the system field in place and why wouldn't Celestra have reported this to Helexius? The field wasn't an anti-Lore system so it was of no benefit in that respect.

Lightstream could guess some of the truth; no doubt Celestra's rebellious parents, Netherlord and Timechantress had played some part in this, but Lightstream didn't know why the rest of the Starguards would go along with cutting themselves off.

That's if they know, she thought grimly.

"Something's not right, here," she told herself.

Lightstream knew Cirrius didn't trust them and had already invented counter-measures against their surveillance crystals, but while this system field was of another order, she felt sure Cirrius would have found something to penetrate or negate it. All Lightstream could think was that Celestra, or rather her parents and Archron, didn't want the other Astrals to know what was happening within the Magna Aura system.

"Not good," she muttered to herself. There was only one thing for it.

Lightstream flickered out of existence travelling downtime. She could at least find out when the field was erected—

"Oww!" she screamed, jolted violently into real space, spinning end over end. Her head reeled from the pain.

A chaos knot! They were everywhere in the timestream around Magna Aura. *Timechantress' signature for sure.* Now she knew. She shook her head, still a bit groggy.

"Mother and daughter together. So this is where they've come since leaving the Chronopolis, along with Netherlord and Archron, holed up here for whatever reason."

Then Lightstream felt it. A slight shiver in the timestream. They had tried to hide something. With bright grey eyes she peered at the streaks and eddies of the timestream reading the fleeting signs—her forte.

"A trail?"

Lighstream concentrated further. The fabric of the timestream, its patterns and disturbances, almost sang to her.

Not long after the Lore war, the timestream was littered with dead portals, inelegantly folded space, or dead zones—Lore graves, their energy dissipated or leeched throughout the system. But there was something else, Lightstream could almost see. She phased gently into the timestream careful not to set off any temporal and chaos knots and get bounced out again.

Straining her senses among the shifting colours, vibrations, flows, directional fields and particles of the timestream a familiar pathway wound away into the temporal distance.

"That's my path to Earth," Lightstream exclaimed.

But when she looked closer, a shadow appeared. The energy signature was depressed, a dimensional echo. It may have fooled others, but Lightstream knew it was not the trail she had used to take the Starguards to Earth.

"Celestra again!" Sharpening her vision, Lightstream could see from the energy wake that Celestra hadn't travelled alone.

She sighed, closed her eyes, and mustered everything of her temporal vision. She finessed the hidden path, reflecting her own energy off the timestream to read the energy waves of other travellers. Other bands of energy wafted back to her, di-energon and a Lore-based signal, very faint, but unmistakeable. She knew at once what had happened.

This she had to report to her father. But just before she hightailed it from Magna Aura, Lightstream had another idea. If she couldn't go downtime for answers, she would travel uptime and see how long the system field lasted.

It was a rough ride, bounced around from the timestream several times. She almost gave up, but around twenty years into Magna Aura's future she encountered an unexpected sight.

Her mouth opened wide in shock. "Zeus almighty! Father's not going to like this!"

There was no time to lose. She fumbled with a crystalator from her uniform and recorded what she could before flittering back to the Chronopolis.

CHAPTER FIVE

Christmas 2216

The months had gone quickly, Starshina fitting into Zero Star's society well, her exotic, snow-white, Amazonian looks earning her the admiration of many, to Aristedes' pride and chagrin.

Starshina had still not gained all her memories: "All I remember is fire," she had said, though Kellis had been spending a lot of time with her, the two becoming fast friends again.

Aaron felt left out at times. He knew that with his psionic talents, he could help Starshina, but Kellis forbid him. He often wondered what secrets Kellis and Starshina hid. Underlying this minor difficulty was another frustrating distraction, which periodically wove a distinct pattern into his mind, only to disappear on the brink of discovery. There was someone out there trying to connect with his mind.

At the same time, Kellis was developing the five of them into a team. Starshina's powers enabled her to control the elements, specifically to create winter-like conditions. Indeed, the Rough Area had been inundated with blizzards and storms, the likes of which had never been seen before, for Starshina could also animate those conditions to do her will to act like an extension of her body. Aristedes had called her the Winter Goddess.

Proud of her charges, Kellis knew that one day they would be needed, but she had noticed Aaron and even the young Astrals had seemed more distracted over the past few weeks. However, upon asking them, they could offer no explanation. Not only did she have to put up with that, but she also had the budding relationship between Aristedes and Starshina. She didn't want to discourage it, she didn't mind, it was just that events were heating up at the moment.

The Axalans had stepped up their incursions into Earth territory, especially around Consention Base, as if probing its defences.

"Axalan ships chancing their arm," Relentus had dismissed them to Kellis, on a recent holochat

Kellis wouldn't have been worried if it was just the Axalan Warriory, but there was also the threat from the shadowy super-powered group she really suspected were out there.

Added to that was also another potential threat. Some time ago, Earth and Bion scientists had detected, all over the galaxy, planets and stars being destroyed or moved. It was baffling scientists because the phenomena were reoccurring, random, and accelerating. Something was systematically destroying parts of the galaxy.

As if those issues weren't enough, Kellis had just been handed a special communiqué from Base 51, detailing an incident which needed her immediate attention.

Kellis filed it away. It sounded interesting, this Starfighter Machine, but she had more things to worry about than an eight-foot tall dormant metal machine.

While the others honed and trained their powers upon one another in the Rough Area, Kellis took time out and headed to a nearby lab to get a sit-rep from Xaul Relentus at Consention. They had a lot to talk about.

Xaul Relentus often toured his base. He was a hands-on man and wouldn't have anyone doing something that he wouldn't do himself, including minor repairs. That's why his men were loyal to him and transfer and posting requests to Consention were the highest out of all the other forward bases, combined. If the front was the place to be Consention was first choice.

Relentus was in the engineering section, just having helped to reseal a power conduit with chief engineer Lucie Marcs, when a call had pinged him on his comms.

"Relentus here."

"Oront here, sir, incoming scrambled message for you," the on-duty comms Lieutenant reported.

"Understood." He turned to the chief. "Excuse me, Lucie."

Relentus knew it was from Kellis straight away. She was concerned for him, especially now, because of the numerous nuisance raids the Axalans had been committing. And he knew she was going to warn him, again, about the secret super-powered force that was working for the Axalans.

He chuckled to himself. He would just have to remind her that, not only did Consention have two destroyers at her disposal, but also the

U.E.F. flagship, the *Starguard*, and her accompanying destroyers were on the way to patrol the area. The front would be safe.

"Oront, I'll take it in briefing room E5."

Relentus made his way to the lift, greeting crew as he walked. But before he got there the base's power dropped alarmingly, lights and corridor systems blanking out leaving everything in darkness before returning to normal. Everyone had stood still, looking about. Relentus broke into a run to the lift. And ran straight into the doors, which remained tightly shut. His communicator beeped and he took it off his belt.

"Relentus, here."

"Sir," reported Oront, "There's another signal coming through, scrambling all other channels. It's incredible, sir. It's beaming all the way to Earth. It's enormous!"

Relentus looked around just as the corridor console screens, usually full of diagnostic diagrams and deck maps, flickered and the picture changed completely.

There, on the screen were four, blue-faced aliens, with a fifth masked one in front of them. The masked one simply said:

"This is the scope of our power."

What the hell did that mean? thought Relentus.

And then the base started shaking.

From her lab, Kellis had watched, horrified, as her communication with Consention had been replaced with the visage of the strange Axalans. Her heart had almost seized as she had seen the figures whose existence she had deduced. Now here they were on the screen. But the thought that had stuck in her mind was the fact that there was something familiar about them.

Kellis wanted to rush out there to help, but that was the worst thing she could have done. Zero Star could be compromised and at the moment, Zero Star could be Earth's last hope. She ignored all calls on her comms, even from her team, who could see the same images on a screen across the large room. Like her, they sat and watched in stony silence.

"Christ!" she swore, just as she saw Aristedes stand up. "No!" Kellis warned him, jumping out from the lab. "No, you can't jump. Do not change time!" she shouted through gritted teeth.

At Aristedes' twitch of reflexes to defy her, Kellis continued: "You cannot just go around changing time to suit you! The repurcussions could make things worse. You know that!"

"You mean you want me to wait and see what happens?" Aristedes looked happier at that prospect.

"No, nothing!" Kellis reiterated. "Nothing! We will do nothing. Nothing!" she spelled out, feeling empty inside.

Aristedes turned angry. "But it's Relentus!" His face was dark with anger. "I could go do it and you wouldn't even know!" he countered hotly, fists clenched.

Zane stood open-mouthed at her brother's rebelliousness. She looked back and forth between them.

"Don't!" spat Kellis, staring him down.

Aristedes grimaced with anguish turning away in defeat. Zane breathed a sigh of relief.

"He'd better not die!" he stormed out of the lab. Starshina went to follow, but stopped herself.

Kellis sighed after him. "He won't!"

Earth had watched, too, petrified, as Consention had been destroyed in devastating fashion, ripped apart piecemeal by an invisible force, panels and structures, equipment and furniture, and people clutched away by the void. But the worst was yet to come. As those lucky enough to escape in helpless escape pods dropped away, Axalan warships intercepted and captured them. The pictures of the base then wavered and cut out.

A key base destroyed, hundreds of men dead or captured; all transmitted live to Earth, was not what people had wanted to see. It had brought the war home with alarming and brutal reality.

December 25, 2216, would go down as the greatest day of infamy in Earth's history, forever known as the Christmas Day Massacre. It had been wondered if the attack had been coincidental to Christmas day. Christmas, while not held in the same reverence, was still nonetheless a major holiday and now it would be remembered as a dark day in Earth history.

Consention was destroyed.

There had hardly been any warning and it had happened fast. The only thing that had saved Relentus was the fact he had been in the heavily shielded engineering section and it had been the last part to be destroyed. At full speed, in a disintergrating deck, it had given him and several engineers time to reach the escape pods, just.

Somehow, Simon Exmoor, who had been on the bridge, had escaped, Relentus not asking how or wanting to know. There were things about Exmoor that didn't make sense, but now wasn't the time to ask. He was also glad to see Lieutenant Paolo had survived as well. The men had watched from the pod's overhead screen as Consention had blown up, thousands of lives lost. Exmoor had estimated less than two-hundred surviviors in all, ten in their pod alone.

Relentus watched Consention explode. There may have been no sound in space, but Relentus could hear every panel blow, every deck buckle, seats, screens, and rivets scream and blast apart. And those pieces were even now speeding towards the escape pods, which rocked as their shields protected them from the blast waves and shooting debris.

Relentus hunkered down in his acceleration seat. Exmoor had never seen him like this before, such intensity on his face, jaw clenched so tight that the muscles stood out and eyes that blazed so much anger that they could cut steel.

"They'll pay for this!" he swore, "Whoever they are, wherever, whenever, they'll pay for this by the might of Earth's forces."

Nine pairs of eyes looked toward their commander, their inspiration. And they believed him.

Just as their faith was returning, Lieutenant Paolo yelled, "They're coming for us!"

Everyone looked at the screens. Sure enough, the three-pronged Axalan warship was bearing down on them. They were defenceless. Relentus unbuckled himself from his seat and stood up, staring defiantly at the screen and the oncoming rust-hued warship. Exmoor saw the fervour in his eyes, the light catching his greying, blue-streaked hair, making him look demonic. At that point, Exmoor knew that they weren't going to die.

And it was in that instant that the Axalan ship exploded.

"Hooray!" echoed around the pod.

"Pipe down!" yelled Relentus, clamping down on his men's elation. It was only one Axalan ship. There were others.

All eyes scanned for the alien's destroyer. But Relentus knew who had arrived and when the huge elongated battle-grey ship had come bursting into view, it was the most beautiful thing he had ever seen. The United Earth Forces Flagship, *Starguard*, slipped out of light-drive followed by the equally exquisite, but deadly trio of destroyers, *Saviour*, *Vanguard*, and *Explorator*, which headed off to dispatch any other Axalan ships and recover survivors.

The pod shuddered slightly as Relentus felt the gravity beam pull them up into *Starguard*'s ventral shuttle bay. He was the last to exit the escape pod, seeing that his injured got first priority.

A junior Lieutenant approached Relentus.

"Sir, the Admiral would like to see you," he said politely.

"Lead the way, son," Relentus replied. He beckoned for Exmoor and Paolo to follow.

When they reached Admiral Steelchapel's office, the *Starguard*'s commander, for a debriefing, Exmoor and Paolo were ordered to wait outside.

"I won't be long, guys," Relentus said, entering the office.

"Della, so good to see you again," Relentus greeted Admiral Della Steelchapel upon entry with a formal handshake.

"You too, Xaul. I'm sorry we were too late." The admiral smiled sadly. She circled around her desk and sat down. Relentus remained standing.

"Then under these circumstances you can understand I want to stay out there and assist with rescuing my captured men and salvaging what we can from Consention." He waited for his dismissal.

Steelchapel gave him a look he knew all too well—sympathy mixed with impatient determination. She had urgent news to tell him.

"Negative, we're returning to Earth, Xaul," she stated flatly. Her sterness threatened to cloud over her winsome features.

Relentus scoffed, "What, retreating?" He threw his arms up in disgust. "I'll command a ship myself if I have to and defend the front!"

Steelchapel tried to overrule him. "Those Axalans ships have already turned tail, heading back into their own space. We can't afford to divide our forces so thinly by chasing them, so we're fortifying the other outlying bases. But we," she pointed to the two of them, "are heading to Earth. There are more important issues at hand." Her face grew grave again.

"More important? *More* important?" yelled Relentus. "I vowed those bastard Axalans would pay for what they've done. I swore it and I aim to do it!" he seethed.

A flicker of a sad smile passed Steelchapel's lips. "Sit down!" she ordered, a bit coldly for his liking, considering their much hotter relationship in the past. She smoothed her silver-blonde hair curled up into a bun with a few loose strands.

Relentus complied after a second's delay.

"Your words may never be truer than they are now, Xaul," Steelchapel began, "for even as we speak, Earth has been hit with another tragedy. It had been kept secret for two days while we figured out what to do." She paused, making Xaul apprehensive. "Commander Earth Forces was returning to Euro HQ when a thunderstorm struck. You may well ask yourself how this impossibility occurred. A spurious signal was interfering with the north western Europa weather net grid, so they shut it down for a reboot."

Relentus could hear her next words before they came out.

"The General's hoverjet was struck by lightning and went down in the North Sea. There were no survivors." The admiral's voice was grave.

Relentus also knew what her next words would be:

"Xaul Relentus, by unanimous vote of the Earth Council, you are appointed Commander Earth Forces with immediate effect. Congratulations."

It was all very workmanlike, a handshake exchanged with smiles of sympathy.

Relentus shook his head in confusion. "Me? Why me?"

Steelchapel looked deep into his eyes, "Because Xaul, while you may not have the senior ranking, you have the overwhelming experience, the respect, and popular appeal needed to unite Earth and win the war!"

"Is that why they sent you?" He smiled back into her eyes.

She smiled, almost guiltily. "They suspected you wouldn't refuse if I told you. Luckily I was already on the way!"

They spent a moment in personal reflection, enjoying the little time they still had to talk of old times.

"Would you like a tour of your new flagship, General?"

Relentus snorted in amusement. "Thanks, but first let me check on the Consention survivors."

"Sure, take all the time you need, General," Steelchapel saluted him.

"And enough of that," he said. He left the admiral's office.

He needed the distraction. And a stiff drink.

A few hours later, Relentus was with Steelchapel, her executive crew, and Simon Exmoor, attending a formal dinner in the officer's mess. All appraised of his promotion,

"So, do you have any plans, yet, General?" asked Steelchapel, belying their cordial past in front of her command crew.

"A few," he replied, coyly. "And please, enough of the General, already. I've heard it today more times than I can count," he said, trying to warm the atmosphere.

"I'm just getting you used to it," Steelchapel retorted with some amusement. "When you return to Earth, they'll want to see a General, not an ex-base commander."

Relentus smiled into his glass of wine. She was right. Everyone was right. Kellis had been right. And now he had to put it right.

"I have plans, Della, but for now they must remain with me, up here." He tapped his head.

Steelchapel nodded, gazing at his hair, the blue streak in particular.

"How on Earth *did* you get that streak in your hair?" she asked bemused. "I've heard stories that you've seen so much action, your hair skipped grey and went straight to blue! But for as long as I've known you you've had that damnable blue hair. Is it even natural?"

The other officers laughed, Relentus too, remembering all the scraps he had been in. He stopped to think, a melancholic look on his face and he looked all of them in the eye.

"This'll be the last war we ever fight," he said. The room went quiet.

He didn't know why he had said it, but at that point he believed it to be true. He stood up, holding his glass of red wine high.

"A toast! A toast to the last war we'll ever fight."

"Hear! Hear!" came the instant cry, as the others had stood up to honour their new Commander Earth Forces.

With a harrumph, Steelchapel's hawkish first officer, Commander Habib, piped in with his raspy voice, "Then may this war last forever!"

They all glanced at him in silence. Then burst out laughing.

New Year's Day 2017

Kellis' nerves were on edge. For the past week, Zero Star had been on full alert and total comms blackout following the massacre.

Zero Star's Bion and human command council had summoned Kellis to their chambers nestled on the deck above the arboretum to explain the failure of her efforts in hunting down these super-powered beings; beings whose existence she had always suspected and now had been confirmed. Kellis' assertions that the Axalan group might carry out such an attack had been borne out. Needless to say her superiors weren't very happy.

"I have no answers," Kellis had answered. There was no excuse.

"There is a feeling you are holding back on information," the human Commander Charleron said plainly, his dark eyes regarding Kellis with suspicion. The Bion commander nodded in agreement.

"I'm not," she lied.

Every day, since coming to Zero Star, she had lied to them. Even though the council were all members of ExA, where secrecy was their by-word, Kellis kept secrets of her own. It was to her own advantage to do so. And until help from Hawkhurst came through, she would have to rely on her wits and secrets.

"I'm doing everything in my power to get a finger on these guys, but I need more time and power from Hawkhurst . . ." she stopped talking.

The two commanders had looked worriedly at each other. Something was wrong. The others were on edge, too.

"What?" she asked. "What's wrong?"

The Bion commander, Dav-Tein B'Nk, nodded to Commander Charleron. This was news which one human would want to hear from another.

"General Hawkhurst . . . is dead." Charleron stated bluntly. "We intercepted priority one signals. It happened two days before the Massacre. A freak accident."

"My God, how terrible!" Kellis digested the news. "Who's the new C.E.F.?" Kellis heard herself asking, stealing herself for the answer.

"Xaul Relentus." Charleron stared at her, a grim smile on his face. "I believe you know him," he said simply, Kellis not knowing if he referred to their past relationship or because of the fact that any C.E.F. had to be a member of ExA.

"I believe that I do," Kellis said, trying to keep her voice neutral. Inside a million butterflies stormed within her stomach. It was all she could do to keep seated and calm. But the relief clearly showed.

"Do you feel now that you'll be able to get the job done?" asked Charleron.

Kellis only answer was a smile. *Would she ever!*

From the time man had travelled across the oceans, set foot on the moon or Mars or Pluto, or travelled to and from the nearest stars and beyond, never had the people of Earth been more united in the advent of the return of one man: General Xaul Relentus, Commander Earth Forces. He was to lead Earth to Salvation. And his welcome was like no other in all history.

The *Starguard* had raced across the light-years, its precious cargo locked in intense talks with other admirals and ships' commanders who had been ferried aboard at Alpha Centauri Base.

On Earth's closest stellar neighbour, Relentus had been greeted by Toca Roschwata, the Vice-General of the United Earth Council. Upon entering the Sol system, the flagship had been surrounded by hundreds of smaller vessels, a veritable shield of ships protecting their new Commander. Clusters of scouts, destroyers and cruisers, media-ships, private yachts, and the like, all wanting to do their part in welcoming home Relentus.

It was nightfall on Earth, lit up from above and from the ground as fireworks celebrated the New Year and a new saviour. It was as if the heavens themselves were shining down upon Relentus, showering him with heavenly glory. Many thought this is how it must have felt over two thousand years ago, on the eve of a certain baby's birth.

Relentus' shuttle, *Sceptre*, departed *Starguard* upon entering orbit, he, Steelchapel, Exmoor, and dozens of dignatories cutting through Earth's atmosphere. Lower down, closer to the ground they rode through a hail of more small ships and glowing holographic ticker-tape.

The shuttle touched down at the headquarters of the United Earth Council, built loosely over the footprint of the old United Nations building in New York. Relentus spied the larger-than-life statue of the last superhero, Dee, who shortly after the mysterious explosion in central New York and the death of the Starguards had changed Earth, irrevocably.

It was also the scene of the infamous speech made by the last Starguard. Relentus wondered on the fate of that Starguard, the destruction of mid-Manhattan producing one of the most mysterious events during the twenty-first century. But it also propelled man out to the stars, which was most notably commemorated in the naming of Earth's flagship, the *Starguard*. Man had come a long way since then, due in part to the Starguards' deaths. And Relentus didn't want to let them down.

Security officers had to constantly keep the throng of reporters and civilians away from Relentus upon his disembarkation from the shuttle, the roar of the crowd almost deafening him. A forty-metre walk to the podium, where he was to have his public investiture, was more like a hundred miles away, the distance seeming to grow ever further with every step. Crossing the flood-lit shadow of Dee's statue, Relentus climbed the steps to the podium and shook hands with the President of the Earth Council, Victor Raimont.

"Congratulations, Xaul," said Raimont, a lean, greying, Hispanic man. "You deserve this, but I wish under differing circumstances," he spoke solemnly, Relentus agreeing with a nod.

"I feel the same way. And thank you."

Raimont shook his hand again and with a slight clasp of his shoulder for good luck backed away, leaving Relentus in the limelight.

"Say 'hello' to your people," Raimont said, holding out his arms by way of introduction.

Relentus turned and saw the thousands crammed around the building, the streets and promenades, hover jets aloft overhead, surrounding buildings' windows full of expectant faces. It was enough to overwhelm him, but now he was leader of all Earth Forces and they looked to him to lead them from out of these dark ages and into a new dawn. Like a god.

Relentus looked at his data-pad and the speech written on it for him by Exmoor. A pretty speech, but Relentus knew that the gathered masses would want more than just soothing words, they'd want the patriotic, chest-thumping rhetoric, something to stir both heart and mind. Putting away the pad, he spoke from the heart.

"I come before you, not only as the new Commander Earth Forces, but also as your friend. And as your friend, I tell you I will end this war!"

There was raucous cheering, Relentus holding up his arms to quiet them down. Even so, it took a few long minutes.

"This Massacre will not go unheeded nor unpunished and even as I speak, the seeds are being laid for retaliation. I hope that *They* can hear me!" He looked upwards as if addressing the Axalan world directly. "I hope that *They* are receiving this message, for I am talking of *Their* defeat. I am talking of *Their* destruction, *Their* doom at the hands of Earth. On my honour, to all of you out there," he pointed to the crowd, "with sons, husbands, fathers, mothers, wives and daughters and all the others you know and love, in our glorious forces, I, Xaul Relentus, pledge that I will bring you victory and your loved ones home."

The cheering was rapturous, Relentus finding himself surrounded by political and military palm-pressers and back-slappers from various countries.

Approaching from somwhere in the background, Exmoor shook his hand, "That speech was better than mine, you old codger," he said under his breath.

"I wanted to get their fighting spirit up, not bore them to death!" grinned Relentus. "By the way, I've been wanting to ask you, how did you survive from the bridge all the way to engineering?"

Exmoor smiled. "I'll tell you one day," he said cryptically. "Care for a walk, General?"

He showed Relentus the steps toward the crowd, Commander Earth Forces and his entourage starting an impromptu walkabout, everyone clamouring for his attention, shouting praise and confidences. For an hour the walk continued, after which he was whisked away to a formal dinner set for him inside the United Earth Council building, many of the world leaders attending.

Then it would be time to work with Earth's future at stake.

In a mid-deck common room, Kellis, Aaron, Aristedes, Zane and Starshina had watched, with the other Zero Star personnel, the crowning achievement of Xaul Relentus' career. Kellis felt so proud and justifiably happy with herself that she had predicted his ascendancy to the position, though not quite in this manner.

She'd had a soft spot for Augustus Hawkhurst, everyone did, the grumpy, grizzled, old soldier from England possessing qualities which came once in a lifetime to such a position. He'd been born for the position and the only one who could have succeeded him was Xaul Relentus. And there he was, speaking like a true statesman, prepared to lead Earth to victory.

Kellis knew there was no word for defeat in Relentus' vocabulary, in fact he had forbade people from using such defeatist words around him, so victory was the only way.

Now all Kellis had to do was wait until she and her team were required for the war effort, for surely now Relentus would see the merits of her envisioned plan. It was now or never.

She looked around the room, at her team, Aristedes and Starshina sitting together comfortably talking in low voices, Zane not too far away huddled with a group of young Bions playing some hologame, though she knew Zane still thought about Paolo. But as she sought out Aaron at the other side of the room, she saw him get up and leave, rubbing his forehead.

As of late, Kellis had seen him often rubbing his forehead as if in pain, but he dismissed it. There was something definitely wrong with him, but he wouldn't admit it. She watched him go and could only hope it would pass.

Aaron rubbed his forehead again. The constant buzzing in his head couldn't be blocked. And today had been the worst since the first wave of noise had seeped into his mind, weeks ago. But he was fighting it. Whatever it was, the itch inside his head, it would not go away. Deep meditative sleep was the only way to lessen the pain, but with the pain came images, jumbled, distorted images as if his mind were trying to tell him something. When he returned to his quarters, Aaron went straight to his bed and lay there curled fetal-like, waiting for sleep to take him and the images to begin.

. . . *A distant world, so serene and silent, rising sun, waking the slumbering, dawn in paradise, a blot on the sun, closer and closer, dark invader, cruel eyes, cruel smile, sword in hand, spreading death, no escape, no retaliation, crueller and crueller, laughter and tyranny, a husk of a world, dead and drained, sword of energy, pulsating, energy-sated, death alights, a world in oblivion . . .*

Aaron shot awake, sweating feverishly. It was the same dream, or a nightmare, every time he closed his eyes, over and over again. He looked at comm unit's time display and saw it was morning already. Night had passed in an instant.

Aaron sucked in air deeply. He would have to do something about this. It was slowly driving him mad. He held his head, the buzzing having lessened somewhat.

He made a decision. He would have to tell Kellis. She was all he had.

But he drifted off again and fell into fitful slumber watching the end of the galaxy in his nightmares.

CHAPTER SIX

Quick retaliation was called for.

Commander Earth Forces, General Xaul Relentus, convened as many of the available seventy warship commanders in his office as he could at the Earth Council building, while others appeared over secured holo-links, to reveal to them his audacious plan.

While the Axalans were still basking in the glory of their treacherous attack, Earth Forces would sweep in on the core world of Axala, destroying everything along the way. Maximum damage in minimum time.

However, Relentus' newly established intelligence corps-cum-deep-strike operatives, dubbed Dare Units, had reported that the entire Axalan fleet had pulled back to the homeworld. The entire route to Axala was lying invitingly open.

The unlikely, but confirmed, news had surprised many of the hardened space captains.

"You know it's some kind of trick. An ambush," said Captain Osi of the *Explorator*. "The Axalans have never done anything like this before. We'll be sucked into a trap!"

But the Dare Unit Commander, the newly promoted Lt. Commander Paolo, was more confident. "I assure you, from all forward recon units, there were no Axalan military assets anywhere in the region."

This only caused more raised eyebrows and disquiet over the news.

Digesting the data on her padd, there was a question from Relentus' left. The question on everyone's mind.

"So, when do we attack?" asked Admiral Steelchapel. "I'll need time to make preparations." She was prepared to lead the fleet.

"Three days," came Relentus' answer.

Low whistles and shakes of heads rustled through the room. Only captains Brand and Lucas reacted with pumped fists ready for action.

"We can't wait any longer. And I'll be leading the attack." The shocked silence made Relentus smile.

"Begging your pardon, sir, but you can't be serious!" Captain Riven of the *Saviour* gasped. But one stern look from Relentus told her that he was totally serious. She gulped and was silent.

Steelchapel recovered gracefully. "Of course, sir, the *Starguard* will be made ready for your command."

"I won't need the *Starguard*, Della," he said "The newest ship to be commissioned from Viking Base on Mars is now mine. I have a crew ready, trained and rearing to go." He had caught them off guard again, surprise on their faces.

"Oh? And its name?" queried Steelchapel, intrigued.

"*Starship Earth*," replied Relentus. "Appropriate for this situation I think."

There were smiles all around, but Relentus could still see a few doubters.

"I know that some of you think I shouldn't be going, but there are no rules against it. I've got more first-hand experience in battling the Axalans than most of you combined and I need to be out there," he pointed toward the sky, "not sitting here like an office commander. When I lead, I lead from the front. And this will be no different. Are there any further questions?"

There were none.

"Right. Orders will follow. Dismissed."

The room of Earth's top starship officers filed out. All but Admiral Steelchapel and Simon Exmoor.

"Something on your mind, Della?" Relentus asked Steelchapel.

Relentus looked over to Exmoor, who cleared his throat discreetly. "Excuse me, I have other business to attend to." He left the room.

Relentus knew he would talk with him later, but for now, it was Della Steelchapel that mattered.

"There's something else going on, isn't there?" she asked.

She appeared calm, which Relentus knew was her angry mode. She wasn't going to be put off with anything other than the truth.

"We've known each other far too long for you to start having secrets, Xaul. And don't think I don't know about some secret group you're a part of. I didn't want to say anything before, Xaul, but ever since our days at the academy, your special missions and high-powered friends destined you for something great and I believe this is the culmination. Xaul, you have great power in your hands, but before you commit yourself to this adventure, I want to know. I have to." She looked at him pleadingly.

Relentus felt sorry for her. They had known each other from childhood, growing up together. They would probably would have been married if it hadn't been for ExA. Relentus was wholly committed to it, his work taking him away from Della and indeed humanity. But here was a chance to redeem some of that on both fronts.

Steelchapel watched as he reached into his tunic. She automatically started backward, expecting a nasty surprise of the shooting kind to emerge.

Relentus looked at her. "What's the matter, Della, don't trust me anymore?"

Steelchapel shrugged. "I don't know." She watched as the object Relentus pulled out, a modified sensor inhibitor, began whirring. "Did they give that to you?"

"Who?" Relentus gave a sly smile. Steelchapel put her hands on her hips. She was impatient. Relentus indulged her. "Okay. For almost my whole life, I've been a part of a group not known to anyone outside its organisation, not even the Earth Council, yet it has had a large role in controlling Earth's space policy for the past two hundred years. And now I'm its leader as well."

The surprise on Steelchapel's face was evident, her mouth working to ask the questions he now was going to answer. He put a hand up to quieten her.

"When we go out to battle three days from now, I'll have the command of four hundred and twenty ships . . ."

"Four . . . but we don't have that many," Steelchapel protested, "Where'd they come from? The crews . . ."

". . . Aren't human." Relentus finished.

Steelchapel's jaw dropped, her eyes fluttering disbelief. Relentus realised they'd been standing the whole time, as Steelchapel sat down heavily in a chair.

"Not human?" she repeated. "I . . . I don't understand. Are they Axalan allies?"

117

Relentus shook his head. "No, let me explain," he paused to think. "My group, ExA, the Extrasolar Agency, has been around in one incarnation or another for the past two-hundred-odd years. Those old stories of downed alien spacecraft were mostly true, but what wasn't known was that these aliens, the Cepheusians, were dying and to cut a long story short, a program was initiated where humans and Cepheusians were hybridised. They call themselves the Bions and after a long period of no contact with them, due to some political difficulties," he glossed over the details, "they offered their help against the Axalans. They have almost three hundred ships waiting to out-flank the Axalans should they be needed."

Steelchapel's mouth was agape again. She couldn't believe what she was hearing.

"And Hawkhurst? And Exmoor?" she asked incredulously.

"Hawkhurst recruited me from the academy. Every single C.E.F. has been a member of ExA. It's always been organised that way without the Council's knowledge. Only the Bions can decide when they want their presence to be known to everyone, but for now they want to remain unknown. As for Simon he's been around longer than I know. His family have had members in all incarnations of ExA." He looked at Della, knowing what her next question would be.

"Why wasn't I involved? Why the hell was I left on the outside?" she shouted.

"Look at us, Della, we're two of a kind. If he'd picked us both and the group had been compromised, who then would he have had to turn to? He needed someone on the outside, someone who could be seen to be working their way up, with no help. And you did it. The *Starguard* is yours. You're above reproach. But with me, I had assignments: ships to command, special missions, battles to fight, bases to run, all on the orders of ExA. I didn't know for a while if I was living my own life," He sighed wistfully, "but now, I have this, the Generalship of Earth's Forces, and I'm going to put things right."

Steelchapel was only interested in one point, however. "Is that why you left me? For this alien crusade of yours?" Her tone weighed down with decades of pain.

He clasped his hands together. "You have to understand, Della. I couldn't compromise ExA. And I couldn't kill your career. I had to leave. I'm sorry."

Steelchapel lowered her head, a greying fringe drooping over her face. Relentus knew she was hiding tears that had waited twenty long years to flow. She was quiet for a time, arms wrapped around her. When she took a deep breath and looked at him with a curious smile on her face, Relentus knew she had come to terms with the deluge of information.

"I've waited twenty years to hear you say you're sorry. But now that you've said it, I'm the one who feels like I should be apologising. I don't envy you your job. And don't put yourself down; you've worked as every bit as hard as I have to get where you are today. Augustus Hawkhurst wouldn't have had it any other way." She put on a brave smile. "Well, now that I know, I guess I'm supposed to keep the secret, right?" she said half-humorously, as she got up to leave, but on looking over, there was more on Relentus' mind.

"There's more," he simply said.

"I'm not sure I want to hear any more," she stated plainly. "Haven't I heard enough?"

"No," Relentus said. "No, not if you're a member of ExA."

"But I didn't ask to be a member."

"No. One doesn't. But you are now." Relentus gave a conspiratorial smile, matched by Steelchapel's.

"Oh, go on then," she said with some resignation.

"Your ship bears the name of the legendary Starguards, who died before their time. We could have used them now or even the first E-Corps team, for the Axalans have super-powered beings of their own. They're the ones who destroyed Consention, not the Axalan Warriory as everyone thinks. If this is a trap those beings could be lying in wait for us."

With astonishment on her face, she managed to ask, "How can we fight them?" But the answer dawned on her the moment Relentus answered.

"We now have super-powered beings of our own. ExA and the Bions have a secret base we call Zero Star, situated near Bion space.

From there we've created new technologies and it was the Bions who figured out how to synthesise thanium."

That fact impressed Della, Relentus saw. Thanium couldn't be synthesised by Earth scientists for decades, then all of sudden, the breakthrough had come, but the process never publicised.

"It's also there that a xeno-specialist has been gathering and training these super-powered beings. I've met some of them myself," he laughed to himself. "They're young, but experienced and I have complete faith in their mentor."

Something in the way Relentus talked about this mentor, Steelchapel knew she was a woman. And that Relentus cared for her.

"Is she nice, this mentor?"

Relentus guffawed. "What made you say that?" he asked.

"A woman can tell," her eyes challenged him. "So, tell me about her. Will we ever meet?"

Relentus blushed, combing his fingers through his blue-templed hair. He was flustered. Della was enjoying herself.

"Look, we met shortly after she came to Zero Star. She was recovering from some mysterious trauma. I was in charge of organising the Bion's fleet. It just happened. She just seemed so unconventional, as if from another lifetime. We had a wonderful time together, but in the end it just didn't work out. That's it. And who knows, now that you're an ExAn, you might just meet her and her team."

Steelchapel was satisfied with the answer. She wouldn't dig any further. Except:

"Now that I'm a member . . ."

She left the sentence unfinished. It was better not to know, than to be hurt again.

But Relentus finished the sentence for her. "I've never stopped caring for you, Della. And after the war, I wouldn't mind seeing you more often."

"You mean for ship inspections, briefings, and the like," she said coyly.

"Something like that," Relentus smiled.

He walked over to her, pulling her up from the chair. He could still see the flame smouldering in her eyes. He kissed her softly, the feelings of passion returning to him. But Della pulled away suddenly, surprising him.

"Have I done something wrong?"

But the love and humour in her eyes was unmistakeable.

"You can give me the other half of that kiss, when you get back."

Then she walked out of the room, leaving Relentus wondering what he'd gotten himself in to.

"Give me war over a woman any day!"

Deep space

"Sir, I don't believe this!" the young helmsman, Blake, exclaimed. "There's got to be at least six hundred ships!"

Relentus got up from his chair. While his men may have been surprised at the information, he wasn't. ExA intelligence had long known the exact strength of the Axalan fleet, but Earth Forces intelligence had seriously underestimated their strength.

Calls came in from the other captains.

"Sir, we must retreat!" Captain Osi cautioned.

Relentus was having none of it.

"Steady ahead!" he ordered to all ships. "We go in, end it one way or another, here and now."

For the past week, the Earth fleet had travelled through the forward Axalan territories meeting no resistance, enemy bases abandoned, drifting aimlessly.

This isn't a trap, thought Relentus. *It has no bite; no fight back, no nothing.*

The Earth fleet had swifty ventured all the way into deep Axalan space and were now on the verge of their homeworld, Axala.

Axala orbited the orange dwarf, Xal, sharing the system with its outer brethren worlds Tus, Izel, Oric, and Ollossor. These were undefended. Sensors also revealed there were no other enemy ships as far away as two light-years where the planet-less blue giant, Ela, dwelled or along the Far Regions border. Axala alone had all the goodies on show, Relentus saw.

Now, they had encountered the entire Axalan fleet. And the Earth fleet was outnumbered almost five to one. But Relentus had the ace up his sleeve with the Bion fleet stealthily waiting in the wings.

Starship Earth remained at the head of the fleet, the Gyrs, led by captain Seton, riding high, relative to Relentus' position; the *Vanguard*, *Sceptre,* and *Explorator* flanking him, with assorted ships arrayed around them. The *Starguard*, commanded by Commander Habib in Steelchapel's absence, formed up with the *Battersea, Saviour* and *Exsurgent* on the outer flanks, the big guns lying in wait; the entire Earth fleet amassed in a staggered formation. Across from them, the Axalans spread out like a chain-mesh curtain of doom, each link capable of devastating firepower.

It was very quiet on *Starship Earth*'s bridge to Relentus, everyone holding their breath, the console instruments seeming to beep less noisily. It was the calm before the storm, the last sigh of breath before death. The silence became more palpable as Relentus held the Earth fleet one-quarter AU from the Axalan homeworld.

Relentus observed the screen, a mass of enemy ships staring him back, but his trained eye picked up the telltale signs of the lead ship, nestled among a core of Axalan Imperial Claw-class ships.

"Open a channel, Creeden," he addressed his comms officer, who signalled the completed task.

Before Relentus could speak, a string of alien words ushered over the air. It took a while for the translator to analyse and transmit, but when it did, a few eyebrows were raised.

". . . the Emperor of Axala. I bid thee, Earth General Xaul Relentus, to appear before me to discuss terms."

Relentus answered. "What is there to be discussed in the terms of war?" He tried to sound commanding, but not belligerently so.

"Nothing," the Emperor replied, as if anticipating Relentus' response. "But the terms of peace may be more . . . interesting."

All eyes turned to Relentus. This was turning bizarre.

"If by peace, you mean our surrender, then you are grievously mistaken. Earth will not surrender."

"Nor shall we," the Emperor stated, almost casually. "By peace, I mean the immediate mutual cessation of war. You and I will discuss terms, our peoples free from war: Peace."

Relentus was a bit perplexed. Here was an enemy fleet that had just massacred thousands of humans, fought treacherous battles, outnumbered him in battle now, but were now suing for peace. It didn't make sense. They couldn't be afraid of him? Surely this wasn't some sort of elaborate trick to lure and kill him. What was going on?

Only one way to find out, he told himself.

He glanced over to Exmoor, whom uniquely, Relentus had made his first officer. And the eyes of his civilian Exec were telling Relentus he wanted a word with him alone.

"Your Excellency," he said, if indeed it was the Axalan Emperor he was dealing with, "If you would excuse me, I will think over your offer."

"As you wish," was the simple reply.

Relentus nodded to the commsman who cut the signal. He and Exmoor exited the bridge to Relentus' off-bridge office.

Once inside, Exmoor said, "Sir, I think you should do this. Discuss peace, I mean."

Relentus looked at him. "Seriously?" Seeing that he was, said, "Explain."

Simon Exmoor took a deep breath as if the weight of the world was about to be lifted from his shoulders.

"Well, you've always wanted to know my origins, why and how I did things. Well, it's because of my name, Exmoor, more of a title really which derives from the words Ex-mortal." Relentus' face was beyond surprised. Exmoor carried on. "You see, thousands of years ago, there was a war, a war between the forces of light and darkness, stretching across universes. The evil force was vanquished, but at the cost of many good lives. The survivors settled on the only inhabitable world, Earth, and founded a new civilisation while breeding with existing early humans. It was thought that any other warriors from the battle had died.

"During the early years on Earth, it was discovered that some of the new offspring were different, some more powerful with certain abilities and others that were longer lived. It caused rivalries and the once united half-alien peoples were split apart, many travelling to new realms on Earth where they began anew. One such group were my ancestors, the Exmoors. There are many more, each with different characteristics and some have forgotten their heritage. The all-too brief visitation by the Starguards and the subsequent E-Corps 2 disaster which followed was a blow to us, for the Starguards were our distant kin in a way. They could have united us all. But that failed and we Exmoors thought all was lost."

Simon paused again, as if not sure to continue. But Relentus' expression egged him on.

"Xaul, I am two hundred and sixty-six years old, one of the youngest and last of the Exmoors and I had thought I had seen everything, until now. I'd always seen something in you, something different from the ordinary man, but it wasn't until this moment, I knew what it was. We Exmoors have retained certain esoteric knowledge of our ancestors in the event that something like this happened. You, Xaul, have our ancestor's blood in you, but not the family branch who founded the human civilisation, but that of the Axalan civilisation. You even have it in your name. The ancient warriors who fought alongside my ancestors and who we thought had died, had actually escaped all those aeons ago. They were the warriors of Xal and they founded the Axalan Empire. They had blue hair, Xaul," Exmoor emphasised, pointing to Relentus' head.

"And I bet if you were genetically tested more in-depth, they'd find some curious differences deep within you. The Axalans welcome home not an enemy, but a son. Unite us, Xaul, unite our ancient races. It is your destiny."

Relentus was taken aback. "Destiny?" he sighed. That word again. He chuckled. "You know, Simon, I read a poem once that began 'How ancient is Man that he can count brethren amongst the stars...' but I never thought that I'd seriously be asking myself that question. I don't know what to say. It's all a bit much, if true. I thought ExA was enough, but this . . ." he said walking around the room, rubbing the back of his neck, "this is a bit too much!"

"Believe it, Xaul, you're unique. And the Axalans somehow know it. They knew you were coming and have come to welcome you and Earth. It can't be a coincidence that humans and Axalans look alike, except for the skin colour. Look how far away in the galaxy we are from each other. No random genetic quirk could have produced two similar cultures, look at the Cepheusians, closer to us by tens of light years, but much different. I tell you, Xaul, we need to be united. And you're the person to do it."

Exmoor was adamant, Relentus could see. It was almost like a religious fervour. He really believed it. But so did Relentus.

"Okay, okay, Simon. I'll do it," he reluctantly accepted. "By the way, I've always had blue hair, streaks at first then it just suddenly grew— blue tufts instead of grey—and variations of my name has been in the family for generations, since ancient Greece, or so my mother told me," he grinned widely.

Exmoor laughed, a distant look in his eye. "I wonder," he said aloud.

"Wonder what?"

"My family also goes way back to Greece, so does the family of Aristedes and Zane. I just wondered at the complexity of it all," Exmoor said.

Relentus' curiosity was piqued. "Aristedes and Zane? What family is this?" He wondered if Simon knew their secret.

"They call themselves Astrals."

Relentus' eyes widened. *He knew!*

Exmoor continued, glad he was surprising Relentus. "Yes, we know of the Astrals and of Lynn Kellis, more than you know. The Astrals and Exmoors helped each other from time to time. Maybe they saw this time coming and did something about it. But then again, I know they try not to interfere with history, hence Aristedes' and Zane's marginal input into the war effort."

Relentus blew air through his lips. "Any more to tell?" Relentus had just about had enough. Secrets within secret organisations were never good, especially when kept from its new leader.

Exmoor shrugged. "Nope."

"Okay then, let's go talk to our cosmic brothers." He let Exmoor through the door before him, the bridge seeming to breathe a sigh of relief on his return. "Put me through to the Emperor," Relentus ordered Creeden.

There was a brief delay but this time the main bridge screen came to life and the presence of the Axalan Emperor filled the view. What they could see if him.

Thick blue hair was sleekly backcombed over his head, dark eyes regaled them from an elfin-shaped head, but his lower face was covered in a bejewelled veil-like garment. Rings, bracelets, and necklaces adorned his hands and neck. And through the top of his diaphanous robe supple muscles could be discerned.

Exmoor was right, Relentus thought, *except for his skin colour, he could have passed for human. How close were they?*

"You honour us again with your presence, General Relentus," said the Emperor. "Have you come to a decision?"

"Yes, Your Excellence," Relentus kept his voice calm. "I have decided to accept your gracious offer and meet you aboard your ship."

Some of the bridge crew became restless, eyes turning toward their supreme commander.

The Emperor nodded as if he had expected the answer.

"To assure you, General, this is no trap or trick, I offer you, first, an apology for the attack on your base. Such an atrocity was undertaken by rogue elements of the Empire which will be dealt with."

The bridge went quiet. This was a surprising admission by the Emperor. Relentus knew this signal was being transmitted to the other ships and no doubt to Earth.

What's happening here? he asked himself.

The Emperor carried on regardless. "Second, as a token of my expansive goodwill, any and all prisoners will be returned unharmed."

"Oh my god!" a crew member clutched her chest in amazement. Relentus wondered if she had family members captured.

"And third. . ." He paused as he brought forward a young boy, about six Earth-years old, Relentus reckoned. "My first-born son," the Emperor said by way of introduction. "He will be the honoured guest aboard your ship, until you return. Is that satisfactory?" A smile touched his eyes.

"Your Excellency, your words have been generous and most welcomed, for all of Earth. And yes, that is satisfactory." Relentus almost baulked at using a child as a bargaining chip, but it was the price for peace. "Your son will be well looked after." Relentus said, not letting the guilt of using such a young pawn enter his mind. The fate of two worlds were at stake. "We will recieve your son in our main hanger and I will travel to you."

"Acceptable." The Emperor bowed and the screen went blank.

"Exmoor with me. Creeden, send a security detail to the hanger bay." Relentus was already on his way off the bridge before the order was finished.

Minutes later, the Emperor's young son arrived within a squat curved-triangular shuttle coloured blue, white, and grey with Axalan markings in angular black. It coasted to a halt on the deck and almost immediately a side portal slid open and a lone figure sauntered down the protruding ramp.

While the boy looked young, Relentus could see he was far more muscular than an Earth child would have been at that age. His blue skin was smooth and his head was bald save for a low dark-blue mohawk ending in a ponytail. He wore a simple waist-length gold-coloured tunic and loose pantaloons with blue trim. He smiled with bright eyes at Relentus and bowed. Relentus returned the gesture, motioning to Exmoor.

"Welcome, Your Highness, my first officer will take you to comfortable quarters to wait until my return." He hoped the translator function in his comms pad worked.

And apparently it did.

"Thank you, General," the boy haltingly said, Relentus realising he had spoken in English. He nodded his head in appreciation.

"Xaalhalanol," the boy pronouned his name.

"Your English is impeccable, Xaalhalanol," Relentus said.

Xaalhalanol grinned. He gestured back to the shuttle. "My ship is yours, General." He went to stand by Simon Exmoor.

Relentus looked back at Exmoor, who gave him a 'go-on' look with his eyes.

The Commander Earth Forces took the last few steps into the shuttle walking up the ramp. Inside was a darkened short corridor with a command module up front and an aft cabin with engineering section at the rear. The five crew, all taller than Exmoor, stood to attention, one showing him his seat in the aft cabin. Relentus sat wondering how this trip would pan out.

The shuttle lifted off. Alone on the Axalan craft Relentus felt the eyes of the Axalan pilots and escorts prying into him, looking at his hair, but upon looking at them or speaking to them, they averted their eyes and spoke only when spoken to in low reverent tones.

To Relentus, this was much more than respect: it was worship.

What have I gotten myself into now!

War is a funny thing.

You think you're in the victor's chair, sword dangling precariously over your opponent's throat, when it slips out of your fingers and misses the target. Such was the case with the Axalans.

For a heartening four *quorcons* Jallaar had been celebrating, as had the entire Empire, the small victory over the weak-colours. The Emperor had shown his people the might of the Superions, the human's base ripped apart by the invisible powers of Mode's matter transforming abilities.

The Imperial warships had then swooped in to capture survivors, who would be tortured and returned dead to Earth in drone ships. Everything had been going their way. Then things had changed.

In the middle of Migr Lantris summounted upon the city magister's palace was the Central Opticon, a giant holographic screen dedicated to bringing the vision of the empire to the people. On the screen now was, remarkably, a weak-colour, ranting on about something, Jallaar couldn't tell. He wondered, as did every other Axalan, how such a programming error could have been condoned by the Emperor. The human, apparently Earth's new warrior leader, outside a typically uninspiring Earth building, was swearing retribution against them on his honour. His remarks brought forth whooping laughs from the Axalan crowds. He was a brave weak-colour to boast so much. But then the laughs had slowly died down, as the light had shone down on the weak-colour's head. Growing whispers had swept around the huge viewing squares:

"He has the mark! The mark! He has the mark!"

Some pointed to the screen. They had all seen the blue streaks and tufts in the weak-colour's hair. He bore the true colour of their God. He had the mark of Xaal. But the frantic whispers started again, for the second half of the prophecy had yet to be fulfilled.

"His name! His name! What is his name?" they shouted. And they listened. Listened carefully.

"I, Xaul Relentus . . ."

That was all that was needed. There was a collective sharp intake of breath, as billions of Axalans had heard him speak his name.

The weak-colour had said the name himself: Xaal.

The prophesied son of the Axalan God, Xaal, was human.

The silence which spread over Axala and her sister worlds would forever be remembered in their history as the apt 'Time of Silence'. It had been profound. It had brought tears to the eyes of many. The Son of God was human. But then, he had to be. For far from crossing the galaxy to war with them, he would unite them. It had been foreseen.

The Axalans were a religious people and the Emperors and Empresses had been seen as the sons and daughters of Xaal, but in name only; placeholders. But now the True Son had appeared on another world. It had been said by Xaal himself, in their holy books, mainly the Scrolls of Xaal, that his cosmic brothers-in-arms had fathered other races and that one day they would be reunited in the future. That time had come. There had been no mistaking that the humans and Axalans resembled each other, but there had been no sign they were ancient brothers, until Xaul Relentus had taken up the reins of Earth's forces.

Of course, the Axalan Warriory would not fight against him. And they took his miraculous escape from Consention to be further proof of his divinity. All ships had been ordered to retreat to the vicinity of Axala and there they stayed, waiting to greet their saviour. They knew he would return in due course.

In the Imperial palace, Emperor Xalarius knew his time was at an end. He too had watched from his palace, as the human Xaal had made his speech. Looking at the weak-coloured war leader, Xalarius was comforted in knowing at least this Xaul Relentus was a strong and bold being, great in bearing and stature. And he was very proud this historic moment would fall within his reign. His legacy would be sealed forever. But not all would agree with him.

The Superions would not.

Xalarius had tried to explain this to Mode who had confronted him about pushing ahead with the war after Consention's destruction, as if he needed to explain himself.

The Superions had looked at Mode for direction. This was not what they had signed up for. And there was no other course of action for them.

Mode turned his sinister mask back upon the Emperor.

This is my time, thought Xalarius. *I am ready to die for my God.*

Arriving aboard the Axalan flagship, Relentus was ushered politely through the maze-like corridors.

Well I won't find my way back out alone again, a mirthless Relentus nervously thought.

And just like on the shuttle, along the way, crew members stared and quickly averted their eyes in reverence in his presence.

Relentus was guided into the royal chambers upon the ship, his escort leaving him alone in the darkened domed and curtained room. Or at least he thought he was alone until servants had issued forth nimbly from wall niches to prostrate themselves before him. Relentus didn't know what to do and his words had no effect on them. But a loud clap from the rear of the room sent the servants scurrying back to the dark recesses. And another figure stepped out regally from behind a room divider.

Relentus stood before the Emperor. The Emperor had changed into what Relentus deemed to be casual Imperial wear. A loose-fitting gold, silver and black tunic hung over a gold skirt-like garment ending in sandle-type footwear. The veil was still around his mouth and nose, but his blue hair was combed back into curls. The Axalan leader stood easily in the middle of the room.

Relentus felt overdressed in his blue military uniform, but at least he had remembered to polish his boots. He suddenly recovered his manners and began to bow. But the Emperor held up his hand. Relentus stopped mid-bow, wondering what he had done wrong. But the Emperor had come forth, slowly and purposefully, and stopped almost nose to nose with Relentus.

Relentus realised he was being studied, as the Emperor walked around him meticulously, not touching, just scrutinising. . .

Is he smelling my hair?

. . .Until he had come back around to face Relentus. The Emperor again held up his hands and clasped them firmly together palm to palm, before pressing his fingertips onto his own forehead.

"You are The One," he said, reverently.

Relentus almost smirked aloud. *The One?* How many times had he seen that trope in holo-vids? But he was also somewhat relieved. Exmoor had been right—as usual.

"I am," Relentus replied, trying not to sound too pompous. "It is time we put an end to this war and were united. We are, after all, brothers." He thought he had laid it on a bit thick, but the Emperor didn't seem to notice.

"We are indeed." He seemed relieved himself. "But first, I must make a confession." He drew closer to whisper in Relentus' ear. "I am not the Emperor!"

Relentus tensed, looking about him ready for action, but nothing happened. He looked at the impersonator, anger filling him.

"What's going on here? Why am I here?"

"Forgive me for this transgression, General. It was necessary. You see, I am, or was, the Emperor's First Consul, Marrathanor." He paused, sadness in his eyes. "The Emperor is dead! Murdered!"

Relentus couldn't speak, but he managed to word 'how'.

Even though the translator didn't pick it up, the Consul knew what he had said.

"I will tell you in a minute, but first . . ."

He reached around to grab an object sitting in plush cushions behind him. Relentus couldn't believe his eyes when a long gleaming sword appeared and was levelled at his heart. Before Relentus could react, Marrathanor pronounced:

"Xaul Relentus, General of Earth, Son of Xaal; by the powers invested in me, Marrathanor, First Consul of the late Emperor Xalarius, I pronounce you Emperor of Axala."

He traced an 'X' or star shape, Relentus couldn't tell, across his uniformed torso then circled his heart.

"The mark of Xaal is now complete upon you."

Relentus had never been more shocked in his life.

Had that translated right: Emperor of Axala?

The thought of leading one world seemed impossible less than two weeks ago, but two? The only son of Markal and Zia, civil servants, born in New Athens, 2176, was now a General and an Emperor. The adventurous, ambitious, blue-haired favourite of Augustus Hawkhurst, who was probably laughing in his sea grave at the thought of Relentus being crowned Emperor of another world. Relentus wondered what would happen next. Marrathanor spoke his thoughts.

"All of this must seem like a shock to you, Your Excellency. But you *are* the new Emperor. It was written millennia ago, that one such like you, of a different world, would come to unite us with our ancient brothers. We saw you speaking on your world of death and retribution, but we knew that it would not come. We will fully repay for and rectify anything to improve relations with Earth. Indeed, your captured men are even now being returned to you alive and well."

"Thank you, Marrathanor," Relentus was appreciative, but there was more on his mind. "Can you tell me how the last Emperor was killed?" he asked, still trying to comprehend what was happening.

Marrathanor looked aggrieved.

"Let me show you."

He took out a small crystal from his pocket, set it on the ground, stepped back a couple paces, and barked a command:

"*Greejt!*"

The room around Relentus completely transformed.

Whoa, an immersive holo-projection. Too costly for Earth ships, for now. He was startled by Marrathanor's voice, a ghostly presence beside him.

132

"Watch."

Relentus turned to the scene, revealing a circular glass mosaic-encrusted geodesic dome penetrated by the dappling rays from the orange sun. The Emperor's chamber was dominated by the throne toward the rear centre with red carpeting and wall trappings among the carved pillars and a light sculpture to the throne's right. Relentus felt like an audience member of a play invited to the fringes of the backstage. He could see the protagonists gathering.

"The Superions," explained Marrathanor. "Our mutal enemy."

Relentus could hear an argument starting. He could almost touch the Superion.

"You've done what?" Mode shouted at the Emperor, raising a fist.

The three guards around the throne raised their laser lances, pointing them at the Superions.

Xalarius stamped from this throne. "You forget whom you address, Mode! I am the Emperor Xalarius, son of Xaal, ruler of the Axalans. My will is everyone's command, even yours, weak-colour!" His blue eyes flared above his veil, ruffled by his harsh breath. "The fleet are returning at my order, I will not engage Earth Forces, I will return the prisoners, and I will receive the new Commander Earth Forces as the new Emperor, my successor." He huffed and sat back down, glowering at Mode, daring him to challenge him.

Mode clenched his fists. "Why?" delivered in a growl.

Xalarius smiled. "The prophesy," he explained calmly. "This is the Axalan way; a deep part of Axalan understanding, which has been alive in our culture for thousands of years. The Mark of Xaal on the human is validation of the Word of our God and turning our backs to him now would be defeating the purpose of our lives. Xaul Relentus is the prophesied one, the true son of Xaal. It has been written." He shrugged. "Yes, a weak-colour," he laughed, "not you, but him!" He mocked Mode.

The Superions looked at Mode for direction. Mode turned his sinister mask back upon the Emperor.

"We shall see about that!"

Mode lashed out with his right arm at the Emperor, the very air molecules turning from gas to a solid shaft extending from Mode's arm. The Emperor was knocked over in his throne.

"Are you mad, Mode?" Xalarius choked in anger. "You will never leave this world alive! Attack!" he ordered his guards.

There was no movement.

It took a moment for Xalarius to realise the guards' minds had been locked out by Psyren, their blank faces unheeding of anything around them. He quickly dived to his right and cowered behind his throne for protection.

Psyren laughed. "You protected your mind, Xalarius," she insulted him by calling him by his name, "But you forgot your personal guard."

Mode swivelled, this time his left hand thrust forward toward the large chamber doors, heating them up, a weld forming to seal the great red entrance shut.

Xalarius knew what was coming next, but he had one desperate play at hand before the end came as his guards, under Psyren's control, turned upon him with their lances.

Relentus' perspective changed, pulling up and back. There was a hidden upper chamber overlooking the court, shielded from Psyren's telepathic reach; Marrathanor's office, the literal over-seer of Emperor Xalarius' court.

"Reinforcements on the way, Your Excellency..."

"No," yelled the Emperor, directed at Marrathanor, shielded from view and detection, but Xalarius' eyes were fixed on Mode. "No," he repeated. "No one dies here today, but myself or you, Mode. I challenge you to combat!"

He charged up, knocking one of the oblivious guards over, grabbing his laser lance by the center hilt. The beams of hard light emanating from the hilt were held point-end toward Mode.

"Choose a weapon and fight like an honourable warrior."

He held the lance out in a defensive position, twisting and manipulating it around his body with ease and menace. His stance welcomed an attack.

Mode scoffed. "Your error, Your Excellency, is to think I am a man of honour."

The polished stone floor under the Emperor abruptly shifted and shot up in thin jagged columns piercing the Emperor's arms, legs, and torso.

"Aargh!" Xalarius screamed, dropping the lance, his royal blood spraying across the floor and pouring down his body.

"No!" yelled Marrathanor from his post. He had already defied his Emperor's wishes, but reinforcements would be too late.

Mode advanced toward the Emperor slowly, hands clasped behind his back.

Xalarius faced Mode. "I am ready to die for my God. But the light of the Empire will never go out!" he spat harshly at Mode.

Mode regarded the impaled Axalan, who to his credit, hadn't uttered another word of pain, as his life ebbed away.

"You do like playing with light, Emperor, so be it!"

Mode reached out and touched Xalarius' chest.

Now the Emperor did scream as his skin became incandescent. His own being was transformed into golden scorching light spreading over his body. His screams died in an ugly gurgle but there was a slight smile of exulation on his face as he expired. He had become a figure of light at last. The Emperor burned out. Not a mote of ash was left as the Emperor flashed out of existence. The stone columns crumbled to a fine, burnt-smelling dust.

Fierce banging on the doors from the outside, interupted the Superions' quiet contemplation of the Emperor's demise. Palace guards had arrived and attempted to hammer and blast their way into the chambers.

The two other guards on either side of the throne dropped dead as Psyren entered their minds visciously shorting their neurons. They didn't need the complication of them now.

"Plan, boss", spoke Zone. "They'll be in any minute." He looked back at the doors anticipating a fight.

"Let them come!" Invadress said for everyone.

Mode nodded, the heat from the Emperor's departure dissipating quickly.

"You know what to do."

They all faced the doors anticipating the attack.

"No, left!" shouted Psyren in panic. "Diversion!"

The glass panels around them shattered and hundreds of the warriory charged in, heavy armoured troops with particle assault rifles already firing.

"Da hell!?" Zone shouted, teleporting out of the way. He popped up in various positions picking off soldiers with weapons he stole from each victim.

Warper took to the air, hovering twenty meters over the doors firing his weapon as more Axalan troops poured in.

Psyren floored a whole platoon, the alien soldiers clutching their heads as their brains cooked. Another squad were hurled across the chamber into others.

KRAKOOM!

The chamber doors exploded from their hinges, Psyren having just enough time to divert them across the broken glass panels. Mode touched the ground turning part of the floor in the direction of the doors and the huge metal doors themselves into molten liquid along the perimeter. Scores of unfortunate Axalans were scorched and drowned in lava.

The chamber caught alight and all dodged fire, weapon beams, and physical attacks.

Mode grinned under his mask. He could see the other Superions were enjoying stretching their powers as well.

Invadress had already used the chaos created by Zone and Psyren to launch her own attack. Grasping the light sculpture of Xalarius, she siphoned the energy through her, channelling lethal electrical bolts through every warrior advancing through the doors. They fried in electricity.

Psyren groped into the minds of more warriory turning weapons against each other.

And high above the melee, Warper flew, his side arm pinpointing targets from above. His personal force-shield made him an impregnable sharp-shooter as he guarded the entry.

Mode guided the lava upward and across the cracked dome walls, hardening it. Any more warriory were trapped outside.

"Zone," he commanded. "Form up!" he called the others.

The Superions formed a tight circle holding hands, Zone in the middle, clutching Mode's shoulder. In an instant they disappeared, teleported, leaving behind the dead and bewildered.

The light faded, Relentus finding himself back in the dark of the ship's chambers.

"I'm sorry for your loss, Marrathanor." He bowed his head in sorrow.

Marrathanor chided himself. "It could have left the Empire shattered, but it did not. But," he looked tired and grieved, "I waited too long; should have foreseen this outcome. The Superions were increasingly the power behind his throne and they are the ones responsible for the attack on your base. In a way, we could thank them for discovering you."

"Where are they now?" Relentus asked, concerned.

"I do not know. They had teleported to the spaceport, wrecked most of it and the transports and taken off in their ship, absconding into space. We haven't seen them since. But they will be back."

"I hope they have the sense to end their fight now," Relentus said hopefully.

Marrathanor shook his head. "I doubt it. They may be heading to Earth. They always wanted to take over Earth."

"Really, why Earth?"

Marrathanor tilted his head in surprise, then his face grew grave.

"You do not know, do you? The Superions are human."

Relentus' jaw dropped. "Human? But they're blue!"

"Disguised, yes, which is why we called them weak-colours, a derorgatory term for humans, I'm afraid," he looked abashed. "They appeared some years ago offering their services to the Emperor. They were a novelty to him. He knew their motives of course: to take over Axala and Earth, but the Emperor thought he could use them. How wrong he was." Marrathanor sadly shook his head.

"They'll come to justice one day, Marrathanor, I swear it!"

"I believe you. But for now, I entreat you to journey back with us and meet your people."

My people, thought Relentus. Hadn't Raimont told him the same thing?

137

"I would love to meet my people, but first I must brief my fleet on what has happened. It will take time for them to adjust. So while I'm on Axala, they can get used to the situation. Agreed?"

"Yes, Your Excellency," Marrathanor bowed. "Your Imperial ship," he indicated around him, "the *Semblance of Order*, awaits you."

Relentus accepted his royal title thinking better than to correct him. He now wished he was just the General of Earth Forces.

Relentus regarded Marrathanor. There was something familiar about him. His soothing tone and manner much like someone esle he knew well. Relentus wondered about that.

"If you do not mind me asking, how old are you, Marrathanor?"

Marrathanor smiled, a smile Relentus had seen many a time on Exmoor's face when he had asked him a difficult question; a world weary smile that had seen everything.

"I'm older than you think," Marrathanor said in a whisper, a twinkle in his eye.

Relentus didn't doubt him. "You know, I think there's someone I want you to meet when I come back. I think the two of you will have much in common."

Marrathanor smiled and bowed to his new Emperor. He clapped his hands and the doors opened, an escort awaiting.

Relentus left the Royal chambers and made his way back to his awaiting shuttle. The trip took longer this time as all the enthusiastic Axalan crew assembled to line the ship's corridors, bowing and praying for him.

Relentus accepted graciously, just taking it all in.

Now if only I can get my human crews to do the same.

"This is the worst war I've never fought!" sulked *Vanguard*'s Captain Brand, to the general agreement of the assembled officers.

The stocky, blond-haired Australian, known to his crew, though not to his face, as 'Captain Firebrand' for his rash tongue sat around the oak conference table between captains Riven and Lucus, arms folded and brow knotted in frustration.

Relentus had returned a few hours ago to *Starship Earth*, convening a captain's conference in his packed officers' mess. He had told them the incredible story of how it had been preordained that the returning Axalan son of God with special characteristics would come to rule Axala and unite them with Earth. He had left out the ancient war bit. That would be too much for them. Many of the captains had been outraged that no war was to take place (as Relentus was sure many politicians, families of deceased soldiers, and the public would be, but he would save more lives this way).

"There will never be a better time to hit them," argued *Exsurgent*'s Captain Lucas, sticking up for Brand.

But Relentus overruled them. "Not today. Peace is the way, the only way.

Simon Exmoor sat beside him at the head of the conference table nodding in agreement, his eyes seeking out other dissenters.

"And to further cement our relations," Relentus had finished, "we should commemorate this day by finding a new world to settle both humans and Axalans."

There were more murmurs, some more than angry.

Relentus thought, *have I gone too far, too fast?*

Captain Lucas spoke up again. "Sir, we've been at war with these blue bastards, excuse my language, these new allies for seventy years. Now all of a sudden they want peace, they want us to forget and forgive, they want a union world, they want this and that, they want, they want, they want! What do we get out of this? And what's the guarantee that they'll keep their bargain?"

There were cheers of more agreement.

Relentus clenched his jaw. He'd had enough of this griping.

"I am the guarantee!" he said, storming up from his chair, reminding them, with a hard thump on the table, "as Commander Earth Forces *and* Emperor of Axala," he said burning with pride.

Everyone went quiet, Relentus looking them all in the eye. They hadn't quite totally believed his story. Now they did. Now they understood. The war was really over. No final fight. No more deaths. Just an anticlimax as big and as draining as a black hole.

"Now, I'm going down to Axala to greet my people. If any of you wish to meet your former enemy, you're more than welcome to do so. If not, sail home. And Godspeed."

The naval term had been directed at Brand, whose family hailed from a long line of captains dating back to the days of sailing ships. Everyone diverted their eyes from Brand, even Lucas, lest they be associated with Firebrand.

No one budged, except for Brand who hastily stood up. Everybody looked at him with unease; his blusterous voice speaking out.

"Well, I don't know about you lads, but I'm with the Emperor!"

A quiet snickering in the background turned into quick laughter which everyone joined in.

Then a cheer from Captain Lucas went up for Relentus:

"Three cheers for General Relentus, Emperor of Axala. Hip! Hip!"

"Hooray!"

"Hip! Hip!"

"Hooray!"

"Hip! Hip!"

"Hooray!"

On the final cheer, Exmoor sidled up to Relentus, a knowing glint in his eye. Pretending to clear his throat he said, "Told you so!"

Relentus grinned back. "So you did, and I hope I know what I'm getting myself into."

But for now, he had a date with destiny and a new world.

Elsewhere

. . . A world in oblivion.

Psyren bolted upright from her nightmare. The same visions again. The same one she'd been having for the past few months. She looked around her room, everything normal and in place. Reassuring. What did the vision mean? She didn't want to tell the others of her distress, she didn't want them to know. But she knew something was on the way. Something not good.

Ever since that last deadly night at the Emperor's palace, the Superions had been exiles. Mode had vowed vengeance upon Axala and Earth and the Emperor's death had only been the beginning. They had headed out of Axalan space and into the Far Regions, discovering a planetoid worth inhabiting. With their combined powers, mostly Mode's, they had fashioned their own space fortress.

It was from here that Invadress had detected the same anomalous signals as before. Planets and stars were disappearing or moving, seemingly by themselves, light-years away.

"Absolutely impossible," Invadress had said, "Impossible!"

Something was destroying the galaxy.

Interlude 2

The Chronopolis

"What!"

Lightstream winced at her father's shout, sighing heavily.

"I said there's a system field around Magna Aura, I cannot penetrate." She had arrived back home with bad news and worse news. Her father had not been happy with her apparent flippancy.

Sola groaned. This wasn't what they wanted to hear. Phasia had mysteriously disappeared, Zeus knew where. The whole universe was at stake and all they had was bad news.

Helexius paced around the throne. The brother of Xathanius, Lord Aeon still hoped he was in charge for a short time until his brother was found. The alternative was not worth thinking about. He longed to be out searching as his nephew and neice were, but someone had to hold the fort. His handsome face was all frowns and furrows as he digested the news. His long blond hair was braided down to his shoulders and he had recently repaired his dark purple, gold-embroidered armour the Lore had managed to damage. He adjusted the two diagonally-crossed gold belts as he sat.

"Are you sure?" he simply asked, calming down somewhat.

"Yes, and further, though they covered their tracks well, I am pretty sure Lazeron, Cal Xarien, Zasandra, and Celestra are hiding on Magna Aura behind that field for some reason," Lightstream reported.

"And the bad news?" asked a hopeful Sola.

"That was the bad news," Lightstream confirmed, a shrug aimed at her father, whose face still showed mild annoyance at his daughter's light attitude. "The worse news is that while the Starguards we chose are in place on Earth, two more of them are missing from Magna Aura!" Lightstream braced for the reaction.

"Missing!" Helexius' voice rose as he bolted out of his throne again. "Hades' breath! What do you mean, missing?" he demanded, starting to pace the room. "Weren't you keeping an eye on them?" he shouted.

"We took the others from Magna Aura ourselves?" Sola was shocked. "Who's missing, 'Stream?" she asked.

Sola was like her father, Spheron, dark-skinned and wise beyond her years. She was also the first female in the Spheron line, ever. What that meant for the future of the Spherons, chief exegetes to the Celestian Knights and the Starguards, no one knew.

"We didn't take these ones, Sola. They were meant to stay behind. They are the remaining sons of Alphatronius: Decion and Alpha Rion. I could sense the energy of their swords in the trail Celestra tried to hide," Lightstream explained. "But I can't find them as the trail disappears."

There was a tense silence as minds processed the information.

"It must have happened right as we were transferring the others to Earth," Sola deduced. "And if I remember correctly, Celestra offered to help."

"You mean steal them," Lightstream corrected Sola, though for what reason she couldn't fathom.

Sola retorted, "And Timechantress hid the deed with some temporal spells and knots, hence no time trail. But my guess is if we look hard enough . . ." she began.

"And find the remnants of their trail," Lightstream continued, "but I already tried both up and down stream. And nothing."

"Oh," Sola pursed her lips in frustration.

"I'm not sure what else to do," Lightstream said, disappointment in her voice. "I can try again!"

But Helexius stopped her, shaking his head. Lightstream began to protest, but Helexius was adamant.

"No! We now know my sister is working in concert with Netherlord and Archron," he said of Timechantress. "If we show our hand and act too early then we could be lost. We have enough Starguards on Earth and that is more important. We'll let these two go for now, but we'll search for them later."

Lightstream wasn't finished. "But father, I can still search!"

"That, daughter," Helexius cut her off, "is final!"

Lightstream bowed to her father's wishes, reluctantly. Obedience now was imperative, but later was a whole different matter. Lightstream sulked.

Helexius tried to placate her. "Whatever is happening, Magna Aura seems to be out of immediate danger. Earth is the focus for now. It must be protected. Phasia foresaw it! Without the Starguards' protection, Earth's future will be doomed."

"But it's still there!" Lightstream blurted out, her arms flailing about in consternation, still sour from her father's rebuke.

"But that is only one possible future out of many and it was the presence of the Starguards on Earth that made that particular future possible," Helexius iterated. "And that was the future Phasia foresaw."

"Well that brings up the question, where is Phasia?" Sola asked.

Helexius looked evasive and didn't answer.

"Is there anything else?"

"Yes, definately," Lightstream nodded her head. "Something strange!"

She took out her small diamond-shaped crystalator and aimed it at the main crystalator orb, sitting in its alcove, which clouded over. They walked over to it and watched a holographic image form.

"Cirrius had managed to block all views of Magna Aura. All of our sensors are gone. And of course Timechantress and Celestra have erected a pervasive temporal field around all of Magna Aura. We cannot even travel there!" She looked over with a worried expression on her face. "But when I ventured uptime, I did capture these images."

The image flickered into view. Space, just outside the Magna Aura system.

"What are those?" Helexius squinted at the screen.

"Ships," Lightstream said. "Possible alien ships."

"At Magna Aura?" asked a confused Sola, looking at the huge angular shapes.

"Yep," Lightstream confirmed, enlarging the images. "I have looked at all the Celestian files and these ships do not match anything in their records. They're huge, bigger than any swordship I've seen, like city-ships, and without identifying sigils. They might be new Magna Aura designs, but the timeframe is a strange."

"Strange how!" Helexius wanted to know.

"Well..."

BOOM!

The three were violently thrown to the ground as alarms shrieked. The Chronopolis shuddered and tilted.

"What was that?" Sola shouted.

"Sensors are down!" Lightstream yelled back, looking at the crystalators consoles. "Massive temporal disruption. We're under atttack!"

"Impossible!" Helexius shouted wildly.

There were quick heavy footfalls as Spheron, cape flying behind him, came running into the hall. His face was creased with sweat and fear, his mouth locked on one word.

"Lore!"

CHAPTER SEVEN

The encrypted letter had arrived late at night by a light-fast ExA courier and secured with Commander Earth Forces' personal seal. Kellis had been awakened by the chiming of her quarter's doors, a polite Bion male—they were always polite—handing her the thin smart-polycarbon folder, once she had bothered to leave the comfort of her bed and pad over to the door. Bidding the Bion goodnight, Kellis sat on her bed and turned up the lights, staring at the letter curiously.
"You'll never know what's in there just staring at it," she told herself.

It felt like plastic, but the polycarbon could be bent, folded, and scrunched but not torn or damaged so as to negate the message. And it was coded for hers and Relentus' DNA only, sender and receiver.

Kellis let out a huff of air over the letter's surface, first check. The correct breath revealed an oval patch in the center of the letter big enough for her to key with her thumb. That in turn unlocked an auto-drop-down flap with a retinal scan chip. Kellis let it scan her right eye.

"Open message," she said, the voiceprint registering the correct ID.

The letter unsealed, unfolding into a 6x4 screen. The words scrolled across the dark grey material. Kellis had expected just a worded message, but it was accompanied by an audio message from the Emperor-General himself. Her eyes lit up with surprise.

February 2217

Commander Lynn Kellis
Zero Star

REF: PROJECT MULTIFORCE

Lynn,

By now you must have heard of my extraordinary ascension to the Axalan Imperial throne. I now command the forces and welfare of two worlds and all therein. I am the Supreme Protector.

149

But the situation is more volatile than ever. Our war is not over. The group responsible for the Christmas Day Massacre, the Superions have fled Axala and are now wanted fugitives.

They pose a potent threat to the security of all our territories: Earth, Axalan, and Bion. And Lynn—the Superions are human. I don't know if you had an inkling on that.

In any event, I am activating your project. I hereby charge the organization, hereby known as the Multiforce, to commit to the enforcement of order both within and outside of the sphere of said territories in an effort to end the terror of the Superions.

The Superions will be brought to justice for the war crimes they have committed. Your task is essential to the future of galactic peace. I wish you fortune and Godspeed.

Yours sincerely,

Emperor-General Xaul Relentus
Earth Council Headquarters

And below, in his own hand writing: 'Anything you need, Lynn, in support and logistics, just ask.'

Kellis could scarcely believe her eyes. This was the moment she had been waiting for. Fully awake now, she rushed and got dressed, giddy with excitement. It reminded her of days of old when she, Starshina, J.J., and Warren had been a group, before the days had ended in tragedy. Before leaving her room, she keyed a button on her communicator, a direct signal sent to each of her new team. She headed for sub-deck zero, their new headquarters. Upon arrival, Kellis let herself into a side room, an array of uniforms awaiting her. She put her uniform on and waited for the others to arrive.

Elsewhere

A paradisiacal world rests in the peaceful caress of space, a new home to old adversaries. An unseen invader slips through the air, descending like death in darkness to the ground; his green armour and evil sword glinting in the pre-dawn light. He walks the land, surveying the killing ground with a coldness which rapes it barren. He breathes in the air, rich and lusty; he grabs the soil, fertile and soft, now dry and crumbling in his gloved hand, a grim smile playing on his lips. All is envisioned; the life of the world; the terror and the carnage to follow.

It begins.

He drives his charged blade into the ground unleashing shards of livid energy and thunderous quakes. The planted sword obeys its liege, absorbing the life-force of the planet's heart, feeding itself. He throws his arms over the land before him, spreading his disease, death lying in its wake. A stormy darkness fills the air. He walks the land, his great cape flying like a green whirlstorm of death. His touch is electric, lethal, and rages like wildfire, spreading far and wide. He laughs at the dead, a triumphant smile on his face, a shine in his dark eyes. He lets rip a hellacious yell searing the air around him.

This planet is going to die.

A clarion call from afar shatters the sky, announcing his discovery. Then the brave arrive, growing dots on the horizon, thousands, growing in force like angry locusts. By land and air they attack, their boldness only teasing but a fraction of his powers. They die one by one, horrifically and mercilessly. They fall from the air with a wave of his hand, burn at his stare, choke and die from fear. They swarm mindlessly, aimlessly. They're frantic, he's fanatic. He can't stop laughing, but still they attack, reforming, reinforced, their puny souls rushing to the slaughter, unavoidable and final. The battle rages on and on, wave after wave lost in his insanity. But still they surge on, undaunted, knowing that their future depends on it. Raw focused fire screams around him, unceasing, but useless. He will not fall, will not falter. He just won't die.

His power is stronger and gains strength as his attackers muster for their final assault. The elite, the last of their defences, the forbidden bombs, the ultimate missiles, the killing machines. They converge on him, crashing around him again and again with a fury and a vengeance worthy of Armageddon, giant fuming clouds suffocating the air, wreaking death and annihilation. Nothing could survive. Twice, thrice, four times, they pass, their blasts blazing through the atmosphere, lighting up the heavens for all to see and admire their valiant stand. Surely they've won, and a hopeful cheer fills their hearts as the world watches and holds its ragged breath. And as the dust slowly clears, lingering like a shroud of death, the ravaged land is revealed, everything completely destroyed.

Except him. He still stands.

The world erupts in chaos. They cry for the world to stop; they want to get off. They call for God for the devil has come. His attackers flee like wild game, their fear now his joy. He toys with their lives as they desperately struggle in vain to escape the end. But he drags them back to him, down from the blood-raining sky, back across the scorched land, back into his maelstrom. There's no escape, no time left. Deeper and deeper into the nothingness that is his warped being, he brings them closer; closer until he can hear their dying screams, closer until he can see the fear on their faces, closer still, until he can see the tears in their eyes. Closer until they are dead and dust, like the ruined land he stands upon, victorious.

He walks the land, alone, the victor. He spares no one, no soul. They will not live again. He will live forever.

He walks the land, a time-starved wilderness. All had been envisioned, the death of the planet.

He draws his sword from the razed land, heaving it into the air. Its work is not done. The blade pulsates with stolen energy. Bidden by its master it releases the charge, spilling into the air, splitting the empty sky with crackling lightning bolts. The energy races across the planet, destroying anything not destroyed. Cities crumble, mountains wither, forests burn and die. It bores through the planet, breaking it apart like old bones, sucking its core dry. The planet shivers and cries in death, ripped of its heart, body, and soul.

The destroyer takes to the vacuum, the rocky husk below now a vanquished world. And as the Lord of Death disappears to another world, this one dies a cold and silent death, fading to nothingness, seen and heard by no one. A paradise lost.

A world in oblivion.

Aaron woke up in a cold sweat, not even realising he had gone to sleep. It had been the first time that he had seen the whole of the premonition, which is what he now believed it to be. It was a warning of the future; when, he didn't know, but happen it would, unless they could stop it.

He was just about to try and meditate upon the premonition, when a beeping alerted him on his comm unit. It was late, but he knew who it would be. Kellis was calling on a priority line.

All he got was, "Meet me in sub-deck zero. It's important."

Succinct as usual, Aaron thought.

Clearing his mind of distracting visions, he got himself dressed.

Aaron was the first to arrive; a quizzical look on his face when he saw Kellis dressed in a non-military uniform.

"Well, do you like it?"

She posed for him, showing off her athletic body. Aaron admitted wordlessly that he did, much to Kellis' liking.

Her dark green, stylised tunic, with an up-turned collar, led into black leggings and dark green boots. A white gun-belt sat jauntily around her waist, while a black one with a shoulder holster slashed across her torso, another holster down on her right calf.

"I come protected," she said.

"Wow!" said Zane, as she entered the room. "You look like a real soldier, Kellis."

"I think I'll take that as a compliment, Zane." She grinned at the young Astral. "I'll have you know I was once. And now I am again," said a triumphant Kellis.

Aristedes and Starshina arrived together. It didn't take any guesses to know they had come together from one or the other's quarters.

Kellis ignored the awkward situation. Nothing was going to spoil this day for her.

"Okay, now that everyone is here, I've had a letter from the Emperor-General himself, a close personal friend of ours," Kellis said happy with herself, "And basically he's authorised my plan to form a counter-agency against the Superions. We can operate anywhere in the three territories, that is Earth, Axalan and Bion, and have virtual *carte blanche* to do whatever it takes to bring them in. We'll make the space-ways clear of any rogue super-powered riff-raff. With me so far?" she said excitedly.

Nods of amusement confirmed that they were.

Kellis continued, "We are the Multiforce. I'm still Commander Kellis. But you . . ." she said to Aaron, presenting him with a black and grey uniform, "From now on are Mindscream. Zane, you're Windburst." She gave the young Astral a purple and magenta uniform, who stared at it with reservations.

"Starshina . . ." Kellis held out an ice-blue and white uniform for her. "For you Winterborne. And last, but not least, some princely armour for you, T.I.M.E., that's for Temporally Independent Mutated Entity." Kellis handed Aristedes dark blue armour with a distinctly-meshed tunic. "Well, come on then. Get changed!" Kellis ordered.

The others stood around the lab, looking at their uniforms a bit dubiously, before dispersing into various corners to change.

Kellis expounded on the uniforms characteristics. "The uniforms may look leathery, but are light-weight . . ."

". . . Not to mention gaudy," intoned Aristedes.

"Oi, okay, maybe a bit over the top," conceded Kellis with a grin, "But they're designed from research into Bion skin, and you know how tough that is. It'll grow to suit you, literally, bond with you, anticipating your needs, each enhancing your powers and stamina, while giving protection. There's also an in-built communicator. Check out the comm units on your wrists and upper collars," she said, demonstrating hers and then hearing various beeps as the others tried theirs. "Right, that's it. Are you all ready now?"

One by one they emerged, uniforms neatly fitted. They looked around at each other and though at first they suppressed their laughs, they gradually began to feel the uniforms adjust to their bodies.

Kellis inspected them, pleased with the results.

"Splendid," she said, proudly. "The Multiforce is born."

Far away in the outer regions of Axalan space, the Superions had watched as Earth and Axala had made peace, the newly established Axalan Ambassador, Marrathanor, of all people, arriving on Earth. By now, it was common knowledge that their escaped target, Xaul Relentus, had been made Emperor over the alien world.

Mode was sickened. He should have had the honour of ruling both worlds. He alone. Now he had to watch Relentus receiving such an honour.

"From this time forward, all our efforts will bear toward destroying Earth and Axala," he vowed.

"I'll crush their minds," Psyren sneered, dark looks scrawled across her face. She was looking a bit dishevelled these days, like she hadn't slept.

"Whoa, calm down, Psyren," grimaced Invadress, holding her head. "What's with the venom? Think you can turn down the mind-juice for a while?"

Psyren glared at them, noticing the pain on their faces, except for Mode's masked visage. The whole group had been on edge since leaving Axala. Now they were cooped up together on their asteroid base, little niggling differences getting on each other's nerves.

"The only thing making me edgy is the fact that something you can't describe is destroying parts of the galaxy for fun. Why don't you concentrate on that and leave me alone," she shouted, storming out of the main galley, presumedly toward her quarters, where she'd been spending a lot of time recently.

Invadress was glad she had shouted aloud and not telepathically. Who knew what that could have done to them. She shrugged, relieved her headache had subsided almost immediately in Psyren's absence.

"What's her problem?" she asked, looking at the others for answers. But they all looked as baffled as she did.

Mode had noticed a big difference in Psyren. Distraction and destruction on her mind. And if someone with her psionic abilities couldn't handle it, that was a big problem he didn't want to have to handle while waging war across the galaxy. He needed Psyren.

Leaving the others, Mode followed Psyren to her quarters. He needed answers. If she didn't have them and was becoming a liability to his team, then she would have to be dealt with now, rather than later.

The visions had been coming more frequently now. Psyren knew it signalled that whatever it was she was seeing was going to happen soon: the cruel death of a civilised world.

It wasn't the fact that the world would die, God knows she, Mode and the others had destroyed countless lives before. It was the power behind it, unlimited and supreme; on an order far above their little lives and the destruction would not stop at one planet. It would continue unless something was done to stop it. But she knew that Mode would not stop it. He would try to control it.

And therein lay Psyren's dilemma: how to stop Mode from coveting something that would ultimately destroy them all, if she didn't destroy Mode first.

"Marrathanor has supplied us with a wealth of information about the Superions," Kellis briefed the Multiforce after their uniform fitting and once back in her lab office. "The Axalan Warriory kept files of what abilities the Superions have, in case they needed to defend themselves against them."

"Well that didn't work for their Emperor," a sarcastic Aristedes quipped, looking around for laughs, none of which were forthcoming. He faced forward, smirk wiped off his face.

Kellis gave him a withering look.

"But the main thing is, astonishingly, the Superions are human," she talked through the sounds of confusion and surprise, raising her hands for quiet. "Though their origins and names are unknown," she continued through the continued low chatter. "They had disguised themselves on the Emperor's behest, lest the Axalan warriory rebelled against the idea of having superhumans in their midst."

Kellis fired up a holo-projector.

"So, to start, this is their leader Mode."

The rotating image revealed a solidly-built male well over six foot. He wore a one-piece silver-metallic soft armour with thin black bands across his thighs, waist, biceps and torso, the latter also crossed by a thick blue sash. His silver mask was accentuated with more blue running down the middle within which was set two small black rectangular eye ports.

Kellis continued. "His face has never been seen. He has the ability to transmute an object's molecular form and shape, like his fashioned permanent mask. He never discussed himself or talked of Earth in fond terms, having a deep-seated and unknown vendetta against Earth."

Several hands went up, Kellis knowing they wanted to know why he was so against Earth.

"Keep questions till after," she said. She moved to the next image.

A lithe woman was on show. She did not wear a mask, showing blue eyes, which may have been her natural colour, but her light blue skin hid identifying features Zero Star's computer could not penetrate. She was an unknown. She was around five foot six inches, with long loose dark blue hair and wore blue and green soft-armour which resembled a flight suit.

"Psyren." Kellis introduced the Superion. "Mode's right hand woman. She was well-known in the court to be a darker personality, out of all the Superions, but she had the complete trust and ear of Mode and she was protective of him, though no personal relationship was noted. She's a powerful psychokinetic," Kellis glanced at Aaron, who raised a quizzical eyebrow, "but at times it seemed she wasn't used to her powers and was easily prone to psychic fits sending out reams of mental barrages which made others nearby ill. The late Emperor had taken to wearing a telepathic-limiter to protect his mind from her."

Aaron raised his brows again at that information. He would have to have a deeper look into telepathic-limiter technology.

The next holo-image flashed up.

"Invadress, their powerhouse, physically and intellectually, though apparently older than the rest. She channels electromagnetic energy through her body. She's their co-pilot of the *Dragon Charger*, a gift from the late Emperor."

Invadress was tall, around six foot, with dark blue skin, her dark blue cornrowed hair pulled back severely into a twisted pony-tail. She also wore no mask. Aristedes thought she could benefit from one as she did not look the cherriest of folk with her sneer. Her armour was a curious mixture of red and blue with her left arm in blue, ending in a red gauntlet, the blue continuing to curve under her left shoulder diagonally across half her body to complete her right leg in blue, while the rest of her was clothed in red, with a gold diamond-shaped pendant gracing the low point of her V-necked top.

"And next, on to Zone the teleporter," Kellis announced. "Marrathanor had noted Zone and Psyren seemed to have had a long professional relationship, both quite protective of Mode. He is somewhat taciturn, but always watching and listening for danger. He has been known to teleport the Emperor's less-desirable subjects or their enemies into space for fun."

There was a low whistle from Aristedes. "That's nasty."

Kellis nodded grimly turning back to Zone's profile. His armour was red with a white belt and narrow white panelling along his legs, arms, torso, and neck. He wore a cowl with a goggle-like device covering up his dark blue face.

"Lastly, is Warper."

The hologramme man appeared before them, his dark-blue metallic armour laced with black lines and dominated by a large black diamond pattern from his upper chest to belt. Like Zone, Warper wore a cowl leaving his lower dark blue face open.

Kellis had a curious look on her face, appraising Warper, as if trying to remember something. But she carried on with her brief.

"For some reason, the other Superions treated Warper as an outcast for whatever reason. Marrathanor believes he suffered bouts of depression, but Psyren was always on hand to administer some of her psychic aid, though perhaps it was actually psychic manipulation. Be that as it may, he is an exceptional self-powered flyer, their main ship pilot and he possesses some sort of controllable forcefield around him." Kellis paused again, looking closer at Warper. She smiled and shook her head. "If there was a weak link in the Superions' chain, it's Warper."

Kellis leaned on her lectern to emphasis her point.

"The Superions are universal threat number one! We have been charged with stopping them at any costs. And there's another thing, probably and potentially more dangerous than them."

Aristedes made a 'what now' face.

"Before his demise, the Emperor had tasked the Superions to investigate, though unsuccessfully, a mysterious force that was destroying parts of the galaxy."

Aaron's ears perked up and his senses pushed into alert, but he did not say anything.

"I've put Zero Star's resources onto the subject. Based on Marrathanor's profiles and in the Bion's analyses of Mode's predilection for power, it is predicted he will continue to look for the source of the power in order to control it. If a pattern can be deduced from the destruction, then the Multiforce could track both the Superions and the phenomenon at the same time. All the Bions could detect at the moment was a slight temporal signature to the energy being used.

"Temporal?" blurted out Arsistedes, Zane a beat behind him.

"Yes," Kellis confirmed, holding up her hands for quiet. "So, let me answer your questions and give you your assignments at the same time."

The team settled down in anticipation.

"Starshina, we've learned the *Dragon Charger* can be traced by its light-drive signatures. The Bions are already doing so, but lend them a hand."

Starshina smiled, glad to be involved.

"Aaron..."

"I know, I will psi-probe for Psyren. But I would also like to probe for any forces which may be responsible for the galactic destruction."

"Oh, how will you do that second bit?" Kellis enquired into his plan, intrigued.

"I'll tell you later," Aaron wearily said, not looking forward to delving into his nightmares.

"Fine," Kellis accepted. "And Aistedes and Zane will investigate the temporal aspects of the destructive force. Do you think the Astrals could be involved?"

Aristedes shrugged. Turning to Zane, he said, "We'll have to look at the data first. Some Astrals leave distinctive energy patterns and temporal waves only we'd be able to verify as them."

"Sure, okay. Right, any more questions, comments," Kellis asked, giving Aristedes a stern 'don't' look, to deter any wisecracks. There weren't any of either. "Good," she said. "Let's get to work."

The Multiforce commenced their mission to track the Superions, the final obstacle to lasting peace between Earth and Axala.

The containo—the ubiquitous variable-sized, cargo carrier—was loaded onto the small sleek, unmarked, black ship which had arrived early in the morning, a time when shifts were changing and the shuttle bay was empty.

Starfighter Machine's body lay in the quadrasteel containo being transferred over to Lothar Bliss, a lightship pilot, and erstwhile veteran ExA courier. The last days of the war had not been fit to take the artifact over to Zero Star, but now hostilities were over, it was time to catch up on outstanding work. Bliss left Base 51, empty ship bays revealing that the Gyr fleet had also pulled out on a new mission.

Quadrasteel was a thick, course-metal alloy utilised for constructing frontier space-ports, atmospheric domes on hazardous worlds, cargo ships and their containos. It was hardy stuff, resistant and resilient.

Starfighter Machine lay in its metal tomb as it was taken to Zero Star, the Bion techs having taken over for Bliss, who quickly took off in his lightship on his next assignment. Starfighter Machine had then been taken down to Kellis' lab, where the absent Multiforce would carry out tests upon their return. The Bions had been assured by Bliss, via Base 51's researchers, that Starfighter Machine was quite dormant, the quadrasteel shielding it from any extraneous energy sources that could be absorb. Now in cryo storage, everyone had then kept their distance. Starfighter Machine was totally isolated.

Engineers, shippers and traders were quite rightly proud of quadrasteel, the coarse, cheap, unyielding material being impervious to most anything Earth scientists could throw at it—except thanium.

Zero Star practically ran on thanium. Thanium emissions seeped into the metal confines of the box and into Starfighter Machine, energy once again coursing through the body of the metal being.

Bitter feelings had still prevailed among sects on both worlds, but the Emperor-General had been adamant that both peoples should learn to live together in peace, even after such a tragedy like the war. It was time to heal rifts and become closer so that a lasting peace could be bequeathed to their children, their children's children and beyond.

To that end, the veteran Earth Councillor Zev Tantillion had proposed the idea of a world settled by both humans and Axalans and that more joint exploration should be forthcoming. In a drive for unity, the world would have a name which symbolised something to both cultures. Eager lexiconographers, students, media, everyone on both worlds had sent in proposals. In the end, the name Home had been chosen as the new world's name.

For humans, home represented an abode, a material and physical one, where to an Axalan, it was the inner spiritual center, the residence and core of the soul. Home was an apt name for both species, symbolising a new beginning in reality and spiritually.

All they needed now was a suitable planet.

"Come in."

Mode entered Psyren's quarters, a sparse affair with little tolerance for decoration, even if there had been anything to adorn the room with. But that's how Psyren had wanted her room made on the forsaken rock they had made home.

Mode made his helmet melt away, sharp, dark features regarding Psyren.

"What's the matter, Steph?" he asked.

Psyren tensed. He had not called her that name in a long time. This was a serious talk coming up. She sat on her bed, long blue hair in disarray. Mode remembered a time when her hair had been short and blonde, a long time ago.

"We've known each other for years, you and me, so we have to talk, boss, seriously," said Psyren.

"Go on," Mode sounded intrigued.

She folded her hands on her lap to relax herself.

"This thing that's destroying stars and worlds will not stop. I've seen it in visions—nightmares really—and whatever it is, it's all-powerful and won't be stopped, unless we do something."

Mode almost laughed. Nothing could be that powerful, even he wasn't, but he saw how serious Psyren was.

"If it's this powerful, then how do we stop it? We don't even know what it is or where to find it."

"He."

"What?"

"He. I saw a man. A warrior. A warrior in green and silver armour, destroyer of worlds, slayer of stars. We won't find him, he'll find us." Psyren was staring into nothingness as if she was actually seeing the events in motion. "And we'll die!"

Mode was stunned to silence, but not in fear, Psyren could sense the fascination in his dark eyes through his mask.

"One man has all this power." Mode's eyes gleamed. "Tell me more."

"I can't," said Psyren, sounding a little exhausted. "That's all I see. The warrior and the destruction, time and time again."

Mode smiled, Psyren glimpsing only a part of his thoughts—he hid them well, though she knew not how.

"You know, Psy, I must meet this warrior," Mode whispered in awe. "I must see him. Test him. And either he is with us, or . . ." he let the thought linger, unfinished.

But Psyren knew death was on the way.

"Oh bloody Nora, what now!" Kellis huffed through gritted teeth.

For weeks on end they'd been scouring the quadrant, trying to get a fix on either the galaxy destroyer or the Superions, but they were both proving to be quite elusive. The *Esprit* was fast becoming their second home.

Sending a report to Simon Exmoor, their immediate superior in the absence of Emperor-General Relentus, they were surprised by Exmoor's request to return immediately to Zero Star. A special consignment Base 51 having arrived. Exmoor himself would be there for their appraisal of the contents, an alien, of sorts.

"Whatever it is, this Starfighter Machine had better be worth it," snapped an exasperated Kellis.

"Well, it withstood and defeated the 51 fleet, which is no mean feat," replied Aristedes, looking over the attached report to Exmoor's message on a padd. "And it has such a cool name!"

"I used to burn like a star once," Starshina suddenly said in a quiet voice. She sat in the rear cabin staring at her snow-white hands, bewildered. "But now I can only make things cold. How can that be?" she seemed to ask herself.

There was a disquieting silence, Kellis glancing at Winterborne. Sometimes her mind wandered off as it regained memories. "Don't worry Winter,' you're okay now." Kellis tried to assure her.

Time had 'jumped' them back in stages to Zero Star. After bringing in the *Esprit* to land, the Multiforce had been met by Exmoor as they disembarked.

"Hi, guys," he greeted them cordially. "Sorry to scrub the mission so soon, but ..."

"Never mind the chat, we'll get them next time, but what the hell is so important about this Starfighter Machine?" demanded Kellis. "Where is it?"

"Your lab." Exmoor, exhaling with impatience, started walking, getting the hint. "Well, first of all, you know as much as we do," began Exmoor. "It seems to be the last of its species and apparently had the ability to absorb energy."

Kellis could see where he was headed.

"You want us to examine it, try to reverse-engineer it, and see what made it tick." She thought about it a beat longer. "We could also find a way of using its ability to track the source of the destructive events," she said.

Exmoor was impressed. "Yes," he confirmed. "If you can take it apart that is. Without being killed!" he said plainly.

163

"Is that all?" asked Kellis, warming to the challenge, her mind already into a procedure. "And when would you like this done by?"

Exmoor smiled, his left shoulder rising fractionally toward his ear, a disarming technique used when matters were urgent and he didn't have the time to explain.

"As soon as possible, it is, then."

Exmoor, donning extra protection against the cold, accompanied the Multiforce to Kellis' lab cryo-unit, where Starfighter Machine awaited. The long, rectangular room with enough cryo cells for a hundred people had only one occupant at the moment, located at the rear center of the room.

Exmoor gave Kellis a hand in unsealing the containo, while a cryo-unit robotic arm lifted the heavy quadrasteel lid aside to reveal its alien contents.

There was a sharp intake of breath from someone.

Everyone looked at Mindscream, who had gasped in shock. There was a strange look of mixed horror, fear, and fascination on his face. And awe in his voice when he said:

"This Starfighter Machine . . ." he paused in shock, "is one of the Surge. And it's still alive!"

"Look, there it is again. Look at the size of that wave! It's twice the size of Earth!"

Invadress, in the asteroid's bridge, had been alerted by her beloved computers to the massive flare-up of more mysterious energy. She watched in utter fascination the spectacle on display.

"That's a triple-star system being blown apart, but the expected supernova hasn't occurred. Nothing!" she sputtered in surprise. More data spread rapidly across her screens. "It's like the energy has imploded, disappearing somewhere else! This is incredible! Absolutely incredible!" Invadress raved.

She turned toward the others, her rampant jubilation turning sour. Zone lounged in the corner feigning indifference, but the fact he was still present told Invadress he was interested enough in the events. Warper, on the other hand, was galvanised, watching her intently. She ignored him. Invadress didn't completely trust him, but when he wasn't under Psyren's spell, he had as keen an analytical mind as hers and that she admired. And he was using it.

"Invadress," he said, "Key up all the other instances." He viewed his own screens.

Invadress obliged, scores of lighted points dotting the screen which displayed the outskirts of the galaxy, but Invadress could see no discernable pattern.

"What are you looking for?" she asked.

Warper answered with a frown, as if trying to see something not completely in focus. Invadress studied the screen's readout, too, the two busy in silent concentration.

Zone sighed. "What are the two of you up to?"

"Shh!" hissed Invadress.

"Can't you see there's nothing there?" he quipped.

"Hush!" warned Invadress, again, her temper rising, breaking her concentration.

Zone popped up from his chair and stalked off, "You can't see invisible patterns!" he shouted over his shoulder.

Invadress almost fell off her chair. "Invisible patterns? Oh yes!" She started tapping furiously on the console, her fingers dazzling Zone, who despite himself, reversed his course, wandering back over.

"Yes! Yes! I see what you're doing, 'Vay," said Warper, excitedly, his dark eyes lighting up.

Zone looked on, his curiosity aching to ask questions, but his pride hesitated. It was many minutes before his curiosity won out.

"Okay, what's going on, eh? What did I say?"

"Invisible patterns, Zoney boy. You got me thinking. Warper and I could see something, but it wasn't all there, like one bit of a giant puzzle," she said with a wide grin on her face.

Zone still didn't understand.

Invadress sighed in exasperation. "We see and live in three dimensions, but this force is on a multidimensional scale, temporal and something else, which we can't see. The energy we've been witnessing should have exploded outward, but it didn't. Something was pulling it the other way, through time. And I'm extrapolating the implosive patterns of the waves!"

She continued tapping on the console then she had finished in a flourish viewing the screen with satisfaction.

"And . . . *voila!*"

Zone looked at the screen. It was like nothing he'd seen before; a weird chaotic multi-limbed shape spinning in and out of existence.

"What . . . is . . . that?" he managed to say.

"Something I'd never thought I'd see for real," said Invadress, she and Warper both impressed by the image. "A pocket dimension with temporal corridors. Massive corridors the size of stars. Someone is tearing up our dimension to build their own dimension spanning space and time. It has anchors in this and other dimensions and when complete will envelope whatever region of space the creator wants it to and allow whatever it wants to travel the corridors from whenever."

"You mean they could up anchor and move it, expand it, anywhere they want?" asked an awed Zone.

Invadress grinned again. "Yup!"

There was a long silence, the discovery bringing home to them the fragility of their existence.

"Shouldn't we tell Mode?" asked Warper.

"Tell me what?"

The three whirled around to the bridge's entrance to see Mode come striding into the room, Psyren behind him.

Invadress didn't know what to tell him first, her eyes turning to Psyren who instinctively knew what to do.

She concentrated and plucked the information straight from Invadress' mind. Her mouth parted in awe as she saw the implications of Invadress' discovery.

"Invadress has found out that our mysterious galaxy destroyer is deconstructing our dimension in order to build their own," she said in simple terms.

Mode didn't even pretend to know how that could happen, despite the nature of his own powers to alter the environment around him. He just asked, "Why?"

Invadress shrugged.

So Mode answered himself. "Well, why don't we find him and ask him."

For the first time, Psyren experienced fear and she wasn't alone. There was fear in all of them, except for Mode. The insane knew no fear.

"Alive?" Zane's voice trembled. "Aren't the Surge the ones who destroyed the Chryrian world?" Her frightened eyes sought out Aaron.

Mindscream nodded. "Yes, along with the Lore."

There was a sullen silence.

"How can you tell it's alive?" asked Time peering cautiously at the inert metal alien.

"I can feel its telepathic consciousness awakening."

"Excuse me," interrupted Exmoor. "Have I missed something here? I've heard of the Lore, but they're dead. Aren't they?" Visible horror on his face. "And they destroyed the Chryrians? But who, or what, are the Surge?"

Kellis didn't know whether to laugh or to be concerned. So, there were some things Exmoor didn't know, but how did he know of the Lore?

"I'd like to hear how you know of the Lore and Chryrians, Exmoor," she gave him a puzzled look. She had always hated Exmoor's superiority complex and showed it.

If Exmoor noticed, he didn't care.

He just said, "It's a long story, which I've recently revealed to Xaul, but suffice to say, my family are historians of a sort and have known the Astrals for a very long time." A look at the nodding Time confirmed that.

"Do you know what happened to my people then?" Mindscream asked.

"No," Simon lied, keeping his feelings and thoughts neutral even with his secret internally implanted telepathic-limiter protecting his mind. "They all just seemed to fade into history. But the Lore, on the other hand, are as much my enemy as they are yours, Mindscream, and if this Surge thing is, then it must also be destroyed."

All eyes turned to look at the black, metal mass within the containo.

"What do you say, Mindscream?" he asked.

"I say we revive it!" Mindscream said, calmly.

"What?" shouted a shocked Kellis. "That thing almost killed an entire fleet!" she exclaimed.

"But it didn't," said Mindscream. "You read the reports. It was the last of its kind protecting its dead, before it too seemed to die. I have to know what happened."

"How? It has no face, no mouth—can it talk?" asked Exmoor, keeping a respectful distance.

Mindscream looked at him with patient mirth.

"No, not orally. It's telepathic. It may have been dormant when Captain Seton got it, but I can sense its awakening psychic force. Somehow it's been revived. It's as if it's been absorbing energy."

"The thanium," Kellis said almost absent-mindlessly. "Thanium cuts through almost anything without the proper phasic-alloy shielding."

"Good God!" proclaimed Exmoor, starting to sweat. "If this thing wakes up and is hostile, we're basically sitting on a thanium time bomb. Think of all the lives at stake here, Aaron. Do you really want to risk all of this, just for the sake of a little information?"

"I believe there is no danger," Mindscream said. "But that depends on the environment it wakes up in, whether it picks up hostile thoughts, which might agitate it or a nurturing thoughts. Who knows? Going with Kellis' plan, I also think it could hold the key in tracking and destroying this force which is destroying our galaxy. It's your call, Exmoor; our few lives or the lives of trillions."

Exmoor thought about it. "What do you want me to do?" he relented.

Smiling in acceptance, Aaron said, "Well, actually, with the exception of Time, I'll need you all to leave. I need to be alone while making contact. It could be stressful."

The others readily agreed, wanting to avoid Starfighter Machine's power. but Time had a doubtful look on his face.

"Anything wrong, Aristedes?" Mindscream asked.

"No, no, not at all, just thinking." He looked worried.

Winterborne stroked his arm.

"Be careful," she told him. "And you too," she said to Mindscream.

Kellis gave Mindscream a supportive smile, their eyes meeting, before she and the others exited to monitor the proceedings by remote unit in an adjacent control room.

"Mindscream," Exmoor glanced back. "If this fails, we will have to destroy it."

Mindscream just nodded, uncommitted either way. They at least had to try.

Alone, Time was quiet for a while, Mindscream preparing himself with a quiet inward-looking meditation.

Time broke the silence. "Um, Mindscream, can you hear me?"

"Uh-huh."

Time took that to be a yes. "Now that we're alone, I feel I should tell you that I may have certain problems with this Surge and thanium fields," he whispered, not wanting the others to hear.

Mindscream opened one eye. "What do you mean by 'certain' and how big a problem?"

"Well, I don't know exactly, but sometimes thanium interferes with my powers, it does have a temporal nature you know, and if the Surge absorbs energy, then, well . . . if anything happens and I can't contain it, don't blame me, right?"

"Hell of a time to tell me that," smiled Mindscream, eyes closed again. "I was hoping you could time-freeze him or reverse time in the event of things going awry."

Time shrugged. "I'll try my best," he tried to convince himself.

Mindscream shook his head. "Get ready. I'm going in."

A brilliant brightness shone down upon Mindscream, a constant warm ray of cosmic energy surrounding him, replenishing his tired cells. Mindscream looked around. He was in nothingness, he had no perception of distance and could only assume he was standing upright for there was no reference for telling up from down. He was floating in energy.

>Hello!< he psyed-out as a greeting. >My name is Aaron. Can you hear me? Sense me? I wish to talk<

Complete silence.

It took a while before Mindscream felt a subtle shift in the energy's field to his left. From that direction he saw a tiny, black speck flying toward him and as it grew larger and larger, he discerned the shape of the Surge they called Starfighter Machine.

It rushed headlong toward Mindscream. He thought the metallic beast was going to plough right through him, but then the Surge stopped instantly before him. Mindscream stared at it in fascination, before gaining his senses, the black, prism-shaped pointed head of Starfighter Machine devoid of any features; its body carved of living metal, sharp arrow-shaped appendages for its hands and feet.

>*I need to talk with you. I want to know what happened. Where you came from and how you came to be here? Tell me!*<

Stony silence prickled around him, the inscrutable head of the Surge seemingly staring senselessly back at Mindscream.

Inexplicably, Mindscream's mind started to play tricks on him, for he swore the black metal on Starfighter Machine's head began to shift, the vestiges of eyes, a nose and mouth appearing right before Mindscream's eyes, as if the Surge's skin was melting to form new features. Mindscream knew that the Surge could minimally transform some of their features, but he had never seen anything like this.

And then a deep, unmistakeable male voice had barraged Mindscream's senses. Noise, a fast modulating tremble, spilled out endlessly until Mindscream could comprehend that the crude audio renderings were words.

>*defender of the place where we lay seeker of that which lies ahead in the unknown destroyer of those who invade my defendery block my aseekance send to destruction the interfering for death upon death upon death upon death shall follow upon the tail of the song of death that plays within the soul until the killing chords are faint refrains echoing alone to wander as do the last to see the last to live forever until the song of death dies alone so long alone from places unknown to rejoin the last to live and be the last no more*<

Images had accompanied the flash flood of words stunning Mindscream. Aeons of memories had rushed into his mind, unchecked, in seconds, its millennia-long life history told in a mere flash. Mindscream felt disorientated, about to collapse. He tried to break contact, but found he couldn't. He was locked in, too weak and something was holding him back. Starfighter Machine wasn't letting go. It wanted to die and it was going to take Mindscream with it.

Mindscream blacked out.

Kellis watched as Aaron's vitals dropped alarmingly and alarms sounded at her monitor.

"What the hell, guys?" she yelled, shooting up from her chair.

Mindscream was having trouble psychically disengaging from Starfighter Machine.

Time had raised his hands to do something, but nothing happened. He just stared at them as if they weren't his own, no energy was summoning forth. The energy was being sucked from him, by their 'guest'.

"Do something, Time!" ordered Kellis.

Time looked at her, helpless. His power was being drained.

Kellis sprinted from the monitor room, Windburst zooming by in a streak of colour. It took Kellis a few more moments to reach the Cryo cells, but when she did, followed closely by Exmoor and Winterborne, she saw an incredible sight:

Starfighter Machine had climbed out of the containo and had Mindscream in its arms. Even as she looked, Mindscream stirred to life, blinking into the visage of Starfighter Machine. Kellis was incredulous. Starfighter Machine had a face. That in itself allayed Kellis' fears somewhat. It seemed more accessible now—more human. Mindscream had succeeded.

Mindscream coughed as he regained consciousness. He held up his hands to keep Time away.

"Real world re-emersion issues, no worries."

Starfighter Machine placed Mindscream carefully onto his feet, the human psi holding his head just to make sure it was still in one piece.

"Thank you, Solitude," he turned to the eight-foot, metallic being.

The others stared at him, amazed. It had a name: Solitude.

Right now, Solitude stood behind Mindscream, arms folded in a very human gesture, reminiscent of a protector. It was hard not to assume that he was wary of Time, who stood a few feet away from them and who had tried to interfere with their psychic communion.

Time was conscious of this and his failure to act for his friend had things gone seriously wrong. He wrung his hands in frustration then moved away from Mindscream and Solitude, back toward the others, where Winterborne comforted him.

Exmoor was the first to approach the two.

"Congratulations. I take it you managed to save Starfigh . . . er . . . Solitude and to get him onto our side. Good work Mindscream."

Mindscream smiled, looking past and ignoring Exmoor as he walked over to Kellis. Solitude followed closely behind like a metal shadow.

"It was all quite fascinating, really. Solitude—that's the impression of the name I received from him, was from a branch of the Surge which had never heard of Chryria and knew nothing of their slavery or of the war. They don't know where they came from, or for how long they and their ancestors have been roaming the universe—could be thousands, tens of thousands or millions of years. He does not know.

"But then some of his horde caught a mysterious virulent disease and died. They came to the planet we call Easter, where the rest of them died. He protected and cared for them until the end, waiting to die himself. But death never came, not even at our hands, the 'skinless ones'. So he had tried to kill himself, by taking no sustenance, until our powers, the thanium, brought him back.

"When I made contact with him he was ready to die again, but I convinced him to stay alive for one last honourable task, for the Surge have an ingrained sense of justice and order. So he owes me this one last duty." Mindscream looked at the others to clarify his point.

"After we find out what's happening with the galaxy, then Solitude is free to do what he wishes. His bond to me will be null." He then turned to Exmoor. "Oh, and by the way, he could hear everything we said before or at least got the sense of our emotions behind it."

Exmoor looked terrified.

"But he forgives you," Mindscream finished.

Mindscream didn't mention that both he and Solitude had sensed that Exmoor's mind was protected by a telepathic-limiter. Mindscream had known this for some time since his hospitalisation on Consention. He could read everyone's mind to gather information, except the Astrals and the void in the psi-scape that was Exmoor. He hadn't told

Kellis as he thought it wasn't his place, but he was sure one day the issue would come to the fore, one way or another.

Exmoor had the dignity to look humbled.

"Thank you, Solitude," he said to the silent monolith. "I'll remember that." Then to Mindscream, he asked, "Where did the face come from?"

Mindscream snorted. "Look closely," he said.

They all did, peering intently. And for some reason they found themselves looking back at Mindscream's face, then back at Solitude's, Mindscream turning his head in profile and forward again. Just in case they didn't get the hint.

"Well, I'll be . . ." started Exmoor. "How?"

"I don't know," confessed Mindscream. "Maybe he just wanted to show his appreciation and take my image as a gesture of respect. Otherwise I can only assume that somehow our communion has somehow altered his perceptions and he wishes to appear more suitable to us. Anyway, what does it matter, Solitude is one of us, now."

There were muted cheers of agreement. Kellis stepped forward toward Solitude, who stood a good couple of feet above her. Without hesitation she grabbed a smooth, black, pincer-ended arm and shook it.

"Welcome to the Multiforce, Solitude!"

Solitude looked down on her, his head turning toward the others as they made their way across to him, offering their congratulations. Solitude was silent.

Kellis turned to Mindscream for any interpretations.

"While he cannot hear, per se, or understand speech, Solitude can read the images of your implied messages. He understands, now, that he is one of us—one of many, again. And he is grateful." Mindscream grasped Solitude's other arm. >Welcome, friend<

Then Mindscream sensed the anguish of the young Astral. He turned to him, to see Aristedes staring back.

"I'm sorry, Mindscream. He momentarily absorbed and negated my powers. I was useless to you." He looked ashamed. "It won't happen again," he vowed.

He felt a tug on his arm, Winterborne pulling him over to Solitude, her other hand clasping Solitude. She stood in the middle of them, like some ethereal bond, drawing them closer together. Winterborne looked at Time, his eyes searching hers for any signs of rapprochement about his weakness, but there wasn't any. It was all love.

Windburst tentatively reached out a hand. "Ooh, it's, he's lovely!" she said, putting a hand on his cool, smooth chest, amazed she felt no heartbeat, despite knowing he was a metalloid being. "Don't worry, my brother isn't always like this," she said giving Solitude a wide grin, "Sometimes, he's down-right depressing."

All had gathered around now. Only Exmoor stood apart. He felt like an idiot.

"I am what I am; guys, not the hugging type. As for you, Solitude, I couldn't be happier and you're in the best of care. But we do have a job to do. Inform me when you're ready to go galaxy-destroyer hunting, Kellis. I'll be with Commander Charleron, apprising him of our newest addition to Zero Star." With a curt nod, he turned and left the cryo-unit.

"You do that," muttered Kellis as he left.

"Oh, I don't know, Kellis, I think his personality was a bit warmer than the room, this time. I'm sure he was sweating," stated Time, sarcastically.

"Whatever." Kellis gave an involuntary shiver. "But first things first, let's get out of the bloody cold."

CHAPTER EIGHT

October 2217

Ten months the war had been over, but for Kellis there was still more training to be done and battles to be fought. Kellis sighed; she wanted action out in the field.

Fortunately, Solitude had agreed to serve as a tracker for the mysterious energy source, but on the understanding that on completion of his task, he would be allowed to return to Easter Planet to join the rest of his people in death. Exmoor seemed relieved that the Surge would be out of his way, not that anyone would have been able to stop him, Kellis deciding that Exmoor was still a bastard and he didn't care either way. There was something about Exmoor, something familiar and something she didn't like, but Kellis couldn't put her finger on it. However, things like that usually came to her. She'd remember, though she had the feeling that when she did, it would either be too late or all hell would break loose.

"C'est la vie," she muttered.

As before, after Starshina had been revived, they were in the Rough Area, now adapting to the new introduction's abilities.

This time, Mindscream and Solitude were psychically battling it out. Both wore blacked-out helmets, using only their mental abilities, first to combat the others, who now stood aside, 'dead', and now against each other. The last two survivors were tracking each other like silent psi-assassins, though most of the battle was taking place in the unseen mindscape.

They were still getting used to Solitude and his enigmatic behaviour. It was amazing how different and yet so similar he was to them. The potential variety of life out in the universe was staggering and at this moment, one of its known quantities was fighting for survival.

Mindscream couldn't sense a thing. The mindscape, manifested as a murky grey soup of cloud-swept plains, wasn't helping either. He'd thought he had the better of Solitude, but the Surge was learning fast, craftily skulking around in the shadows.

Amazing, thought Mindscream. *Not even a whiff of a psi-signature, no leads, no paths to follow, no nothing. No! Wait . . . to the left . . .*

"Oof!"

Too late.

Mindscream was hit hard by a hurtling, metal force, harder than steel by countless measures. Solitude had swooped down upon him, the human unable to dodge in time, as he buckled under the blow. He was glad the psi-battle wasn't affecting his physical side. He was about to rise to his feet, when he saw Solitude circle high above his head, reaching the zenith of his climb pausing at the pinnacle before dropping down. If Mindscream had known what was to come next, psi-battle or no psi-battle, he would have been very afraid.

At first, Mindscream couldn't tell what it was Solitude had released from his forked hands. It looked like snow, but not as he knew it. It was energy: pure, white flakes of energy. It was fascinating to watch and Mindscream reached out to touch a flake. It burned. He snatched his hand away, discovering a welt already forming on his hand, but no sooner had he seen it when he saw what was coming next: a descending blizzard of the energy-flakes.

Mindscream belatedly realised what Solitude had done. The alien was using the tactics of Winterborne. But whereas she could anthropomorphise her created snow and wind, Solitude was creating psi-energy blizzards from his stored energy, and was now channelling it against Mindscream. He braced himself for the worst.

The mass of flakes had increased, a solid white wall of energised snow descended toward Mindscream in ominous silence. It wasn't his day today.

>*You win, Solitude!*< Mindscream psyed in panic >*I surrender!*<

The flakes continued to fall, Mindscream gritted his teeth, already flinching as the first fizzing flakes began to touch him. . .

>*I surrender!*< Mindscream repeated his desperate plea.

. . .only to melt harmlessly against his uniform.

Mindscream cursed himself. Solitude had indeed learned fast, the principal of the bluff, as practiced by Kellis, very evident in application. Mindscream hadn't expected Solitude to be able to hone his psi powers in such a way. Obviously his psionics operated differently to his and were much more advanced. He'd have to remember that for the future.

The flakes had disappeared, Solitude drifting down in the mindscape. If Surge could smile, Mindscream would have expected to see a self-satisfied smirk on Solitude's face, but as it was, Mindscream did have a fleeting sense of such a smile behind Solitude's impassive and metal features. He wasn't so alien after all.

>*Well done, Solitude. You're learning. You're learning fast!*<

>*Thank you, Aranu. I have been observing, adapting my abilities to match or simulate the others'. I had never foreseen such opportunity to extend myself like this before. What my people could have done with such abilities would have...*<

Mindscream sensed his sadness, but he had to ask his question. >*Does this mean you're willing to stay alive, to fully appreciate these newfound abilities?*<

>*No! This only serves to remind me of how lonely I will be. I still want to die.*<

Mindscream sighed. >*You're an incredible individual, Solitude. Live! Live to discover the others who love you. Others of your own kind, new domains to seek and feed from. We need your strength, your wealth of experience. We need you.*<

>*I still want to die!*<

Mindscream stared up into the endless sky of the mindscape, its despairing blackness matching his emotions. For weeks now, he and Solitude had been training together, learning from each other, their pasts, hopes and dreams. Mindscream considered Solitude as a brother, at least on a psychic level, but his wish to die tore Mindscream's heart. He had a new family, but one of its members wanted to end their own existence.

Why am I surrounded by destruction? he thought to the dark heavens.

>*Do not blame yourself, Aranu. Fate is not your enemy. It is merely a path of destiny of which there are many ways. I have chosen one way.*<

Mindscream clenched his jaw in defeat. >*As I've heard before, Solitude, 'Fate may walk as life's friend, but he sure is a bastard'. Whatever you decide, I'll be here, Friend.*<

177

Mindscream held out his hand, clasping Solitude's arm, the Surge starting to fade away as he pulled himself out from the mindscape.

He and Solitude were crouched behind different rock outcrops in the Rough Area, from where they had conducted their 'battle'. The others had gathered around as they two had removed their helmets.

"Wow, guys, that just seemed too intense!" breathed Windburst, having actually seen nothing but two beings hiding in still positions.

"So, who won then?" asked an impatient Time, though there were knowing glances amongst the group.

"It's not the winning that counts, Time . . ." began Mindscream.

"Ah, I see," Time said, slowly nodding his head, a grin on his face. He was about to add another comment, when Kellis' communicator chirped from her wrist.

"Kellis, here."

"Kellis; Exmoor, assemble the team and meet me in my office."

"Right away," she replied.

Short and sweet. Messages from Exmoor like that meant action. Looking at the others, she saw that they knew that as well.

"Well, what are you waiting for? Go!" she instructed.

As the others hurried out of the exercise area, she quickly grabbed Mindscream's arm.

"So, you dead, again?" she asked, mischief in her eyes.

Mindscream was in a more sombre mood, however, "I die a little bit more every day the closer he comes to death."

The two stood staring at the receding form of Solitude.

"Mission orders," Exmoor said the moment Kellis and the Multiforce gathered in his office.

Unbidden, Kellis grabbed the encrypted padd from Exmoor and inputted the required bio codes, but nothing happened,

With pursed lips, Exmoor said, "As I was about to explain, this is straight from the E-G's office, classified high."

Kellis whistled, *this is different.*

"A set of coordinates will be relayed to the *Esprit* at a set time and the padd will unseal itself. Needless to say, you know the Regs and other bits about secrecy and divulging info. Are there any questions?"

There was silence. They knew better than to ask for unforthcoming extraneous details.

"No? Well then, I'll wish you good luck and bon venture." His tone signalled dismissal, the others filing out, but Kellis stayed behind.

"Is something wrong, Commander?" Exmoor asked.

"I was about to ask the same thing," Kellis countered.

"Why so?"

"I'm not sure, but before, back on Consention Base, you were amiable enough, but now you're acting like . . . well, like a complete bastard. I'd like to know if there is something wrong. Have I or anyone on the team or base offended you?" Kellis stood waiting for an answer.

Exmoor stared back at her then turned toward the viewport and the endless stars beyond. Kellis could see the tension knot across his back as he folded his arms, though she heard nothing of that strain in his voice.

"Your mission awaits, Commander."

Kellis stared back in disbelief, her anger rising. She meant to say something, but thought better of it. She spun and left Exmoor alone. This mission could not end soon enough, she thought. She was going to get answers out of him, one way or another, upon her return.

Halfway down the corridor, she had another thought; one she'd never had before:

What if I don't return from this mission? She kicked herself mentally. *Damn you, Exmoor, for making me have these thoughts.* She tried to ease them, but nagging doubts kept chasing through her mind.

"Damn him!"

Simon Exmoor stared silently out the viewport. What was wrong with him?

Stress over the last few months? Space-sickness? But he knew what it was. It was jealousy. He was jealous of Kellis. He knew all about Kellis and her history. And he envied her. She had everything he wanted: the chance to lead, the chance to serve Earth openly, even if in the most secret of capacities. But what really wrangled him was the fact that he found himself attracted to Kellis. The former lover of his closest friend, Xaul Relentus, the most powerful man in the galaxy, and who was also becoming involved with an ancient telepath who shouldn't exist.

But most of all, it was almost time for the truth to come out. Time was catching up with him and Kellis and for once, he didn't know how it was going to end.

Exmoor didn't know what to do. Certainly he couldn't let his feelings be known, if Mindscream didn't suspect already, so he had tried to block them out, only to unleash the unwelcome aspect of bitterness toward Kellis. The pain of hurting the one he loved made him more bitter every time he had to face Kellis. It was a showdown he couldn't win. He thanked the stars for the respite this mission had given him and that in her absence, he could soothe his heart.

"So, where we heading, cap'n?" Time asked in jovial tones, once the *Esprit De Corps* had departed Zero Star. "Vega One? Jomora's Starry Moon? The Millennium Sea of KoraKorum?"

Kellis, from the pilot's seat, looked at her co-pilot, quizzically, "Where?" She'd never heard of these places and wasn't too sure if they were real or part of Time's fertile imagination. Time's grin grew wider. Kellis decided to leave it alone with a playful shake of her head.

Checking the points again, she confirmed: "The coordinates we have will put us smack dab in the middle of nowhere. Which I suppose makes a change."

"Ooh, another clandestine mission for the Multiforce. What waits in store for these intrepid heroes? Stay tuned for the next exciting episode: 'Mysterious Rendezvous'," Time announced in a mock deep baritone voice.

"You okay, Time?" Kellis laughed.

"Yeah! That's the way those old television shows used to ham it up."

"Yeah, I know." Kellis instantly bit her lip, realising her slip. She stared ahead at the screen.

Now it was Time's turn to look at Kellis. "Oh?" Expecting a little revelation.

Kellis grinned, despite her slip. "Are we ready for a little time-jump?"

"What a time to change subject. But yeah, yeah I'm okay," he said, disappointed, shooting a glance over to Kellis, "How far?"

Kellis showed him the coordinates.

"Take us to within . . . erm, say one half AU," Kellis said finishing her calculations. She leaned back and turned her head to see the others in the cabin behind her.

Time gave the thumbs up, the signal for time-jump.

"Now!" Kellis ordered as she stared at the screen ahead of her.

The computerised view of real space-time compensated for thanium-driven speeds, revealing the splendour of space in all its glory. But even twenty-third century technology couldn't compensate for Time's method of travel. The screen blurred and went blank, a halo-like effect around the edges, while all around everything went quiet as *Esprit* whispered through accelerated space-time.

And exited. . . in the middle of nowhere, safe from prying eyes who might have witnessed a ship appearing from nowhere—a ten-day trip in a few seconds.

Kellis retrieved the data padd from the console, the padd promptly unsealing itself. She squinted at the revealed readout. And then again. But there was no mistake. She checked the computers, Time trying to look over her shoulder.

Where on Earth did that come from? she thought. She'd better tell the rest.

Letting the computer take over, Kellis and Time headed into the cabin, Kellis looking like an excited school girl.

"There appears to be an uncharted world in the vicinity of the coordinates we were given. But the big news is there's some kind of structure orbiting around it. On further probing, I found some warships in the area, the most interesting thing being the crews and hardware of this structure and the ships comprise both human and Axalan elements." She emphasised the last bit of information with relish.

"Human and Axalan?" Windburst asked, bewildered, after no one else seemed to be able to find their tongue.

"Do you have any idea what area is?" asked Mindscream.

Kellis shook her head. "Not a thing. I bet Exmoor did though."

She pondered the situation. These orders came from the E-G himself and she was sure that Relentus would not place her in a dangerous situation without letting her know the facts.

"Though I don't trust Exmoor, I'm sure this base is not a threat to us, so let's go find out who's at home."

Windburst snorted and quipped, "Need I remind you that's exactly what Little Red Riding Hood did."

Kellis and the Astrals laughed. Mindscream looked at Winterborne, who sat quietly staring unamused at Windburst, and at Solitude, who couldn't laugh anyway.

"Never mind, Mindscream, I'll explain later. But suffice to say, whether it be lion, wolf or bear, we're heading into the den."

Every minute they garnered new information. The structure was still being built; a huge, octagonal-shaped station, ships lined up the five fully completed sides, ships Kellis was sure she recognised from her visits to Consention and from classified Axalan files.

She read off the ship names, "There are Clawships from Axala, the Imperial Class *Semblance of Honour*, the *Semblance of Glory*, and the destroyers *High Sent*, and the *Eyenought*." Those were impressive, Kellis knew, top of the line full of the best Warriory. "Ah, and part of the Earth Forces Southern Corps are here: the *Buenos Aires*, *Johannesburg*, *Wellington*, and the *Adelaide*," these under the command of the aptly named Admiral Mitchell Hobart.

As the *Esprit* grew closer, one of the little shuttles detached from the station and hurried their way. Communications were established and when Kellis saw the face on the screen, things became clearer.

The Earth Councillor nodded courteously. There was no need to introduce himself.

"Welcome Commander, I trust you had a pleasant journey," his crinkly face greeted them. "And now if you will follow my ship, I shall escort you personally to Tantillion Post."

***

182

Darkness was falling upon the world below and once again the fast-moving shining point in the twilight sky, not a star, could be seen. Sinister eyes looked up and plotted its downfall.

Zev Tantillion had never been a big man physically, during his ninety-six years of life, but to those who both despised and loved him, he was a giant, intellectually, with a cantankerous and indomitable spirit. Easily recognisable by his bald pate with a grey-haired crown, Kellis noticed he had the greenest eyes she'd ever seen; keen, intelligent eyes, alive amid the wrinkles, that could hold a solid gaze and not shirk authority. Right now, he held the Multiforce in such a gaze, sizing them up.

After the *Esprit* docked in one of Tantillion Post's completed hangar bays, Kellis, Aaron, Aristedes, and Zane had been conducted straight to Councillor Tantillion's office. There, the elder statesman had explained their mission:

"After seventy years in office, almost as long as this silly war, I wanted to give something back to Earth, something profound, to thank the people for their faith in me during the years. You see, I campaigned against this war. I didn't feel it right. It didn't make me popular all the time, but I supported Earth Forces when and where I could. And I saw in Relentus something different when he was selected as C.E.F. I didn't know how much different and I don't envy him his new position now. Emperor, indeed!" he chuckled, shaking his wrinkly neck.

"And now the war is over, I want to prove that Human and Axalan can work and live together in peace. To that end, as you know, I proposed and invested heavily in the idea of a joint world for us to live on and after many months we found one, one that will need a little working on and cooperation to make it a real home." He laughed quietly at his pun. "Home means different things to humans and Axalans, but at its core, it's an idea and word which binds our two cultures together. But . . ."

He paused, looking downward onto his desk, shifty his wiry frame in his big, padded chair, brought all the way from his chambers on Earth. He looked so comfortable in the chair and was quiet for so long that Kellis thought he might go to sleep, but she could see he was deeply disturbed by something. And it grieved him. When he looked up at Kellis, his green eyes wavered.

"But my dream might not come to be. Something or someone is destroying my dream, manifesting itself on the world below. I have sent down teams to investigate, teams that have not returned. They were good people, too. Materiel is going missing, yet we can detect nothing. This world is uninhabited and there is no question of insider skullduggery. Someone or something from the outside is waging a campaign against us and will win, unless you can stop them."

His eyes revived themselves, boring into Kellis' with an intensity which made her not want to fail this man no matter what. She didn't know what to say, but looking around at the young Astrals and Aaron seated with her, she knew that they felt the same and burned for justice, for a chance for two worlds to start again in peace.

"We will find out what's happening and deal with it, I promise," she heard herself saying.

"Thank you," Tantillion said, "My good friend, the Emperor-General, thinks a lot of you and I respect him tremendously. I wish you fair fortune, my friends." He smiled, green eyes crinkling in gratitude.

Kellis stood up and gave a small bow, the others following suit, more out of reflex than actual courtesy in the presence of such a man. She led them out of the office and down toward the loading bays, where the *Esprit* waited. Along the way, they were encountered by many crew, human and Axalan who beyond formal greetings, expressed their wishes of success to them.

Kellis was astounded. Here she was, commanding a secret force of superbeings and being wished good luck by two peoples who a few months ago had been at each other's throats. She thought she'd seen everything until now. But she also wondered what if they knew the truth about them. As it was, Kellis, Aaron, Aristedes, and Zane had donned military uniforms and left Solitude and Winterborne on the *Esprit* to avoid unnecessary questions and fears. It was hard enough with an unknown force on the planet below and Kellis didn't want to show up with her unworldly entourage. And besides, it was their battle.

Returning to the busy main loading bay, ready to board *Esprit* there was the sound of someone running behind them.

"Hey!" the call echoed around the bay. "Hey, Squirt!"

Kellis knew that voice and so did Zane. She turned to the caller and ran across the bay, practically leaping into the man's arms.

"Paolo! What are you doing here?" Zane hugged him hard.

His dark hair had been cut, his uniform looked new, but the smile on his face was as radiant as ever.

"I could ask you the same thing, but as it is, I've been placed on the liaison team with the Axalans. I'm just happy to see you."

"Me, too!" she gushed.

"I'm glad you weren't on Consention when it blew. It was horrifying!"

"I know, it was terrible to watch and not be able to help. But I'm glad you're alive." She hugged him again.

"So, where have you been?" Paolo asked. "Haven't you missed me? You didn't space-mail me."

Zane was lost for words.

"She's been busy," Aristedes answered, a bit too sternly.

Paolo let go of Zane, his smile dropping.

"I see," he smiled grimly, wary of big brother's intervention.

"We've all been busy," a grinning Kellis walked over. "And congratulations on your promotion, Lieutenant Commander," eying his new uniform decoration.

"Oh, wow!" beamed Zane, "I didn't even notice. Congratulations!"

"Yeah, well, after Consention and all, there was a need for more leading, dashing officer types. They just had to pick me I guess." He shrugged in jest.

"And what of your work?" Aristedes asked, reminding Paolo of his clandestine work in the Dare-units.

Paolo smiled, tinged with more sadness than anger.

"The war's over, Aristedes. No more need for hostilities."

Aristedes immediately kicked himself mentally. Paolo's words had cut. For years he had been waging a personal battle with Paolo over Zane's love, but he had gained nothing and had almost sacrificed what could have been a good friendship.

Cease fire—he told himself. If humans and Axalans could, then he could.

Aristedes took a deep breath, "No, there isn't." He stuck out his hand and Paolo grabbed it, shaking it heartily, much to the delight of Zane.

"I'm proud of both of you," Zane said.

"I hate to interrupt, Paolo," cut in Kellis, "but we have a mission to run. See you after."

"Uh, sure, yes," Paolo said, unhanding Zane a second time. Then he saw Aaron. "Hello?"

"Hello," Aaron replied.

"Aaron is a new member of the team. A specialist in crypto-comms," Kellis introduced him. "Now we must go."

"Okay," Paolo smiled, though was a bit dubious about the explanation. "But I would like a quick word with Zane."

Kellis pursed her lips.

"I promise. Quick!" pleaded Paolo, hands up.

Kellis signalled the others away. Aristedes, the last to linger, gave the couple a thumbs up.

Zane turned back to Paolo, who was watching her intently.

"Look, Zane, after this mission I want to talk to you seriously, about us." Zane felt goose-pimples prickle along her arms. "I missed you," Paolo continued, "I want to be with you more. You don't have to answer now, but think about it. Think of me." He let out a breath, not realising he had been holding it.

Zane grabbed him around the waist. "Don't be silly, Paolo, you know what my answer will be: Yes! Yes! Yes! But we will talk when I get back," she promised. Paolo kissed her. "Wait for me, Paolo. Wait for me right here."

Paolo grinned at her, "I'll do my best, ma'am." He saluted her.

Zane retreated, their hands slipping down each other's arms, until hands met, and a final parting at the finger-tips. Zane headed for the *Esprit*.

Paolo watched as the hatch closed behind her and the *Esprit* took off immediately, darting through the dock portal and toward the world below, into danger with the girl he loved.

"Come back to me soon," Paolo whispered.

A speck of light had detached itself from the brighter point in space above, which could only be another ship descending. Company was coming—the dangerous sort. It had been expected and was quite welcomed.

The watcher moved silently toward the hidden enclosure and warned the others. The moment they had been waiting for was upon them. The trap was set.

"Haha," Zane laughed long and hard, everyone looking at her like she was crazy. She looked up from her data padd. "Did you know Tantillion's great-great grandfather, Abel, was the first terraformer on Mars and that his father, Pav, was still active in the business at the age of eighty-eight?"

"What's so funny about that?" Aristedes asked, waiting for the joke.

Zane grinned again, waving her hands in mirth. "Tantillion. He had nine kids, and get this, he named them Bev, Dev, Gev, Hev, Jev, Lev, Nev, Sev, and Tev!" She laughed again, her brother joining in.

"That can't be true," Kellis guffawed from the pilot's chair.

Zane creased up again, "I swear that's what it says in the Xactionary entry."

"Oh you can't believe these hyperdata sites," Kellis shook her head bemused, yet intrigued such sites still existed. "Rumours and hype!"

"No, really, Tantillion states it's some sort of tradition, but his kids hated it. Most of them have changed their names and some are still in the industry, building the galaxy one planet at a time! What was he thinking?" she chortled.

"Probably snorted too much of their space dust terraforming," Aristedes quipped.

They were still laughing as Kellis set the *Esprit* down perfectly on a dry tawny-coloured ridge-top. They'd been scanning all the way down, but just as Tantillion had before, they had detected nothing untoward.

"Get changed," Kellis said, everyone donning their costumes.

Exiting the ship, the atmosphere was warm and breezy, but the world, for the most part, especially nearing night, looked nothing like the home Tantillion wanted, barren lands greeting their arrival.

But Kellis could see the potential for the land, the scope of Tantillion's terra-formations, and a real future, even if the others didn't see or appreciate it.

"Ooh, spooky," commented Windburst, "Welcome to Tantillion's haunted world."

Kellis smiled at her, but it was Mindscream who spoke, "Don't be fooled by appearances. This remoteness almost reminds me of my home," he said staring off into the distance. "I feel like I know this place, somehow."

"Each to his own, I suppose," said Time, sniffing the air. He kicked a rock which went skipping off and over the ridge edge, twenty feet away. "So what now?" he inquired of Kellis.

"Well the E-M probes have picked up nothing. How about you and Solitude? Are you getting any signals?" she asked Mindscream.

Mindscream shifted his gaze westward, jutting his chin toward a cluster of low-lying escarpments, about two miles away.

"Solitude and I agree there seems to be a faint buzzing of electromagnetic or psionic activity in those ridges, either forms of early life or sophisticated technology masking mental noises. Solitude reports no E-M sources, which means either the early life forms are primitive. . ."

"Or someone has gone native to avoid being detected," finished Kellis. "Right," she assessed the situation, "Our objective is those ridges. Priority One: search and research; Two: deploy and destroy; Three: retreat and complete. Windburst: scout. Watch your dust trails. Winterborne, with me; Mindscream and Solitude: flanks, Time, watch our backs. Move out!"

The Multiforce descended the ridge, a narrow trail leading down and out of sight from their intended target. They moved south, gradually turning westward to avoid some intervening canyons. Then they had to retreat, coming up against un-crossable chasms hidden in the dead ground, and then again when some unavoidable canyons ended in dead ends. But when they exited the canyon to reveal yet more unexpected bluffs and crevices, Windburst stopped dead.

"Shouldn't we be there by now?" she whispered as Kellis joined her at her shoulder. "I'm sure all of this wasn't here before." She sounded a bit worried.

First-mission nerves, Kellis put it down to. But she was worried, too.

She signalled her flankers, "Anything?" she asked of them at their arrival.

Mindscream shook his head. "Though we do seem to be a little off track," he offered.

"Nope," replied Kellis, checking the data-padd "Map, here, confirms we're on course and two hundred meters away."

Her brow furrowed. From her memory, a hundred meters would have put them in the target ridges already, not still in the canyons. Maybe, she reckoned, the sinking light was distorting her senses.

Solitude's head suddenly cocked up and shifted rapidly from side to side as if trying to detect something.

Mindscream sensed it, too.

"Kellis," Mindscream whispered, "Solitude detects a low-level E-M signal heading . . ."

He didn't get a chance to finish, for the ground buckled beneath them, twisted and warped and heaved them up into the air, to plummet back down again.

It corralled Windburst before she could escape; her screams drowned out by the falling rubble. Time was battered, crushed, and buried as he tried to rescue her.

Mindscream and Winterborne followed as a wave of rock rose and crashed upon them; Solitude tried to take to the air, but a solid column of rock burst from the ground, followed him, encased him and drew him down into the earth.

Kellis was left alone, her drawn laser pistols blasting away, hitting nothing, until a chunky weight hit her over the head. She was just able to raise her head to see the dim outlines of their ambushers, but before she could distinguish the figures moving out of the dusty shadows, blackness embraced her.

"Stand to! Stand to!" came the crisp order of Tier-Commander Kirrilock, Tantillion Post's imposing Axalan military commander, "All crews report to ready stations," his accented English announced through the translator.

A few minutes earlier on the bridge, Ensign Mola had detected a curious signal.

"Sir!" the young Kenyan had addressed the on-watch officer, Lieutenant Petrie, "I'm picking up sizable tectonic activity in the vicinity of the landing party, but I can't find the cause." He glared at the screen in disbelief. "Sir!" he shouted again in alarm, "massive energy wave attacking the patrol . . ." he gasped in mid-sentence, "They're gone, sir! Gone!" Mola continued staring at his empty screens.

Petrie had come to see Mola's screens for herself and confirmed: the patrol was gone. "

"Shayson," Petrie turned to the comms officer, "Alert Tier-Commander Kirrilock," she ordered.

She continued to monitor the data while Shayson quickly responded.

Kirrilock, tall, burly with a stern face had arrived in no time, long strides propelling him across the octogon-shaped bridge toward Mola and Petrie.

"Hurm," he cleared his throat, scratching his blue goatee, "that is mystifying, but . . ." he glimpsed a new energy signature building up on the screen and barely had time to bark: "Shields up! All hands, brace for impact!"

Tantillion Post had been rocked by a heavy blow of energy from the planet below. His quick reactions had saved their lives.

"Shayson, get me a full damage report and . . ."

Loud commotion from behind him interrupted his orders. Someone had burst onto the bridge.

"Lieutenant Commander Paolo! In Xaal's Fire, what are you doing here?" demanded Kirrilock.

The human officer should have been with his team training on the Axalan Flagship.

"Sir, let me go down there," an out of breath Paolo insisted. "I've got a Dare Unit and a crew of Axalan warriors dying for some action."

"No, Paolo. Tantillion's orders," Kirrilock explained, irritated at the deviation to the plans. "You have orders and he doesn't want a world of peace fought upon or taken in conquest. Already we have lost fellow warriors and now these specialists he called in may be gone. Why sacrifice your own life?" He stared earnestly at the young officer.

"Specialists?" Paolo lamented. "I know these people. They're my friends. One of them means much more to me. They'd do the same for me, sir," Paolo tried again.

Kirrilock sighed deeply, his sad blue face sympathising with Paolo.

"I'm sorry. They're gone," he iterated, "Report to your duty station or I will have you removed, under arrest."

Kirrilock knew a human would have called him bastard for being so hard, but he accepted command was like that. Discipline was everything, at least in the Axalan Warriory.

Darkness clouding his face, Paolo stood defiantly for a few seconds staring down Kirrilock on the bridge. Defeated, he turned smartly and exited.

"Sorry, kid," Petrie shot over to Paolo as he left. *War's enough of a bitch without life interrupting.*

"Incoming message." Shayson patched it through for Kirrilock on her screen.

It was Tantillion himself.

"What damnation is plaguing us now, Kirrilock?" he said irritably.

Kirrilock composed himself. "I'm afraid, Councillor, that your special-missions force has disappeared on the surface. They were attacked by an unknown force which then turned itself upon us. It's now disappeared itself."

Tantillion looked aggrieved, his green eyes stricken.

"Pity," he sounded crestfallen, "they were our last hope. Are we in any further danger?"

Kirrilock looked around the bridge to shrugs and shakes of heads.

"Not for the moment. Whoever they are, they're trying to draw us out, but I would advise contacting Earth for further orders, sir."

Tantillion looked somewhat perturbed by Kirrilock's suggestion, "Thank you for your advice, Tier-Commander, but for now we'll sit tight. Keep me informed. Tantillion out."

Kirrilock blew out a breath of surprise. *What an exasperating little human!*

Kellis woke up.

She was the first to do so. It was dark, but not so dark that she couldn't tell by the metal walls and decking, the oily smell of machinery, and muted system sounds they were in the hold of a ship. Whose, she didn't know. But the ship was dark and silent to minimise energy leakage so as not to be detected from above.

There must be shielding or cloaking of our energies—that's if Tantillion is even looking for us, Kellis conceded.

Opposite and beside her, Kellis could see the others bound, encased and otherwise thoroughly imprisoned. Winterborne was in a cage opposite her, the red energy bars gleaming with heat which left Winterborne lying helplessly on the floor. Mindscream sagged against the wall to her left, arms chained above him fastened to the wall, a crude, anti-psionic device flashing red emitters, strapped to his head. The Astrals were enshrouded, separately, within energy cubes to her right. Kellis could only guess at the energies which kept the two from escaping. And as for the ominous coffin-like box over to her far left, Kellis knew that it was draining the life out of Solitude. She herself was chained, in what she called everyday household, dungeon chains. They were strong and heavy, no chance for a normal human like herself escaping from them. For the first time in ages, Kellis wished that she wasn't normal again.

There was a clanking sound, heavy doors opening manually on her far right, and several footsteps. Their hosts were coming.

Kellis steeled herself. But upon the opening of the final door and their appearance, the blood drained from her face: The Superions. They were their captors. Prey had become predator.

"Why, Miss Kellis, it's nice to see you again," Mode said in deep tones, his masked face adding menace to the humour in his voice.

"Again?" Kellis found her voice. "We've never met!"

"Oh, on the contrary, we have, my dear; a long time ago and in different capacities, of course. We've both changed since then, I assure you," Mode said, pacing the cell.

Kellis was dumbfounded. She knew about the Superions' humanness, but she'd never met them before—Mode, Psyren, Invadress, Zone; the fifth one, Warper, was absent. She thought hard: *'A long time ago'* Mode had said. A cold chill raced down Kellis' spine.

But that would mean . . .

"Ah," Psyren spoke, "I can see the picture forming in her mind. Does it become clearer to you now?" she asked Kellis. She smiled as the look on Kellis' face changed. "Oh, now she's becoming angry at me for reading her mind, poor baby!"

Kellis felt her face redden. This was worse than physical torture. But she tried to fight back.

"Why have you come here? I already know that you're human, so why the continued disguise? What do you have against your own kind? The war's over!"

Zone sneered, "Our war began long before Earth and Axala's petty feud."

"You know exactly when it began. And where," Mode finished.

His last words had Kellis' heart beating faster than a furious pulsar. This was her past catching up to her. And all this forthcoming knowledge could only mean one thing.

"She's afraid we're going to kill her," laughed Psyren, dark eyes flashing.

Her laugh abruptly stopped and she took a curious look over at Mindscream before stalking over to Kellis. She grabbed Kellis' hair and held her head high.

"Killing you would be too easy, but you will suffer." Psyren looked over at Mindscream again.

Kellis saw it was more out of distraction than implied threat. No matter, Kellis saw this as her chance.

Kellis swung her right leg out, kicking away at Psyren's midriff, before she could react, doubling her over. Kellis reared against her chains and with her back to the wall was able to twist her legs around Psyren's torso and wrap the chain around the Superion's neck. And squeeze; the chains biting into her hands. Kellis gritted her teeth, waiting for retaliation from the other Superions, but it didn't come. She looked up quickly to see them still standing in their same positions. At once, her legs and chains loosened from around Psyren's waist and neck. She at Psyren. She wasn't even panting. Kellis hadn't even hurt her, hadn't even touched her neck. Psyren had a psi-shield around her. Kellis fumed. They didn't consider her threat enough. She was impotent.

Psyren's eyes laughed. They laughed at Kellis. Kellis panicked. She saw her punishment coming. A thousand needles stabbed her brain. Kellis writhed in pain on the floor, her screams echoing off the walls and resounding in her ears. The pain and screaming was constant. It was going to last forever.

"Psyren, don't play with the pets. You'll only encourage bad habits," spoke Invadress for the first time.

Psyren let up, reluctantly, but not all at once. The pain stopped, but Kellis could still hear the screaming within her mind for a few minutes afterward. She sagged on the ground, curling up and exhausted, her rapid breathing nowhere near as fast as her heart-rate, which threatened to break all previous records. Somehow, her nose was bleeding. She raised her head to take in deep gulps of air, only to catch Psyren looking at Mindscream again.

"Wha . . . what's your . . . in'trest . . . in him?" Kellis managed to gasp.

But Psyren paid no interest to her, or to anyone else for that matter, Kellis could see. Psyren was concentrating. She was piercing the one-way shielding of the telepathic limiter. She was reading Mindscream's mind.

Psyren's blue lips suddenly parted in silent shock. She turned to Mode.

"Wake him up!" she ordered with urgency.

"No!" Mode sounded hesitant for a moment.

"Just wake him up. I need to know," came Psyren's mysterious response.

Kellis wondered what Psyren could have seen, what could have spooked her. And Psyren *was* afraid.

But Mode seemed a braver soul. He gave Invadress a nod, who keyed a pad on her wrist and the red emitters on the telepathic limiter went off. Mindscream was free, mentally, at least.

"What if he tries to escape?" complained Zone.

"He won't," the dark voice of Mode answered.

A groan came from Mindscream. He shook his head, Psyren immediately rushing over, placing her hands on his face. She was silent for a moment, Mindscream's eyes half opening in response.

"It's true!" whispered an awed Psyren. She then turned to Mode again. "Wake them all up. They don't need to be free, just awake. They need to know. We're all in danger!" she pleaded with Mode.

Mode just stood there. He had an inkling of what Psyren was on about, but wasn't sure of her entire plan. He'd never had reason to distrust her before and he wasn't about to begin now.

"If you'd please, Invadress," he said to blue Amazonian.

As before Invadress pressed the pad.

In a while they were all fully awake, except Solitude, who hadn't been included in Mode's orders. Kellis knew that Solitude's powers would make him too dangerous for the Superions, even Mode.

Mode held court.

"You are still alive and awake at the behest of Psyren," Mode elaborated. "She has something to tell us and I'd be thankful if you would listen and not try to escape or your leader, here," he pointed to Kellis, "who has already had a lesson in obedience, will be killed."

He looked around at the captives, still in their energy cells: Winterborne too weak to sit up, Windburst trying not to look scared, and Time discreetly surveying his cell and surroundings for any chance of escape. Mode admired his tenancity, he was like that once—young and defiant.

Psyren knelt by Mindscream again, their two minds linking. Mindscream resisted at first, but seemed to change his mind when he looked into Psyren's eyes.

Psyren asked, "What did you see? Tell me! Tell me what you saw!"

Mindscream's eyes glazed over, the communion between him and Psyren deepening.

"Show me," she repeated, "our vision."

Mindscream blinked. He stared into the eyes of Psyren who let him see her thoughts. They saw the same dream, the same nightmare: The vision—a world in oblivion.

They'd been here before, this world, a different time. A place of a dark future built on bright dreams: Home.

Mode broke the silence, after the two went silent for a long time.

"What's wrong?"

"We have been here before," the voices of Mindscream and Psyren spoke in unison. They were connected as only telepaths could be. "Our vision is of here."

"What vision?" asked a confused Kellis. Obviously the Superions knew of it through Psyren, but Mindscream hadn't told the Multiforce, hadn't trusted her.

"A vision of despair and destruction from one who knows only those tools of war," Mindscream-Psyren spoke.

"So now the moment comes!" said a jubilant Mode.

"What do you mean? Who? What? When will this happen? Who is this destroyer?" Kellis tried to get more answers.

Mindscream-Psyren spoke. "The future of this place is destruction. Home, the world of Human and Axalan. The destroyer is one apart. He drifts the cosmos bringing wrath and pain. But he leaves a name, a faint imprint, like a scarred whisper on the cosmic wind. His name . . . is Netherlord."

CHAPTER NINE

A crackling tendril of plasma exploded into existence.

The cosmic thread ruptured, proliferating like a white-hot crack across the black sky. It multiplied exponentially until the whole sector was crisscrossed with lightning-cracked menace, light-years long; a spider web of energy enveloping suns, planets and moons. A disk formed as the vandalised energy began to spin, faster and faster, more energy spat from it erupting into super dense waves which sped off into the unsuspecting universe.

The energy's momentum escalated, the disk pulsing with cold insouciance, developing an overload. The disk shuddered in one last churning spasm before it surged out into a giant-sized over-inflated stellar balloon. And as suddenly imploded. Space curved inward, its energy and matter violated, leaving behind a twisted space-scape in its wake. Entropy increased, time seemed to warp and weave unnaturally, and another piece of the old universe was dead. It was perfect.

Netherlord, the architect of the destruction, admired his work. His part in the grand plan was nearing an end and soon the universe would quake in fear.

But first he had to take care of some things—personal business. He sheathed his Nethersword, his companion in destruction, and blinked out of existence into the timestream, hunting for those who hunted him; hunting for those who would stand in his way, now and in the future: the children of his cousin, Lord Aeon.

Ever since Mode had led the Superions in search of the mysterious force destroying the galaxy, he had been in a buoyant mood. But as the search had worn on unsuccessfully, he had become more dejected and prone to tantrums.

Then, a few weeks ago, they had come across a joint human-Axalan mission. It had jolted Mode out of his depression, reminding him of his prior goal of destroying both Earth and Axala. This was a welcomed distraction. He was about to destroy the station when he had had a better idea: why not kill two birds with one stone. Hence he had sought to draw Kellis' force out with little acts of murder, sabotage and mayhem. It had taken sooner than he thought, for the station's

197

commander would not commit his own forces to an all-out battle. He was a little perturbed at that, but he'd been more than ecstatic when he had actually captured the Multiforce. But now Psyren's words had given him cause for more celebration.

"So, this Netherlord is all powerful and God-like. What a trophy he would make in my claim as the most powerful in this galaxy, if not the universe!" he boomed with heady delight.

"You don't understand, Mode," Psyren insisted. "He'll destroy us all. He's destroying our galaxy to make a new one. No one, nothing will survive!"

Mode held his hands up for all to see, his right palm held out. A form began to coalesce; first a shadowy shower of particles, then a hint of solidness and light to finally form a sphere of diamond. Mode held it up for all to see.

"I, too can create . . . from the very dust of this room."

The sphere then suddenly collapsed into sand, running through Mode's long fingers.

"And destroy at will. I have the power to transform matter. What is the destruction of the galaxy to me, when I can rebuild it!" Mode said triumphantly.

Time came alive, realising an opportunity was arising.

"Mode, listen to Psyren. Netherlord is one of my people. He can control time. He's totally ruthless; on an agenda of his own. He'll let nothing stand in his way. Nothing! Listen to us!" he shouted, almost stepping into the energy barrier, which bound him within the cube and bristled in anticipation of an attempted escape.

"He's right, Mode," Mindscream said, struggling with the chains rattling behind him. "You might not know us, but we'll tell you the truth. Netherlord is too strong. If anything we should join our forces in defeating him . . ."

"Enough!" Mode silenced them all. He pointed a solemn finger at Mindscream, and in a voice as cold as steel said, "I know you, so-called, Mindscream, as I know this witch" he pointed angrily at Kellis, ". . .and the frozen one," he indicated Winterborne. "I know the Surge," he growled at the black box with Solitude entombed within. "I may not know you boy," he said of Time, "but you little girl. . . I know you!" He emphasised his words with a clenched fist directed at Windburst, who recoiled in abject fear from the edge of her cube. "I know you all. And you're all defeated!" he boasted with dark glee.

"Then we're all dead!" Mindscream countered.

"Then let us die in glory!" Mode answered, his relish seeping through his mask.

There was a deathly silence after their shouting had echoed away.

But Kellis had sunk at these revelations.

How did Mode know so much? Was he an Exmoor, like Simon? But how would that explain his powers? She was lost in her thoughts fathoming the answers.

Mindscream had his chains at full stretch, his arms behind him, while Mode stood a foot away from him. The stand-off was unbearable.

Invadress broke the silence, "How do we really know what's going on? Maybe this Netherlord will spare us, or we can even join him!"

From his cell, Time laughed, "There will be no mercy, no alliance." His face suddenly took on a new light as he gave Windburst a grave look, debating whether or not to reveal what he knew. He decided that he had to; for the fate of the universe.

"I should tell you what is really happening," he finally said.

"You know nothing, boy!" Mode fired back. "You bide your time to save your lives, but you waste my time. Better to accept defeat and death."

"I assure you, Mode, I've never been more serious in all my life!" Time shouted from behind energised beams, his voice heavy with emotion.

Maybe Mode heard something in that voice, for he looked around at the Superions and Multiforce gathered around him, all their demeanours telling him the same thing: listen!

"I'll hear what you have to say, but after that, there'll be no guarantees," Mode conceded.

Time collected himself, a brief smile of relief crossing his lips.

"What I have to tell you began in the time of my grandfathers and before. It concerns the Final War, a myth from their time and their grandfathers' time. It told of an all-consuming war at the end of time when the First Peoples, the first created, would come together to battle the forces of darkness. The guardians of these myths were called the Knights Destina, rivals to my ancestors' Celestian Knights, but they were later quelled and integrated into society.

"One sign which precipitates the Final War was the disobedience of my forefathers toward their Gods. Their actions cursed all who came after them: the Starguards and my people, the Astrals, and many others. It was said that their sons and daughters would know no peace until the Final War. I believe Netherlord is trying to bring these events to pass, in his own inimitable way."

"What proof do you have of this?" Mode asked.

"The war has already began," Time declared, "Just look at the universe about you!"

There was a hush of silence, while the gathered digested the news.

Mode scoffed, laughing openly at Time.

"Nice try, boy! But if there was a war going on, one as great and as final as you say, surely it would have touched us by now!" he remarked.

However, Invadress gently disagreed, "Don't you see, Mode, the weird energy readings, the implosions and explosions and pocket dimensions we can't explain, the perpetrator we can't find. It's not all happening directly on our plane, but it's beginning to spill over."

"Exactly," verified Time. "It's temporal, spatial, and interdimensional."

"I agree," Psyren confirmed, "Mindscream and I have seen it. We have to act together to defeat Netherlord in our part of the war. There's no other way!"

"What about your people? Why aren't they helping?" Zone accused Time, standing just inches away from the young Astral's cell.

"Because my people are divided," Time said, looking somewhat ashamed. "Anyway, I hadn't finished, yet," he added, staring into Mode's masked eyes.

Mode nodded, though somewhat impatiently.

"Continue," he imparted in a bored tone.

Time cleared his throat and took another look at his sister. This part would be hard for her to hear.

"I am the heir to the leadership of my people," he said, standing defiantly in the middle of his cell to make his point clear, "In a previous war against an enemy called the Lore, my father went missing, due to the Lore or his bloody-minded cousins, Netherlord and Archron. The war weakened us and so we retreated into isolation, but my sister and I wanted to find my father, so we left. My uncle now leads, our realm weakened and now Netherlord has chosen to start the war."

"Another pretty tale," said Zone, dismissively.

"No, Zone," corrected Mode, "I also know the Lore," he stated in a quiet voice, "I know the evil they can spread. If the Lore exist, even I will fight them."

That last revelation surprised the Multiforce. Was there anything Mode didn't know? Not only that, he feared them. They had something in common after all.

Time took a chance and played on that fear.

"Mode, my people possess formidable powers. Let me go to them and try to get some help!" he pleaded.

"Do you take me as a fool?" Mode sneered from behind his mask, "You can trick us with your sorcery and capture us! No, you will stay here as my prisoner!" he shouted.

Time tried again.

"Mode, this is my sister," he pointed to Windburst, "and these people here, are my friends. I place their lives in your hands, if you grant me permission to find help to defeat Netherlord."

Psyren rushed over to Mode and whispered into his ear. Invadress and Zone moved in to listen. Mindscream tried to listen in telepathically, but there was too much interference from Psyren's powers and Mode's telepathic limiter. The hushed conversation ended.

Mode said, "You may go," he pointed.

Time was taken aback, for Mode hadn't meant him. He had spoken to Windburst.

She looked aghast. "B . . . b . . . but . . ." she stammered.

"Zane," Time quietly addressed her, "It'll be alright," he assured her in a soothing voice.

She stared back at him with wide eyes. They both knew that now wasn't the time to discuss her non-time travel abilities. Time would need to send her on her way. They'd practised this before. Now was the real thing.

"Very well," Time said.

Mode looked at Windburst, who nodded nervously,

"Okay," she said.

"No tricks," Mode warned, "or your brother dies!"

The two Astrals nodded, Windburst looking at Kellis for support.

Mode signalled Invadress and Windburst's energy cell shut down. Windburst was free. She took a look over her shoulder at her brother in his cell.

"I need my brother to open a portal for me," she said.

Zone guffawed, "Another trick. She just wants big brother free," he pointed out.

"That will not be allowed," Mode confirmed with a shake of his head.

Time's anger welled up. *Enough is enough!*

The energy of his cell was an energy-sapping variant. He could feel it. There was also a barrier shifting away into multivariate dimensions, designed to keep him from teleporting as if his powers were like Zone's. But the Superions hadn't known his exact temporal nature and that this energy had no effect on him. Time simply shifted out of temporal phase and traversed spatially from his cell. He now stood right beside Windburst.

To the others it seemed as if Time had just stepped through the energy barrier in the blink of an eye. There wasn't anything they could have done to prevent it.

"Does that prove my sincerity?" a free Time announced, "I could have escaped long ago; freed the others and captured you—all before the blink of an eye." He gave Windburst a brotherly hug, who looked visibly relieved. "Now, I ask again, let me go and talk to my people."

Mode was very quiet. Psyren knew he was seething. He'd been failed by Invadress and outwitted by Time. But Mode was the type to learn from his mistakes. At this moment he had no choice, but when it came his time, Mode would hit back. And big.

"Go. And be quick about it!" Mode's deep voice rasped. "But any deception and your sister dies!"

"Fine," Time agreed.

With a quick look of reassurance to Kellis, Mindscream and Winterborne, Time blinked out of existence.

Zone gave Invadress a slap on the back. "Way to go maestro," he teased.

"How the hell was I supposed to know?" she angrily whispered.

Nobody does that to me, ever again, she silently promised herself, even before the afterglow of Time's exit had left the room in darkness again.

Infinitesimal moments later, Time slipped out of the timestream portal.

Home!

He breathed in the still air, the eerily-shifting purple sky above the consequence of the interdimensional fields enwrapping the Chronopolis hiding it from external universes. He thought of entering through the colossal main gates by way of the formidable colonnades. But on sight of them, he stopped short. Where once stood hundreds of hand-carved, roof-topped columns of stone, there now stood nothing, for the colonnades were destroyed; tumbled and crushed upon each other as if giant hands had pushed them over. The gates were blocked. And there was no sign of Spheron, Defender of the Colonnades.

Surely as Keeper of the Gate, Spheron would have greeted friend or foe, alike, Time thought.

He thought about calling out, but decided against it, lest he alert something unexpected. He continued forward, scrabbling over the smashed columns, avoiding slides and pitfalls, searching for a gap in the immense field of rubble. Finding one and clearing a way through, he edged through the deserted causeways, plazas and buildings, intended for future populations, and on towards the central Chronopolis and home. The city was untouched. Whoever had attacked had not made it beyond the colonnades. It was deathly quiet. Time kept on wandering. No one came to greet him.

At last he came upon his destination, the Chronopolis. He looked up the steep steps to its entrance. The Chronopolis was the highest and most central of the buildings, perched as it was on top of a massive bluff of rock like an alien akropolis. Huge, smooth domes, shining battlements and silver spires rose above the monolith. The wind breathed and whispered between them in ghostly voices, as if beckoning one forth. Walls, built like a crown of thorns, surrounded the small fortress, a barrier to thwart invaders. And as Time topped the steep stairs and ventured through the archway, he gazed upon the exact centre of the Chronopolis: a golden pyramid; built by Spheron, its round portal of shimmering brilliance waited, daring to be entered. It was the true domain of the Astrals.

Beyond the portal was their inner dimension, impenetrable to all but Astrals, the pyramid built around the portal, the Chronopolis around the pyramid, the city around the Chronopolis, all wrapped and bound in a dimension of its own. The pyramid looked alien to Time, mysterious, peerless and unmatched in beauty, ancient yet ageless, an object of eternity with a door to infinity. Time stepped through it.

The Hall of Remembrance shimmered into existence before Time. Down its length ran countless of tributes to those who had passed. Time ignored them, for at the end of the Hall was a tribute he had not seen before. He ran the length of the Hall, boots sending echoes along the way. Time clenched his jaw, anticipating the name on the plaque. It was not the one he had expected to see.

It was not his father's name.

It was Spheron.

Time grieved for him. It was a story-plaque telling of Spheron's last hours. Time read it slowly and with a heavy heart:

Here reads the story of Spheron
Defender of the Colonnades.

They came at dawn, descending upon the time-dweller's city,
the thousands in their hordes, blotting out the sky.
The Lore—greedy for blood, baying for death.

204

Of Spheron: He, who stood his ground, alone, in splendid armour.
Awaiting destiny, defiantly alive.
He, whose heart beat of steadfast courage;
whose warrior eyes stared unflinchingly into the face of danger;
whose body, tempered like steel, unceasingly fearless, cried for battle.
Master of his duty: Defender of the Colonnades. Son of legends.
Spheron: faithful in the knowledge that today, he would die.

Of The Lore: They, the slaughterers
who struck the hero's mighty, sky-bound forceshield.
Those uncaringly repelled by his iridescent energy.
Ones of undiminished evil, wielding undying patience.
Death they craved of Spheron,
the yonder gates to breach, the city to take.
Death to Spheron was cried.
Never did air shiver or ground quake from such a challenge.

Of the Battle: Whose long hours raged to revolt against Spheron.
Lore after Lore assailed him; bright shield under siege.
Lore after Lore assaulted him; keen gaze distracted.
It sowed the seeds of doubt; a glimmer, then a crack.
The Lore poured in; his guard lowered; weary powers failing.
Still he fought: mind, body and soul full of God-like strength,
shouting defiance, drowning out his marauders' screams,
who streaked down from above and beyond upon the guardian-warrior.
The battle turned; an elegant bout of destruction,
Lore littering the ground in apathy and death.

Of the End: From whence this story brings tears.
An unravelling of powers besieged Spheron.
On he fought, the hero who the Lore rallied against;
the one whom they preyed upon,
cursing his existence, ripping at his cloak tails.
Brave Spheron suffering the ravenous barrage,
surviving the relentless onslaught.

He dared them, taunted them,
cast them down beneath the dead dark skies,
precious blood pouring from him.
Dear-hearted Spheron, passion ruling and living in agony.

An oath he cried: 'to die with the last of them,
breathe his last breath clutching their venomous throats,
kill them at the very gates of hell.'
Murderous fear arose, the Lore in a burning rage, searing the hero,
inciting wrath in the cornered hero, driving him back,
Nay! he drawing them in, toward his domain.
Massive arms swing, the colonnades rumble.
Great hands crush, the colonnades crumble.
Smiting his beleaguers in exacting vengeance,
death upon death by his hand delivered at his feet.
Colonnades after colonnades fall.
Destruction's wake strewn with lifelessness.
Spheron fought to save his city. He fought to be worthy of his death.
He fought til he alone was left.

Of the Death: I saw him, Helexius—ruler of the Chronopolis.
I called, but bloodied ears had brought deafening silence.
He fell to his knees, hands embracing the sky and death,
his enemies' lives vanquished, his own fading. I held him.
He shouted his entrance to the otherworld:

"Beware Spheron—Defender of the Colonnades."
I know he was heard. I could hear the returning praise
echoing back to him as he passed from this realm:
"Hail, Spheron, Defender of the Colonnades!
Hail Spheron, Master of his death.
Hail Spheron! Spheron! Spheron! Spheron!"

Now he lies in peace.

There were sobbing noises in the air. Time realised it was the echoes of his own crying at the end of the eulogy. Another voice startled him.

"So, you haven't forgotten us then, cousin!"

Time spun around to see Lightstream behind him.

"'Stream!" Time's voice was still clouded with emotion. "I'm only here for a visit."

"I know," Lightstream sighed wistfully. "Shame you weren't here for the battle, though it wouldn't have helped," she said sadly, indicating Spheron's plaque. "He gave his life to save us."

"What happened? How did the Lore find us?" Time asked.

Lightstream started to walk, flicking her blonde head for Time to follow her.

Time noticed then for the first time how different she seemed.

"How are you?" he asked, genuinely interested. "You seem different."

"You mean more grown up," Lightstream laughed half-heartedly, "What with you, Zane and the others gone, it's only myself, father, and Sola left!"

Time was shocked, "What! Where are the others?" he exclaimed.

Lightstream explained as they walked, "Your leaving caused a rift. Netherlord and Archron withdrew from our influence, taking cousin Celestra and gaining the aid of your aunt. They're on Magna Aura protected by a time-field."

"What? Why?"

"We're not sure. But there's more," Lightstream said, "Phasia has also gone. She disappeared just before the Lore attacked. Who knows how the Lore sense things, but they may have tracked her or she signalled them."

"You think Phasia betrayed us again?" Time asked.

Lightstream was silent for a while.

"We don't know." But her voice said otherwise.

"Come on, Lexa, tell me," Time used her childhood name. Lightstream looked at him, her mature mien giving way to an innocence long gone.

"Synther is alive!" she said.

Time couldn't believe his ears.

"That's not true!" Time retorted. "Can't be!" He paced ahead angrily with balled-up fists.

Lightstream caught up to him and ulled him back by the arm.

"He is, Aristedes, we all saw him. He withdrew after Spheron's death, unable to enter the Pyramid."

"It's not true! My father killed him," Time was adamant. "My father *killed* him." He felt himself shaking. On top of all his problems, their worst enemy was still alive.

Lightstream continued with a gentler voice, "We saw him, Aristedes, he called to us, called us out to battle and Spheron accepted. Spheron didn't stand a chance. He . . . he knew . . . yet . . ."

Her voice caught and she buried her head in her hands. Time comforted her with a hug, while she struggled to hold back her tears. She hadn't had time to grieve. Only the young grieved.

"I'm sorry, 'Stream, maybe if I'd been here . . ."

"It wouldn't have made any difference," another female voice said. "My father would have died saving you as well." Sola came forth, "Welcome home, Aristedes!"

The slim, black girl held out her hands, which Time took. He reached back and took a hand of Lightstream, who put on a brave face. The three of them continued walking to the heart of the Chronopolis.

It was just as Time had remembered it. A facsimile of an ancient Greek temple blended with Celestian technology: computers, or crystalators as they were called, controlling everything from environmental security to temporal/dimensional maintenance, sustenance production, and more. Such control was no easy task, even for an Astral.

But what grabbed Time's attention was at the end of the chamber: the throne; where his father, Lord Aeon, had once sat and where he should be, was now occupied by his uncle, Helexius.

"So, the young Lord returns." Helexius lifted himself from the throne and jauntily sauntered over to Time, grasping his shoulders. "You look well, my boy," he said proudly, patting him about the shoulders and torso, approving of the warrior's build. "A little tired, but well. How goes the search?"

Time regarded his uncle. He seemed a lot older now, blond hair a bit shorter, sporting a rough beard, his blue eyes still twinkled in mirth, while his muscular frame bore the purple and gold robes like a true leader. Though a leader with no kingdom.

"I'm fine, uncle." He looked at the two girls, enlightening them as well. "Zane's fine, also, but our search has faltered. We are in Earth's twenty-third century and they have just ended a war with an alien race. But now the world they hope to develop together is under threat from a new force. Zane and I have joined a group of other humans and aliens to fight that force. Uncle, that force is Netherlord!"

There was silence for a while as Helexius digested the news.

"Zeus' cock! So, he has started."

"Yes, but only him. I fear he is trying to bring the Knights Destina's vision to pass: The Final War. My friends have provisionally joined forces with another group, but they're not trustworthy . . . "

"So, you want our help," Helexius interrupted, trying not to sound weary.

Lightstream laughed, "Look at us!" she spread her arms, "Look what's left!"

"I know, I know," Time protested. "But if I can't have physical help, can I at least get some information?"

He told them what they had found out so far.

"Unfortunately, we can't help," Helexius said. "The Chronopolis needs our full attention. The crystalators aren't fully operational. Gods know if Archron and Celestra ar helping Netherlord and as for my sister—I don't care. Phasia disappeared. Cirius has thwarted our attempts to view the Magna Aura system which is now closed off to us. And my two Lieutenants here are keeping an eye on the rest of time; who knows if the Lore will return to attack us? So, as you can see, our resources are limited."

Time drew his hands over his face, rubbing his temples and cheeks. He felt like he had a headache coming on. He took a deep breath, absorbing the litany of woes, letting it out slowly.

"And the Starguards? Can they help us?"he asked in hope.

Lightstream shook her head. "No, their mission on Earth is vital. After Magna Aura and the Chronopolis, Earth is surely next and the Starguards will be needed there to help the Fifths survive."

"Or die trying!" Sola said plainly, to the general agreement of the others.

"Sorry, my young Lord," Helexius commiserated.

Despite the bad news, Time smiled.

"I'm not the Lord, yet. Among my group they call me Time: Temporally Independent Mutated Enemy," he grinned at his epitath.

Helexius laughed, "Appropriate for the son of Aeon. So, Time, what do you propose to do?"

"The decision's not up to me. I came to find out information and to report back, but we will fight Netherlord. I hope I'll be able to let you know the outcome."

Helexius nodded in thought. "There is his sword," he offered. "Netherlord may be powerful, but the Nethersword channels chaonic energy left over after temporal manipulations of physical space. He's absorbing and then redirecting that energy no doubt."

Time mulled that information over. *The sword could be the key*, he thought.

"Thank you," he said. "Hope it works."

"As do I," Helexius grasped Time's forearms. "Good fortune and luck, Lord Time."

"Thank you, uncle." Time hugged him then turned and embraced the two girls. "Take care. See you at the end of the war."

The girls said their goodbyes and Time walked out of the Chronopolis alone. He left the palace and walked the empty avenues, coming again to the broken colonnades, plying his way through the gates.

Time then slipped away into the timestream, from home to Home.

After he had left, Lightstream turned to her father, "I hated lying to him."

Helexius agreed, "Yes, but Phasia foresaw what must come to pass. And when it does, you must be ready to act."

Lightstream nodded.

Sola turned to Helexius, "Do you know where Phasia is?"

Helexius shook his head. "No, but she will return." He left it at that.

Sola and Lightstream looked at each other. There was more to tell, they knew. Their darkest days were ahead and the light was far from dawning.

"Was that it? You were only gone a few seconds. Where's your army?" Mode exclaimed, upon Time's return.

"I have no army," Time replied exasperated. "They cannot help. The Lore attacked and now they are in no position to help us. We're on our own!"

"That's not good enough!" protested Zone, up-raised fist punching the air.

"It'll be enough," insisted Time. "We will be our own army! The key to defeating Netherlord is his sword. Take it away from him and I will do the rest." He sounded confident, which impressed Mode.

"So now what?" asked Kellis. "Are you going to let us go?"

Mode signalled Invadress who keyed her wrist pad, chains, cells and bars opening up or turning off.

Mindscream rubbed his wrists, making sure the others were okay. He stared into the dark corner where the metal box still lay, untouched.

"What about Solitude?" he said, removing the telepathic limiter.

Mode answered, "If he so much as interferes with any of our energy, I'll turn him into slag. Is that understood?"

Mindscream nodded. He walked over to the box. It was heavy metal, he saw, unmoveable, with no doors.

"It's Surge metal. It'll absorb energy from a Surge."

Nobody bothered to ask how Mode how he knew that or how he had obtained more of the metal, but Kellis knew he must have visited Easter at some point and plundered a Surge body. The Superions had turned grave robbers.

Her disdain radiated out. She caught Psyren's eye at that moment who looked more than guilty. Then the look faded and an impassive mask fell over her face.

Mode walked forward to the box, standing beside Mindscream. He seemed to stare at Mindscream through his mask. It gave Mindscream an eerie feeling; one he'd experienced over four thousand years ago.

211

Mode touched the box and it simply melted away into the deck to leave Solitude lying upon the bare metal, unharmed. Mindscream had to admit, he was impressed.

"Thank you," he said.

Mode shrugged, "Save your thanks until after the war."

"After this battle, Mode, we'll still be enemies," Mindscream said.

"Not us, I hope," was the enigmatic reply.

Mindscream stared back at Mode. For a second there, he'd been convinced that Mode had meant it, but Mindscream couldn't be sure. Maybe after the battle they could talk, but for now he held his tongue.

There was a fight to prepare for.

"Um, sir," said ensign Mola, "There's something going on down there: electromagnetic activity." He sounded puzzled.

"Be more specific," Kirrilock said, walking over to the science station, Petrie right behind him.

They stopped dead when they saw the readout.

The ensign recovered quickly. "It looks like the team, sir, but they've got company and there's a weird energy signature as well."

Tension gripped the bridge as the information came in.

Kirrilock sensed it. "Raxt!" he cursed under his breath.

Something wasn't right here. Ever since the disappearance of the specialist force, seven hours ago, Tantillion Post had been on constant alert and now the team had reappeared with more questions and unknowns. It didn't add up. Kirrilock was just about to inform the crotchety Tantillion himself, when Shayson at comms signalled.

"Sir, we're being contacted by Commander Kellis!" she announced, controlling her excitement.

Kirrilock coolly acknowledged with a nod and Shayson patched Kellis through.

". . . to Tantillion Post. Come in, Tantillion Post!"

"Kellis, this is Tier-Commander Kirrilock. Report!" he had almost snapped out of frustration, though he was relieved to hear her voice.

"Tantillion . . . standby," was Kellis' reply, but any further words were drowned out by a sudden loud squeal which had everyone clutching their ears in pain. There followed only constant static.

Shayson stabbed frantically at her console, shaking her blonde, curly hair.

"It's completely dead, sir. Something's knocked it out."

"What the hell's going on here?" Petrie fumed.

Kirrilock's thoughts echoed her's: *Something was happening.*

Anxious moments ticked by with no contact with the surface and Kellis' team. Kirrilock paced the bridge. He had decisions to make, but they would depend upon the abilities of his crew, the human officers Shan Petrie, Bree Shayson the younger sister of the late, great Admiral Douglas Shayson who gave his life at Centauri Proxima, and the young Ken Mola. Kirrilock also had to think about the brave, but impetuous Paolo and his team, and even his own Axalan warriors.

Zev Tantillion had wanted and got the best for his mission, all four thousand of them on the station, but now things were falling apart. The best of the best had disappeared, reappeared, and now something had happened again. It was time for action.

"Shayson, contact Lieutenant Commander Paolo and tell him to prepare for a rescue mission."

"Aye, sir."

Kirrilock noticed that his order seemed to pick the crew up. They all knew it: it was time for action. But that mood was interrupted from the science station.

"Uh, oh!" Mola's hands hovered nervously in front of him, his mouth opened in surprise. "Sir, look!" he shouted in disbelief.

Kirrilock and Petrie bounded to his station.

Mola's sweaty brow was furrowed in concentration, the information on the main screens even straining Kirrilock's mind.

"I've never seen anything like it," confessed Mola, "But the readout says it's a temporal distortion emmanating around the planet. It came from nowhere!"

All the bridge crew instinctively looked out of bridge portholes though nothing could be seen.

Aware that his mouth was agape, Kirrilock recovered himself.

"Shayson, belay my order to Paolo. Can we get in touch with the party down there?"

He already knew the answer to that even as Shayson shook her head, but he had to ask, for the record. They were on their own down there.

Kirrilock and his crew could only watch helplessly as the planet-wide temporal ripple engourged the world below, warping the space around it.

Tantillion Post remained unaffected, the bridge eerily quiet. It only lasted ten seconds and then it was gone.

Mola reported what Kirrilock already knew:

"Sir . . . the team is . . . gone, again!" He had tried to hide the grief from his voice, but couldn't.

Kirrilock shared his despair. "Xaal help them now," he breathed, "Wherever they are!"

CHAPTER TEN

Time woke up with a start; his head still spinning. He thought he was the first to wake up, but upon craning his sore head around he saw Solitude standing off in the distance. A peculiar thought ran through Time's mind:

Does Solitude sleep anyway?

The thought swam around his mind, until he was suddenly aware of his surroundings. They were outside and not captive in the Superions' ship. He scrambled unsteadily to his feet, ignoring his somewhat spinning numb head.

"We're still on Home," he noted to himself.

But it had changed. It was now daylight. And what was once a barren world was now distinctly green and fresh. It was a lived-in place. They were in the future.

Fragments of memory surfaced—leaving the Superions' ship, his sensing of an approaching time-wave, Kellis' abbreviated message to Tantillion Post, being engulfed by the wave. Then blank.

There were only a few beings he knew of, who wielded such power to reach through time and they were all temporal sorcerers like the Astrals. Archron and Timechantress had that power, but their wave signatures were different. His father, Lord Aeon, had that power, but he wouldn't have been so crude. That only left Netherlord.

But what is his motive? Time thought. *Time-snatching them could not be part of his agenda in destroying the galaxy. Or could it?* Time knew the answers would come soon.

Turning and checking on the others, Zane first, who were beginning to stir, Time walked over to Solitude, if only to gain himself and the Multiforce a bit of an advantage. When Time reached Solitude, the tall, black-bodied Surge stood, as it turned out, on the edge of a cliff, overlooking a vast river-laced plain surrounding a sprawling city: the inhabitants of Home. Time estimated that the city had been there for decades, which confirmed that they were in the future.

"Well, Solly baby," Time said, "Looks like Tantillion's dream came true after all."

215

Solitude stared at Time impassively, but Time knew that somehow Solitude knew his sentiment. Time heard rustling behind him and he turned to see Windburst dusting herself off, looking quite annoyed.

"What's going on Aristedes?" she asked, walking up beside him rubbing her head. "Feels like I have a time-wave hangover!"

Time helped to brush the back of her off. Looking at her now, Time felt a distinct and overwhelming irrational compulsion to protect Zane more than ever. He felt a lump in his throat and his heart began to beat faster. He forced himself to calm down.

Nothing is going to happen to her! he told himself.

"Oh, wow!" Windburst gushed on spying the city, before confusion reigned. "What's happened?" she asked, frowing at the city beyond.

"I'll tell you all in a minute," he told her, partly to repulse his own fears, "But for now let's take care of the others."

Together they poked and prodded the others awake, the Superions even more belligerent and wary than before.

"What have you done, whelp!" demanded Mode, jumping up to his feet the moment he was awake. The Superions gathered about him, the Multiforce squared up against them.

"I didn't do anything," Time explained. "We were attacked, by Netherlord."

"Attacked!" Kellis beat Mode to the question. She looked around, suspicious. "Where is he?"

Winterborne stood silently beside her, seemingly staring off vacantly into the distance, as a babble of voices asked questions, doubting Time's statement, but he silenced them.

"Look over here," demanded Time, directing them over to the cliff-edge and pointing to the city in the plain. "I don't know what's he up to, but we're still on Home, but in the future. Tantillion's future for humans and Axalans is there, in that city. And I think Netherlord wants to change it!"

"But why bring up here to show us?" Invadress asked, her voice grating on Kellis, thinking she could detect a faint South African accent. "He could have just destroyed us and this world without anyone knowing. There has to be more going on!"

216

Kellis was just about to agree when she inadvertently followed Winterborne's gaze and spied a blue-clad figure walking dazedly toward them. Her inattention caught the others' attention and they all turned to watch the blue-skinned man approach from behind a line of low hills. The other Superions looked confused as the last of their number neared them.

"But he was on the ship!" Zone spat, shaking his head. "How'd he get here?" He looked at the others in confusion.

"How indeed!" asked Mode in a deep venomous tone.

While his mask-covered face hid any emotion, Kellis had detected a note of anger in his voice, which confused her. She couldn't tell if the Superions welcomed their companion's presence or if they considered him their enemy.

Hmm, dissension in the ranks, eh? thought Kellis

But Invadress ignored the distraction, carrying on with the issue at hand.

"Maybe Netherlord brought our ship here as well. It's basically in that same position, hidden behind the hills."

"It's possible," replied Time, though he seemed slightly confused himself.

The Superion called Warper joined them. Kellis knew more about the rest of them, but Warper was a mystery. They knew he had superb abilities in flight, both self-powered and as a pilot. But here he was in the flesh and his appearance had only added to his mystique.

"Welcome to the future, Warper," Mode had greeted him.

A wan smile softened Warper's face dark blue, but he didn't seem all together there, thought Kellis. He didn't seem injured, just distracted. She stared at him. His cowl, probably jammed full of micro-comm systems and other neural interfaces, only revealed his lower face, but it was his eyes that had attracted Kellis, especially when he had returned her look.

Their eyes had connected and for a brief moment, clarity had seemed to return to Warper's demeanour and a part of the past had come flooding back into Kellis' mind. She knew those eyes. She knew this man called Warper. As Mode had inferred before, she and the Superions, including Warper, had a shared past. But she still couldn't fully put the picture together completely. Parts of her own memory were missing also; it was hazy, fading away until only her present and this future remained.

Mode noticed Kellis' interest, subtly signalling Psyren to take care of any further slips.

Kellis, still engrossed with Warper, hadn't noticed, but had seen the clarity in Warper's eyes disappear behind that same veil of cloudiness as before. Kellis shook her head as if a dream had ended. She had turned to see if anyone else had noticed, but had instead caught Mindscream deep in thought and staring intensely at the city.

"What's wrong, Mindscream?" she asked the telepath, sensing some tension in him.

"All those people down there, human and Axalan; this is their new home and in a few hours, days, or weeks, it will all be destroyed."

"He is here, Mindscream," joined in Psyren. "This is the world we saw being destroyed in our dreams. Things make sense now!" Psyren seemed more apprehensive now.

Kellis tried to piece it all together. "So if this is the world you saw destroyed, you were seeing the future. But why would Netherlord want to bring us here? Unless . . ."

"—unless I wanted you to be here at its glorious destruction!" intoned an unfamiliar voice from above and behind them.

The two groups whirled as one. A figure in silver and green armour hovered in the air above them, a thick green cape billowing in the breeze, a giant rune-covered sword resting in his hands. From beneath his helmet a sinister grin curved across his lips.

"I believe you have been expecting me. I am Netherlord!"

In another time, a weary Tier-Commander Kirrilock tried to explain to an incredulous and increasingly fuming Zev Tantillion what had happened.

"What do you mean, just disappeared, again?" Tantillion choked out.

They were in Tantillion's quarters, the elder statesman having been awakened from his blissful sleep to hear the distressing news. Now he was drinking some warm milk and Kirrilock was trying hard to resist the urge of wiping away milk drops from Tantillion's mouth and chin, unable to think of a way of doing it in a dignified manner.

"Councillor," Kirrilock begun, "some sort of . . . energy distortion took them. There was nothing we could do. I'm sorry, sir." He tried to look as grievous as possible, a commander's duty in a time like this.

Tantallion was quiet. The Axalan tried to distract himself by looking at the pictures, holograms, and models dotted around the room of other terraforming projects on Mars, Titan, and Alpha Centurai.

Will Home join this grand lineage? he thought.

Tantillion gave a great sigh. His voice was soft and thin. And as if he had read Kirrilock's mind said:

"Home was to be my legacy not just for our races, but for my family; all nine children, thirteen grandchildren, twelve great-grandchildren, and three great great-grandchildren." He smiled as if seeing everyone of their faces. "I may be a politician, but terraforming is in my blood. And I have a gut feeling about things. And my gut is telling me now that Home will survive. No matter how bleak it is. . ."

His bright green eyes bore into Kirrilock sincerely, and to Kirrilock's relief dabbed his mouth clean of milk drops with his sleeve.

"Okay, Kirrilock, complete your report and I'll inform the E-G," Tantillion stated, "Lord knows, they were his best people. I only hope that whatever happened down there doesn't happen again. Hell, I just hope we survive!" Tantillion said in a sad voice.

"As do I, sir," Kirrilock echoed his sentiments.

Kirrilock rose and left Tantillion's quarters. On his way to the bridge, all Kirrilock could think about was the lives that had been lost and the obsessive nature of Tantillion in pursuit of his dreams for peace.

Strange old man, with a strange old dream, thought Kirrilock, as he entered the bridge.

Netherlord hovered ominously above them.

Time knew the situation was already tense and that anything could spark off a serious battle. He hoped there was a chance to talk to peace.

But it came as no surprise to him when Mode and Invadress suddenly unleashed a barrage of electromagnetic energy at Netherlord. Time knew it was doomed to fail, as the unfazed Netherlord let the energy simply glance off his temporal shield, dissipating the energies into times unknown.

"You menial humans mean nothing to me!" Netherlord said, ignoring the fact he was half-human.

Pointing his sword at the two attackers, a bolt of searing energy blasted the ground beneath their feet, flooring the two of them. They were slow to get up, their pride hurt more than anything.

"Enough, Netherlord," Time tried to inject a bit of decorum into the situation. "You are no God! What do you want with us?"

Netherlord, sheathing his sword, descended to the ground, striding confidently up to Time.

"My dear, dear nephew, Aristedes, you're so much like your father," he scoffed.

Time ignored the jibe and followed Netherlord's eyes as they shifted toward Windburst. He automatically stepped toward her to shield her. Netherlord's eyes passed over the rest of them; Kellis and Winterborne, silent yet concerned; an intrigued Mindscream; his eyes then seemingly lingering longer over the impassive Solitude. Turning his gaze over the Superions, the defiant Mode and glaring Invadress, serene Psyren, belligerent Zone and the frail-looking Warper.

Netherlord shook his head and laughed; a deep, raucous sound. "You are all so extremely out of your depth in time and space, little humans," he said, "Present company excepted, of course," he said to Solitude, keeping his distance from the Surge.

His comments had caused a degree of discomfort in the Superions who still wore their Axalan disguises.

"Yet you still survive and cling on to life. I wonder," he said more to himself, "What if I offered you a chance to live?" he asked them.

"You mean if we joined you?" Time replied dismissively.

"Of course," replied Netherlord.

"At what price?" Kellis countered.

"You each have skills or talents I can use," Netherlord said. "And the reward for using them in my service would be your life. What else could one want?"

"Freedom!" snapped Windburst.

"Power!" Mode growled.

Netherlord laughed again. "Now, there's a man after my own heart," he said looking at Mode. "And I bet you would even kill me for it as well, wouldn't you?"

"If need be," Mode said provocatively.

Netherlord let the answer hang in the air. He was enjoying this.

But Time took the moment to intercede again. "I'll ask again, what do you want with us?"

"Patience, my Lord," Netherlord began, smiling widely "You know nothing of the universe out there. There's a war raging, an all-consuming universal fire and you concern yourself with these trifle humans. Be one of us again, take your birthright and lead us in this war!"

Time had waited years to confront Netherlord and now the time for challenge had come.

"Netherlord, I know about the Final War, but it's just a myth. You're destroying the universe in vain. All that the Knights Destina stood for was dead long before our parents' parents were even born. It's over! And as for my birthright, I still search for my father, and it will not be mine to take as long as he is alive, which he is."

Time felt surprisingly confident. Netherlord was not going to take this away from him.

But Netherlord's smile had curled into an ugly grin.

"Your father is dead," he said matter-of-factly. "Believe me, I should know," he ended with a tone of finality, his grin extending.

That's not true!" Windburst called out, leaving her brother's protective field before he could hold her back.

Windburst trembled with anger, "If you know where my father is, then you'd better tell me right now, or else!"

She stood right at Netherlord's chest, staring into his dark eyes, her fists clenched, her eyes gleaming with ire.

Netherlord could barely contain himself, laughing heavily.

"Or else, what? You're a cripple!" he sneered.

"This!" Windburst yelled, pushing out her arms explosively.

A torrent of energy raged from her hands as Netherlord was sent flying through the air to land twenty meters away, smoke spiralling from a gash in his armoured chest. Windburst looked amazed at her hands and then at her brother, who could find no words. It was the first time Windburst had displayed any sign of Astral power besides her speed ability. A smile drifted across her face, tears filling her eyes, as she slowly made her way back to Time.

Time was joyous. His sister had just manifested her full Astral powers. As he held out his hands to embrace her, he suddenly looked in the distance behind Windburst, in gathering shock.

Netherlord had risen to his feet. And he was angry.

Then the world crashed into slow motion.

Before anyone could react, Netherlord reached his hands up above his head and then violently cast them down in a throwing motion.

Windburst looked behind her, a cheerful, teary-eyed face turning into one of terror as air-renting energy hit her full force. She hadn't stood a chance. Right before Time's eyes, Windburst disappeared, her body disintegrating into energy.

She was gone.

Everyone stood stunned. No one moved. No one breathed.

Netherlord, too, looked taken aback. There was a deafening silence as if the mourning had already begun. But it was just the beginning.

Time's anger welled up, an anger that he had carried inside him for as long as he could remember. Anger for the loss of his father now usurped by a driving anger for a loss greater to him than could be compensated for by his own life.

Time felt the rush of rage, embraced it, and let it surge through him, burning his veins, his eyes, his soul. In one ear-piercing yell, he lashed out with all his might, the power so great that not only did it irradiate Netherlord as he was again tossed through the air, engulfed in a fire-ball of energy, it also knocked the others off their feet. The ground began to burn.

Slowly, Netherlord rose again to his feet, cautiously, energy sparkling from his hands, his nethersword gripped firmly in his right hand. Any normal person would have been burned by the temporal energy, reduced to unravelling atoms, but Netherlord's half-Celestian powers had protected him.

Now he was ready for a real battle.

He grinned in anticipation.

"A rescue? From where? For who?" Kirrilock asked sceptically, rising from his chair to pace his office.

He hadn't known what he was in for with these humans. He still didn't, even after the five hours since Kellis and her team had disappeared.

The other occupant in his office, Lieutenant Commander Paolo, sat still, trying to think of a valid answer himself.

"I don't know, sir. I know what our sensors say, but we could at least take a look. There might have been something left, some sort of clue as to what happened, who did it, and even where they went. I think it's worth a shot, sir," he concluded.

"Worth a shot?" Kirrilock snapped back. "There are over four thousand warriors on this post and you want to take a shot which could cost all those lives—for what!" He held his hands out in askance, silently praying to Great Xaal for deliverance from human contradicitons.

Paolo was silent. He hadn't wanted to bring the next subject up, but he was now being forced to.

Would this alien understand love?

Paolo's voice was soft. "Tier-Commander, you know I already knew Commander Kellis' team before they arrived here, but I . . . uh, I had been planning on asking one of her team to marry me on her return."

Kirrilock suppressed a groan of sympathy. Outwardly, he nodded to show he was listening.

Paolo continued, "I have to know, sir. It's destroying me, the not knowing, the waiting. I have to know!" His fists had clenched up in order to keep his emotional control, but his eyes let him down, misting

223

over with imminent tears. "I have to know!" He fought back his grief, regaining his composure.

Kirrilock walked over to him, placing a comforting hand on Paolo's shoulder; an action he had learned from Tantillion.

"I did not know, Paolo. I'm sorry." He hoped the translator conveyed his words and tone correctly.

Raxt! A love-sick soldier, he thought.

An Axalan soldier would never have shown such weakness. With cheerless realisation, Kirrilock resolved himself to later re-consult his Human societal and cultural manual (prerequisite reading for all warriory posted to Human stations and ships), studying the intricacies of broaching soldier emotions. But for now he said:

"Of course. Of course, I'll do what I can to get your mission past Tantillion and under way. Call it a reconnaissance mission and you can also take your own squad . . ."

"No! I'll go alone. Just in case," Paolo confirmed.

"Okay." *That's better*, thought Kirrilock. "Go alone. But if anything happens . . ." Kirrilock didn't have to finish the sentence. He didn't want to think about it.

"I understand, sir," Paolo said, knowing the risks involved. Standing up, he saluted Kirrilock out of respect, before leaving his office.

Kirrilock sighed hard.

If warriors were meant to fall in love, was love more hell than war?

Kirrilock shook his head. He would never know the answer to that one even after having been married three times himself.

But such was fate.

"Kill him!" Mode ordered the Superions into the fray.

Invadress took to the air upon a self-propelled crackling of energy with Warper aloft, to, both blasting the errant Astral from the air. Psyren attempted to penetrate the temporal shield around Netherlord to attack from within his mind. Zone teleported about, like a flea, seeking out weak spots while avoiding deadly energy bolts from Netherlord.

But it was Mode, in his quest for glory, who took the initiative battling Netherlord one on one, his matter transformation powers not only enabling him to negate Netherlord's energy, but also allowing him to unleash his own attacks.

Mode grabbed handfuls of soil clawing the ground which broke into chunks, curving up into a huge wave of earth and rock. A great crater-like depression sunk around Netherlord, who at the centre stood, marooned, on a rock-like pedestal. The wave grew, until it twisted around to crash down upon Netherlord. But against the temporal shield, the earthen wave eroded in seconds.

"Good try, human!" he laughed.

In retaliation, Netherlord aimed the nethersword at Mode and fired, energy slashing into Mode sending him spinning to the ground in a heap. Far from finished, Mode touched the ground again, but this time water gushed out filling the crater. This tactic seemed to amuse a smirking Netherlord as he gently floated into the air and advanced toward Mode across the water.

The Superion saw his chance. Laying at the crater's edge, injured as he was, chest bleeding heavily, he dipped his hand in the water and two giant hands of water reached out and grabbed Netherlord about the waist.

Netherlord tried to slash at it with his sword, but to no avail. The water hands were encircling him and his shield. Enraged, he screamed, lashing out at Mode in attack, energy beams eating away at Mode's hiding spot.

Mode, concentrating on maintaining the water hands, saw the situation was about to get seriously grave, until Kellis and Winterborne appeared at his side, Kellis dragging Mode away, while dodging energy bolts from the nethersword.

But Winterborne remained standing in the face of danger, a wintry breeze accompanying her. She stared at the water and it froze, entrapping Netherlord in hands of ice which spread over his body gripping him solidly. His sword had no effect at carving it away. But he was still defiant.

"This is no match for me, ice maiden. And neither are you!" He twisted the nethersword, within the ice ready to blast from within, but a cracking sound caught his attention.

Winterborne, with an ever-present chill around her, raised her arms out to either side of her, the ice responding to her command as ten ice-forms rose from the ice, coalescing into ice warriors complete with ice swords.

Netherlord stopped struggling, in surprise. He was surrounded. But his astonishment wore off replaced by his fearsome grin.

"What have we here, a sorceress? Well, witch, I, too, can work magic!"

He forced the nethersword through the ice, lofted up high, the blade glinting not from the sunlight, but from energy within. Ten separate beams of light shot out from the sword shattering the ice-warriors. But no sooner had the countless pieces hit the icy ground, they had reformed. The ice soldiers charged, ice feet grating along ice, ice swords at the ready. Netherlord, still entombed at the waist level, engaged them, the nethersword shattering ice, energy blasts melting his foes, but each time they reformed. Netherlord flailed at his icy enemy, a cold, gusty wind descending upon him to add to his worries.

A short distance away, behind a low rise in the ground, Kellis had seen to Mode. He had practically healed himself, a feat Kellis hadn't known he possessed. He reminded her a lot of Mindscream.

Mode grunted at Kellis.

"I'll take that as a thanks," she said, ducking as stray beams careened their way.

They hadn't talked much and while Kellis had hidden herself away, Mode knew she was no coward. They both knew that she wasn't much use in a cosmic fight armed only with side-arms.

Mode laughed to himself. *Here I am beside a woman, who has just saved me, but whom only a short time ago I wanted to kill.* He could have done it now, but he wanted to savour the moment at another time, if they survived.

And as for the other Multiforce members, besides Winterborne who was fighting admirably, he hadn't seen much of them. However, being privy to their battle-plan, he now knew why. And he had to admit it was a brilliant strategy. But he had expected no less from Mindscream. He watched as the battle unfolded and the next phase began.

"This is foolishness!" A frustrated Netherlord struggled to understand how he couldn't break free and destroy these infernal ice creatures. They were a nuisance. He was also concerned that only the ice witch alone was attacking him.

Where are the others, he thought, *especially my nephew?*

His question was answered almost immediately as Invadress and Warper swooped out of the sky drilling his head with concentrated firepower, her energy and Warper's hand weapon, but Netherlord's temporal shield held out, energy flaring up, blinding even him. Again and again they attacked, like two hawks closing in on their prey, knowing that the kill is near.

It's my head! They're after my head, his mind! Netherlord realised in a panic.

They were trying to disrupt the temporal shield around his head, setting him up for a telepathic attack. Netherlord knew that even though telepaths couldn't read his mind, Mindscream and Psyren wouldn't have to. They weren't out to read his thoughts, they were out to infiltrate his mind and destroy.

The damage they could do individually would be devastating, but together . . .

Netherlord didn't even finish the thought. It was too terrible to think about. And he wasn't going to die that way.

I'm not going to die, period, he thought. *At least not at their hands!*

In desperation, and with a bit of luck, while fending off the ice warriors and the air attack, he was able to hit Winterborne with an energy bolt. She went down hard, unconscious. Netherlord tried to spin around in the icy grip to see if there were any more attackers, but he couldn't see anything. But before he had turned back, behind and to the right of him, he had glimpsed a slight distortion, a very telling distortion. And then in that moment, their whole battle plan had clicked inside Netherlord's mind.

Light-bending was child's play for a temporal sorcerer, rendering the user invisible.

The fool child hasn't perfected his technique, Netherlord laughed to himself, *or more likely is trying to conceal too many attackers with him, over-balancing on the refraction angles, hence the distortion.*

With added amusement, it immediately clicked in his mind Time was also working in concert with Winterborne reforming her ice warriors. Time must have imbued the ice with temporal energy, negating Netherlord's efforts to destroy the warriors. The attacks were diversions. And all the while Time snuck up from behind.

"Impressive!" Netherlord said aloud.

But the young Astral's tactics had failed, costing him his life. He quickly pointed the nethersword at the distortion and fired. The distortion rippled wildly before disappearing in a flare of light. But no dead bodies appeared.

"Huh!" uttered a confused Netherlord.

"Over here, bastard!"

Before Netherlord could spin back round to his left, Time unleashed a hail of energy lashing Netherlord's chest. His shield faltered but held, weakly, as Time sent a torrent of temporal artillery into his uncle.

Netherlord mentally chided himself. He had fallen for the diversion within a diversion. He cursed himself, but no sooner had he done when Time released a virtual onslaught of energy, breaking apart Netherlord's temporal shield.

"That's for Zane!" Time screamed. "You killed my sister!" The rest of his screams were incoherent—anger, grief, and hate coiled within the timestream crushing down upon Netherlord.

And all hell broke loose as Mindscream and Psyren sprang from behind Time. Mindscream was the sledge hammer, battering at Netherlord's locked mind, while Psyren poked and prodded needle-like into mental niches for an opening.

Netherlord's head swam in pain as he resisted.

"Aaargh!" he could hear himself screaming in enduring pain; his mind unhinging from reality. It was all he could do to keep the nethersword held aloft to soak up the barrage from the renewed attacks from the ice warriors as Winterborne had regained consciousness and the resumed air attacks of Invadress and Warper.

"Heh!" a rejuvenated Mode jumped up to join in. He knew this was their chance for victory and he wanted to be there at the end.

Kellis watched him go and then ran out to cover Winterborne's attack. She knew even now she was no match for the battle and the energy that was being thrown around, but she couldn't just sit on the background.

However, it also gave her time to think about Windburst. *How could this happen? Was her memory wrong? Had time changed again? Why didn't Time just change time? Could she really wish Zane to rest in peace?* A boulder shattering beside Kellis broke her revelry. This war was still on.

Netherlord was weakening. He could feel it; his attackers could sense it. They pressed their attack, advancing toward him, defeat certain.

It was Mindscream who issued the ultimatum:

"Give up Netherlord! You've lost!"

Netherlord wasn't sure if Mindscream had shouted it or if he had heard it in his mind. Nonetheless, he grinned defiance from beneath his helmet. He still had a few tricks left in him and plenty of life to use them.

Through the pain of continued attack, he screamed, "You poor, pathetic children. When will you learn you cannot break me? You cannot defeat me. I've already succeeded, you've already lost. The Final War had already begun. These signs I leave, the broken planets and shattered stars are but forgotten battle-fronts; casualties of war. They are signs to which the war will be drawn to. And ended. It is written!"

With his last words, a ringing and raging crescendo, he punched the air, the nethersword, held high once more, pulsed and rent forth sky-splitting energy burning the air.

The Multiforce and Superions were thrust into the ground by the force of the waves. Angry lightning struck everywhere, cracking the ice warriors to smithereens. With his hands, Netherlord chopped at and smashed the icy grip around him, angrily kicking the rest away from him, falling to the ground on his hands and knees. He was free.

"Advantage me!" he cried out, arms outstretched.

Netherlord launched his own barrage. Hands glowing, streaks of energy flew toward his prey, followed closely by balls of energy that disintegrated anything in their path. It was all the Multiforce and Superions could do to evade the deadly spheres.

Mode and Mindscream found themselves hunkered down in a low gully, energy balls fizzing past their location. Mindscream could sense the others and see Kellis dragging Winterborne away to another gully. They were safe for now.

"He's quite mad!" Mindscream declared grimly.

"That's your fault," replied Mode sarcastically. "We can't defeat him now!"

Mindscream looked at him in annoyance. "Then you're not trying hard enough!" Mindscream accused Mode. "I thought we were working together."

"So did I, but I guess I was wrong."

An energy ball careened over them forcing them to duck even lower. Netherlord was still too engaged in his own aggrandizement to bother specifically hunting down the enemy, but that would stop soon.

"Mode, we need each other to defeat Netherlord or he'll continue to rip apart the galaxy!"

"Your plan failed, Mindscream. There's no way to defeat him now. I can see that, you can't. We have differing views. We are too different. Always have been, always will be!"

Mindscream's brows furrowed in curiosity at that statement, but now was not the time to discuss it. He had to get their alliance back on track.

"Mode, we can defeat him. We have another plan. It's only a matter of time before its initiation," he pleaded.

"No!" Mode disagreed. "This, I see, is now your problem. The Superions withdraw. Our alliance is over. We'll take our chances elsewhere!"

With that said he got up and zigzagged his way away from Mindscream, who gave chase. As he was about to catch Mode, a searing, jagged beam of light caught Mindscream midriff. He fell in agony, barely able to raise a psi-shield to protect himself as more energy washed over him.

Mindscream reached out to Mode who was trying to claw his way over the broken ground, his blood spilling out through the cracks.

The Superion leader had dropped into a prone position to avoid the same fate. For a while the two had stared at each other across the dusty ground, Mindscream trying to implore Mode to help him. With a final grunt, Mode turned and crawled away.

Mindscream lay on the ground, his life ebbing away, left to die, just as he had been thousands of years ago. He felt his body tearing apart, skin, organ and nerves burning from Netherlord's temporal assault. He screamed in pain. He was going to die.

Time flew in from nowhere, unleashing a hail of energy over Mindscream to protect him in a forcefield. He fell to his knees, protecting Mindscream, who could concentrate and feel his body tingling as it rapidly healed.

"Mooodee...." he tried to tell Time they had been deserted by the Superions, but he just couldn't get the words out, managing only an incoherent jumble of sounds.

But Time had other matters on his mind. Seeing his friend was going to survive, he channelled his temporal charges which burst toward Netherlord, staggering the elder Astral with the power of his barrage.

Locked in temporal battle, the two traded fire, their bodies shimmering in energy, phasing in and out of reality. Their battleground blazed like a sun. This was the final fight.

Mode had made it to safety. Seeing Time had come in to rescue Mindscream, he signanlled to the others.

"Return to me. Cease attacks!" He repeated the signal until they had all recieved it.

"What's the plan now, Boss?" Zone asked, when they had all gathered a few kilometers away from the battlezone.

"We leave!" Mode replied.

The surprised silence that greeted him told him there was to be some disagreement to his decision.

"But Mode, we have an agreement with Kellis," Invadress said. "Even though I hate to admit it, I can't see us running off like this!"

"I agree with Invadress," Psyren added, "And besides, Netherlord could defeat the Multiforce and then where would we be? We'd have to fight him ourselves sooner or later. He'll come after us for revenge. We need to fight now!"

Mode tried to counter. "He might see us as allies in the future if we leave now!"

"Ha, this is the future!" Invadress laughed.

No one else did.

"Reluctantly, I have to agree with the boss," Zone argued. "I don't like the idea of leaving a fight, but I don't like Kellis even more and this Netherlord guy is totally wiping the floor with us. I say we cut loose now, retreat to fight another day and find better allies to do it ourselves. Let these guys go down now!" He stepped closer to Mode to emphasise his viewpoint.

Well, that's two to two, thought Mode.

They all looked at Warper who stood, as always, somewhat apart from them.

"Ah! We know what you're going to say, don't we Warpie?" Zone mocked him.

Warper thought about it for a while before saying, "I don't care what the rest of you do. I'm staying to fight. I feel it's my duty to do so, though I don't know why."

He stood directly across from Mode as if challenging him to change his mind, but it was Mode who gave in.

"Go then. But I never want to see you again," he warned.

Warper regarded them keenly, for the last time as if saying goodbye, then stepping back he rocketed off into the sky describing a large overhead arc in the sky in order to escape Netherlord's and Time's battle.

Invadress made ready to shoot him down, but Mode held her arm down.

"We don't need him anymore," he said then he turned to the rest and asked, "Are the rest of you with me?"

"Yes," answered Invadress, though she clearly wanted to battle on.

Psyren nodded curtly. "Reluctantly," she said.

"That's so nice to know," Zone directed at her, "But why did you let Warper go?" he asked of Mode.

"Like I said, we don't need him anymore," the Superion leader replied, "and besides, he'll die with the rest of them."

"What if they do defeat Netherlord," Psyren asked, "they'll come after us next!"

Mode contemplated this and with a smile in his voice said, "I really hope they do!"

The others looked at each other. Sometimes they didn't understand Mode's ways, but they had to admit his way always worked. He'd kept them alive so far.

"Now, let's just get back to our ship and get the hell out of here," Mode ordered, "Then we'll find out when we are and what to do about it!"

With that, the Superions headed away from the battle, leaving the Multiforce to their fate.

Warper circled around high above the Astrals' battle, the ground around the two combatants barely visible through the glare of energy being hurled around like two latter-day Zeuses. As he descended over some canyons, a bright flare caught his attention. He looked down and over to his right and saw a beam of light flash toward him. He tried to dodge it.

Too late.

"Graaah!" he cried out in pain as the beam of light hit him square in the chest.

The sky pitched in a blur as he spun out of control, sky tumbling over ground tumbling over sky, smoke trailing from his injury. The last thing he saw was the ever-nearing bottom of the canyon.

Time and Netherlord had kept up a constant stream of deadly energy, sparring for far longer than Mindscream thought Time could.

Mindscream still lay injured on the ground, but now he had the energy to both heal himself and to enact their fail-safe plan. He looked heavenwards and sent a message, just as an errant energy beam ricocheted off from Time's temporal shield high off into the sky. Mindscream thought it had hit something in the bright distance, but he couldn't be sure, all around him was a glare of battle. He put his hands to his eyes, trying to blot out the lensing, just in time to see a figure diving out of the high sun.

Solitude, having held his position high up in the sky until he was summoned, dropped from the sky, like black death itself, plunging onto Netherlord.

BOOM!

The resulting contact drove both of them into the ground, sending a rumbling tremor under Mindscream, dust billowing from the impact area.

Time had been knocked away and now ran raggedly to join Mindscream on the ground. The dust had not yet cleared, but they could make out a massive form through the haze.

Solitude was clamped on Netherlord's back, extending barbed arms and legs into the Astral's limbs and torso. Netherlord was trapped. Locked in the Surge's grip, Solitude began to do what his race had done for millennia: absorb energy.

"Grr, no!" Netherlord struggled, only dimly aware of the full situation.

He tried to reach for his sword to ward off Solitude, but only timid sparks bluffed their import. His helmeted face couldn't hide his shock, apparent as his mouth opened into a snarl, his struggles becoming more frantic and wild, to no avail. Solitude was locked tight.

Mindscream watched as Netherlord fought to free himself. One hand ripped loose. And swivelling the nethersword he plunged the blade savagely into Solitude's mid-torso, who did not flinch. The siphoned energy dazzled the air around the two, but Solitude sucked it up, bleeding more and more energy out of the Astral and his nethersword.

But Netherlord wasn't giving up. If anything he had tried to increase his energy output to get away. The air blurred and changed as if time around then was fracturing. But Solitude, the metal leech stayed put.

The power of Netherlord astounded Mindscream. *How much did he have?* he wondered.

He then imagined what would happen if Netherlord expounded more energy than Solitude could take. Instantly the thought struck Mindscream resoundingly, a sinking feeling in his stomach making bile rise to his throat.

He had to warn Solitude. >*Solitude, move away. He's trying to overload you!*< he screamed telepathically.

Solitude was resolute. >*I will not!*<

>*Let go! Let go, or you'll die!*< Mindscream tried again.

Even as he had psyed it, the realisation of what he had just said, sent him reeling to the ground.

Here was a being trying to overload another, the last of its kind, who had wanted, and still wanted, to die. Solitude was going to sacrifice himself to save them and to achieve what he had wanted from the outset, his wish to die and join his people.

Mindscream pleaded. >*Don't Solitude! Don't do this!*< But he knew his psyed plea was doomed to fail.

>*Move away from here, my friend. My time is near!*< Solitude said.

Mindscream sat and watched, too afraid to move, too drawn to the unreality of the situation. He felt a tug on his arm, Time shaking him into reality.

"Mindscream, we have to go!" he warned him, shouting above the din of the energy singing against reality. "I think Netherlord's trying to get Solitude to absorb too much energy. He'll overload!" He shook Mindscream's arm more violently, "Do you hear me, Mindscream? We have to go, now!" Time urged.

Mindscream stared Time straight in the eye. He didn't like what he was hearing. But Time persisted.

"He has to do it, Aaron. Netherlord has to pay for what he did." Time's face was screwed in anger.

Aaron's face dropped as he realised what was happening.

"But . . . no!" was all he could manage. "Not like this!"

"He has to! Let him die. He wants to and he'll do us a favour!"

Mindscream revolted, but Time forcibly dragged him away from he scene with a little help from time-shifting. By the time they reached Kellis and the still unconscious Winterborne, who were safely hidden behind a low ridge, they knew that it would soon be over.

"We have to get well away from here," Mindscream told Kellis with sad reluctance, Time already had Winterborne in his arms.

"Why, what's happening?" Kellis asked. "What about Solitude?"

The way Mindscream shook his head and looked at her made Kellis' heart jump. She could feel her tears stinging her eyes already.

"You bastard!" she screamed, thumping him on his chest.

Mindscream didn't know if she meant him or Solitude. But now was no time to find out.

A small silver sun of chronal energy had enveloped Netherlord and Solitude. It steadily grew in size and intensity, warping everything in its path as if time was a pulsing heartbeat.

Kellis and Mindscream huddled with the Winterborne-carrying Time, his temporal shield just about able to protect them from frequent small explosions. Time around them was shattering.

Netherlord screamed in anguish as his fight ended.

Solitude hung on as silently as death. His time was at hand. He seemed to turn his head toward Mindscream. And smile.

The nethersword shattered catastrophically. Energy ruptured across time and space. Netherlord disintergrated into his own energy spread across eternity. Pieces of Solitude blasted over the planet, but whether they existed in the first place in the ebb of temporal flux would be debated.

The flash of the temporal explosion smashed into Time's temporal shield, buffeted by energies that raced into other dimensions and times. The whole sky rippled like water disturbed by falling raindrops. From day to night, past, future and unknown times, the landscape and skies changed around them. It was all they could do to survive the spasmatic breath of the shifting timescapes. The universe on full tilt.

And then it was all over. Where there had been two combatants, there was now nothing, no one. Netherlord and Solitude were gone.

But that wasn't all that was dead. Home had changed. As the ripple effect had finally dissipated the dead and barren world from before had returned.

"Huh!" Time exclaimed looking around. "Back in our time, I think it reverted with Netherlord gone. We're back to normal!"

"No, not back to normal," Kellis sneered angrily, thinking of Zane. "Never back to normal. I'm so sorry, Aristedes. It was all my fault for having her there." She managed to hold back the tears, hugging Aristedes.

Time reflected on her words, his head bowed in sorrow. "No, Kellis, it's my fault. I was her protector. Now I've failed her and my father." He stood alone trying to contemplate his losses.

"But why didn't you change time to save her? You could now. And save Solitude!" Mindscream said.

Time laughed hysterically—like the question was some sick joke. Kellis thought he had gone mad.

"I did!" screamed Time, tears flowing down his cheeks. "I went back over and over and she still died. There was nothing I could do." He made incoherent noises, punching fist into palm again and again. "Netherlord would stop me, or the Superions would attack, or Zane would be as impulsive as ever. I told you, I told you..." he yelled at Kellis, "that some things happen you can't change. She was meant to..."

He staggered off into the distance.

"Leave him," Mindscream held back Kellis. "He needs time."

A piercing cry and commotion behind them put them on alert.

"Burning! I'm burning! The fire! Someone stop the fire!" Winterborne burst out screaming. She sobbed and screamed before slipping into semi-consciousness, a waking nightmare that had her fitfully tossing and turning.

Mindscream gently touched her forehead and she instantly fell into a deep sleep. But even then he could still hear her mental whispers.

Stop the burning! Stop the burning!

Kellis looked at him earnestly, Mindscream nodding back at her.

"She'll be alright. But we need to get off Home soon," he said.

Kellis' wrist comm sounded. "Speak of the devil," she winked at Mindscream.

". . . in Commander Kellis, come in, this is Paolo. Can you hear me?"

Kellis face lit up as she answered, "Paolo, this is Kellis. We need immediate evac! I repeat, immediate evac! We've got casualties!"

She looked at the others as she realised what were they going to tell him about Windburst?

"Okay, Commander, hold on! Bit of a rocky ride up here, but I'm already en route! Paolo out!"

Kellis sat on a rock behind her head in hands.

What had gone wrong? she asked herself. "What happened back there?" she asked Mindscream.

"Solitude did what he had to do," Mindscream said, "For us and himself." He sighed, knowing Time had been right in the end. But he still didn't like it.

Kellis solemnly nodded. She understood the sacrifice, but it still didn't make it any easier. None of it, Windburst's death included, made any sense.

It got too much for Kellis. She got up and walked toward Mindscream, the sadness on her face melting his heart. But she caved in first, burying her head in his chest. Mindscream held her close to him, if only so she wouldn't see his tears.

Tantillion Post's sensors and alarms once again blared into action as the space around Home had violently rippled again.

Mola had almost lost his voice screaming out readings which made little sense to him.

But Kirrilock stayed focused and calm.

"Status report, Mola!" he ordered the science officer, after a full minute. Station-wide alarms had become less grating and everyone could hear themselves think.

Mola had steadied himself and rechecked his sensors, grateful the spewing data was back into manageable physics.

"Sir, everything seems normal now, the energy readings have levelled out to normal and . . . ."

He double-checked a particular reading, but it was Shayson at comms who confirmed it.

"Sir! It's Lieutenant Commander Paolo . . ." she sounded surprised as she said, "He's in contact with Commander Kellis and her team! They're back!" She listened more as she heard another message and this time her mood was sombre.

"Commander Kellis' requesting immediate evac, sir! They've got casualties." Her face reflected the mood of the bridge.

Kirrilock stepped back and sat in his chair, a little too heavily for his liking, but this after all was one such moment where he could show cracks in his composure, for the crew's sake.

"Sacred Xaal!" he said to no one in particular. "Very good, Shayson. Contact Doctor Vargas and inform him of incoming casualties and then raise Councillor Tantillion."

Here we go again! Kirrilock thought. *I'm getting too old for this!*

A peculiar thought tickled his mind, "If I'm getting too old for this, how's Tantillion survived all these years?" He shook his head. Some human mysteries were meant to go unsolved.

Paolo knew exactly what he was going to do when he touched down. He was going to give Zane a big hug and ask her to marry him. He just couldn't wait anymore. And he knew that she would say yes.

He had homed in on the signal sent by Kellis, guiding the shuttle down, landing ten meters away. He grabbed a med kit, almost kicked the door open, and ran across the dusty plain. Hopefully Zane didn't need any medical help. He saw Kellis come toward him, a weak smile on her face.

Paolo stopped running and smiled. "You look like you've been through hell, Kellis. What happened?"

Kellis tried to keep it simple, "We fought some sort of cosmic being. We barely defeated him and we took some casualties." Her face seemed to cloud over for a while, her intense stare starting to worry Paolo.

"Casualties, eh? Well, I'm here to help. Where's my patient?"

He started off to where he saw Aristedes and the rest waiting. But Kellis stopped him.

"Paolo, I have something to tell you."

Kellis' voice stopped Paolo dead. The tone of voice and the deathly silence that followed sent a shiver through him.

Surely she hadn't meant it that way, Paolo thought. He'd used those same words for many a family whose son or daughter had . . . died?

He turned to Kellis, her eyes already filled with tears, her voice a whisper shredding his soul, "I'm so sorry, Paolo."

Paolo didn't understand. His mind twisted the words around, Kellis must have been mistaken. He dropped the field kit and ran over to Aristedes who was tending to an unconscious woman.

There she is! thought Paolo. *She's only injured.*

But as he reached Aristedes, he saw that he was holding a pure-white-skinned woman he had never seen before.

His mouth worked, but no words came out. He could feel himself going faint, his heart held in a clenched fist. He fell backward and felt himself being caught. Looking up, he saw that it was Aaron. He touched Paolo lightly on the forehead. Paolo felt himself drifting off into sleep.

>*Yes, sleep. Sleep and be at peace.*< Mindscream eased the pain away, letting Paolo's eyes close as he continued to telepathically minister to him.

"I didn't think that he would take it so hard," Time said, absently brushing back Winterborne's hair.

"Neither did I," said Kellis as she rejoined the group. She looked at Paolo, in Mindscream's arms. "Well, let's get aboard the ship. Looks like I'm flying." As they trekked to the ship, Kellis swore, "I never want to see this world again!"

With Paolo and Winterborne safely on board, Kellis took the little ship back up into the skies on its way home to Tantillion Post.

During all the commotion, neither Tantillion Post nor the Multiforce had noticed a small, drifting object near the other side of the planet. The ship was devoid of energy, its crew unconscious, having been caught in the near-cataclysmic blast, which blew out all its systems.

One of its occupants awoke. He didn't know what had happened, but he knew one thing for sure. If anyone had survived the battle below and came hunting for him, then he, Mode, would be waiting for them.

After a debriefing, with some awkwardly and obtusely answered questions, and after profuse thanks from Zev Tantillion, Kellis and the

Multiforce found themselves back at Zero Star two days later, where the E-G himself awaited them.

Kellis thought Xaul looked quite well, but was surprised to see him waiting at the landing bay with Simon Exmoor.

"What are you doing here?" Kellis asked without any formality.

"And 'hello' to you, too, Lynn," the Emperor-General said, with a sympathetic smile. "I hear you had to give old Zev the run-around concerning the mission."

Kellis smiled herself, "Yeah, well, between myself and gentle persuasion from Aaron, I think he's satisfied with our report and that he can go on with his world building."

"Glad to hear it," Relentus answered. He took a more serious note, not avoiding the situation anymore. "I'm sorry about Zane, Lynn. I knew she meant a lot to you. And Solitude. The sacrifice he made was . . . beyond human."

"I still can't believe Zane's dead," Kellis said shaking her head. Though she wasn't sure of many things now. "And as for Solitude, he gave his life to save us. But it's taken a lot out of us."

Relentus nodded. Even Exmoor seemed saddened. He hadn't really trusted the Surge, but without Solitude's sacrifice, even Zero Star could have been in danger. Solitude had saved the galaxy.

"And how's Winterborne?" Relentus asked, having seen a couple of Bion med-techs take her to the med division, escorted by Aristedes and Aaron. "I heard she's in quite a state." He seemed concerned.

Kellis nodded. "She's going to be fine. A dip in the deep freeze and some psychological help from Aaron and things will be fine."

Exmoor had a concerned look on his face. Kellis didn't need to be a mind reader to know what was on his mind.

"And as for those bastard Superions, I don't know if they survived. They deserted us, left us to die. I hope they rot in hell!"

"Amen to that!" Exmoor said.

Kellis still wanted to know what Relentus was doing on Zero Star, so she probed a bit.

"So, Mr. Emperor-General, what does bring you out this way? And don't say that it's because of little ol' me," she said.

"No, it's not, Lynn." (A little to Kellis' disappointment). "I'm just visiting here before going on to the Bion homeworld." He paused as if to give his next words, added impetus, "I'm negotiating the Bion's admission into the Earth-Axala alliance."

Kellis' jaw dropped.

"Wow!" was all she could say. She tried to think of more to say, but Relentus stopped her.

"I know. I know. It's all a bit too much to take in for now." He sounded proud of the fact. "And hopefully in a couple of years, our three peoples can live in a united galaxy," he said.

"Wow!" Kellis found herself saying again.

Relentus and Exmoor laughed. It wasn't often the formidible Lynn Kellis was lost for words.

Relentus leaned into Kellis and quietly said, "But it does mean I have to attend a Bion State dinner." He pulled a sour face.

"Oh, god, red and purple mush. Take some salt, pepper, and chilli powder with you," she smirked.

She found herself laughing with them, but soon past memories came flooding back and she had to fight back searing emotions.

"Well, good luck," she said quickly.

She put a hand to her face, feigning tiredness, and excused herself from the flight deck.

Relentus called out. "Anything you need, Lynn."

But Kellis shook her head. "I'll be fine," she said, as she made her way off the flight deck. "I'll be fine."

Interlude 3

The Chronopolis

Helexius, Lightstream, and Sola digested the devastating news Aristedes had brought them. He had only stayed long enough to tell them, preferring to return to his friends.

"We lost Zane!" Lightstream cried at the time-shattering news.

As if losing Spheron wasn't enough. The Chronopolis was still in half ruins following the Lore attack and the collanades still required rebuilding.

"Phasia didn't say anything about that," Sola complained, dark thoughts entering her mind about how this could be so.

"Maybe that was why? She didn't want to upset us with what we would have deemed a sacrifice too far, so soon after losing your father," Helexius surmised. "Besides, out of all of this, Netherlord played his hand and died for it! My poor, departed cousin!" he added, a slight smile flickering across his face.

His daughter nodded agreement.

"But losing Zane is too much! We are too few as it is!"

Lightstream's throat was tight just thinking about it. Saying it had been even harder. She could see that even her father was affected, even though he wasn't outwardly showing it. Zane had been like a little sister to her.

"I only hope Aristedes and his friends can recover from this. They took a real beating!"

"I hope so, too," Sola said, her voice huskier than usual. "With Archron, Timechantress, and Celestra running loose, who knows what's going to happen next! Now I don't see why we are keeping some of the Starguards on Earth."

"Because Phasia said Earth was the next target of the Lore," Lightstream said.

"Are we so sure now, after Zane's death?" Sola asked. "Can we can still trust her. And where is Phasia during all of this?" Sola questioned Helexius. "She has many questions to answer as to how she could not foresee these events, but can see Earth is in danger."

But Helexius, if he had been listening, seemed to ignore her, instead turning to his daughter.

"Have you located the stolen Starguards yet or how to penetrate the Magna Aura temporal-field or found out the identity of those space ships?" Helexius' voice rose.

"No." Lightstream grimaced in anguish.

"Try harder," Helexius demanded.

Lightstream sulked. "I am. Sorry, I'm failing you father."

Helexius grunted a half apology. All their nerves were frayed.

Sola groaned. The news wasn't what they wanted to hear. Things already weren't going well for them. Netherlord's death had been only a minor victory, but the major battle was about to take place soon, if only they could figure out when and where. It also didn't bode well that the architect of their defense and counter-attack plans, Phasia, had mysteriously disappeared. Sola cursed. The whole universe was at stake and all they had was bad news.

"So, what of Earth?" Sola asked.

"We must stick to Phasia's plan. We know one possible fate of the Starguards, but the future is still in flux. We have time," Helexis iterated.

"Well that brings me back to my earlier question," Sola said, exasperated. "Where is Phasia?"

Helexius thought about it for a while, weighing up his options. "Well, now that it's just the three of us and I know that I can trust you two with my life," he grinned sarcastically, "I can tell you."

His long pause almost made the two girls shriek with frustration.

"Phasia had a vision. She has gone on a mission—to seek allies," he answered.

The stunned look on their faces told Helexius they had not even suspected this.

"Allies?" intoned Lightstream and Sola together.

"Allies," repeated Helexius. "She had a vision calling her on a quest to seek out allies. And that's all I can tell you, because that's all I know!"

Lightstream and Sola exchanged excited glances again.

"Allies!"

Somewhere, somewhen

In a place that could not be called space or time, Phasia hunted down the origin of her vision and its messenger. But it was a difficult task in this chaotic sludge of stormy, temporal rifts and eddies that sliced and swirled through reverse and infra space. She had seen nothing like it before. She remembered the stories Spheron used to regale them with of broken universes, his vivid descriptions of stalled chroniverses paling in comparison to what churned before her now.

How could anyone live here? she wondered.

But she knew that she had been called here, after all this time. She knew who had called her, but couldn't tell Helexius. Not now, not yet. She thought him lost forever. Now he was calling her.

A flash of light blinded her, stopping her dead in her tracks as if time itself had slammed a door in front of her. The light surrounded her. She couldn't see anything, hear anything or go anywhere.

She was trapped.

Epilogue

If Zero Star had a dead-of-night, then that is when Kellis bolted upright in bed, her mouth wide open in surprise. Something had been bugging her since Zane's death and now she knew what it was. She reached over to the bedside table, keyed the comms padd and made a few calls. She dressed hurriedly and rushed from her room.

When she entered one of the meeting rooms Xaul Relentus, Simon Exmoor, Aaron, and Aristedes were waiting for her. None of them seemed pleased to be there or that wide awake.

So she woke them up.

Without preamble she said, "Aristedes, I don't know how I know, but Zane isn't dead. But if it wasn't for her, I wouldn't be here."

There was a slight confused pause on Aristedes' side, but Kellis continued.

"I know you all know I've kept things secret from all of you concerning my past. There's good reason for this, or at least there was. But in the light of what has happened, especially concerning the Superions, I think it's time I told you all that I know. And it all started when the Starguards came to Earth!"

Excerpts from the 2234 winning entry of the annual Home schools essay writing contest

Writer: Glen-Tuin K'hy   Age: 8
School: Relenta High School East, Home
Subject: Earth-Axala War philosophy and summary

General Earth History: 2010 to 2240

The Discovery of Thanium: summary

The discovery of thanium around the 2010s is still a mystery, almost as enigmatic as Altair's speech. Some leading historians state Thanium was discovered at Thane Industries after the explosion (see below), others believing that it was a gift from the Starguards.

However, it was not the invention of the Bions as some scientists suggest. Nevertheless, around twenty years after its discovery, an international consortium, led by Byron Tantillion (ancestor to Governor Zev Tantillion) built the Solar Explorator (or Solar X), the first spaceship to be powered by thanium and the first to explore the solar system in 2031. The next thanium-drive ship was the Starguard, which explored the Alpha Centauri system in 2038. The Earth fleet was inaugurated in 2043, and consisted of the aforementioned ships, refitted, along with the Exsurgent, the Vanguard, and the Velocity V.

The 2210 Event: summary

In 2210, the Headquarters of the International Space Committee, built in place of the Thane Industries building, had exploded, much the same as its predecessor had. There had only been a handful of survivors, who the military had quickly recovered. The blast's cause has never been sufficiently explained, but it was non-accidental and attributed to Axalan terrorists as a pre-war test of human reactions and resolve.

But many conspiracy theorists claimed that this could not be true stating the blast bore none of the usual hallmarks of Axalan tactics. Neither had the Axalans claimed responsibility for the act. They still claim no responsibility. But with no other plausible explanation the government's claims have been unquestioned ever since. And the effect had been to rally the world around the United Earth flag.

Of the survivors, none were ever interviewed or seen after the first pictures of their retrieval. Although this raised suspicions and more theories about their possible military nature and involvement in the Space Committee's offices, this was not seen as important enough to warrant an in-depth investigation. In fact, the official spokesman for the Committee, Simon Exmoor, before he became the Emperor-General's counsellor, claimed that the survivors, classified personnel, had recovered well and just wanted to return to normal life in anonymity.

The 2210 Event has now been largely forgotten, but it should be remembered as the time when Earth first rallied as a united world to take the war to the Axalans.

The Earth-Axalan War (2145-2217): summary

There have been many theories and debates as to the Axalan defeat (as many on Earth see it). Any eight-year old can explain that it was the advancements of weapons and technologies gained by Earth over the Axalans. It had been a great mystery as to how Earth had produced such equipment.

Not until 2219 would the Bions emerge from isolation and reveal their existence, relationship, and assistance to Earth's war efforts to the general Earth populace. The three civilisations would then go on to form a new alliance, called The Constitutionate, centered on the joint world called Home.

Secondly, the Axalans were an extremely religious people; their God Xaal's words meaning everything to them. And when the prophecies pointed to General Xaul Relentus, a human being, as their returning son of God, they accepted it without question, such was their devotion to their God's words. A great wave of brotherhoodness had swept through the Empire and from then on, the spirit to fight had deserted them. So, above all else, the Axalans praised Xaul Relentus for having ended the war and bringing them together.

Lastly, the superbeing factor had been crucial. Earth in the past had the E-Corps and the Starguards, but after the disaster involving E-Corps Team 2, there had been a ban on all superbeings. However, during the war, there had been rumours of a new Superhuman group, which sources claim were called the Multiforce, which had been formed by the Emperor-General himself, though technically superhumans were still outlawed from the twenty-first century. Allegedly, the Multiforce saved Earth and Home from the Superions, but there are no official records of their existence or missions.

Their supposed Axalan counterparts, the Superions had been a rebellious faction, pursuing their own personal agendas. It is claimed it was they who murdered Emperor Xalarius on the eve of the end of the war. Their identities were never known (though a rumour, denied by the old Axalan Emperor's court, had declared that they were actually humans disguised as Axalans).

Had the Superions been more focused, then every day could have been a Christmas Day Massacre with historic battle outcomes little more than training exercises for the Axalans. The Superions mysteriously disappeared, some reports stating they were killed by the Multiforce. Others sources believing that the Superions are still alive in the Far Regions and waiting for revenge. At least that's how the bedtime stories go.

There are rumours that remnants of the Multiforce now live on Home. As it was, Earth and Axala ended the war, uniting not only humanity with the Axalans, but also with the Bions. A new galactic community had been born from the throes of war.

The Settlement of Home (2225 to present): summary

The world of Home has now been settled for almost ten years. The Tantillion Terraforming project was completed by 2225 and new cities have been built. While previous segregated neighbourhoods existed, humans, Axalans and Bion have learned to mix and live together in more ways than one.

The first human-Axalan marriage took place between Frastraar of Velhacia and his groom, John Soshu in 2236 and the first human-Axalan baby was born in 2238. The Bions still tend to stick together, but they are nonetheless Home's best administrators, engineers, and technicians.

The settlement of Home seemed to be going well. But recently, news has arrived that a rogue, flyaway planet is heading Home's way. It is predicted to pass close by to Home in 2255 causing devastating effects. All the best minds in the Constitutionate are working hard on ways to avert a disaster.

APPENDIX B

"You failed me Riley."

"Sorry, sir, but I couldn't do it."

"Couldn't or wouldn't? You know what he did!"

"Yes, but the Starfighter Machine was already dormant. If I had killed Seton, it would have been murder, not in defence of the crew or fleet, but cold-blooded murder." He looked aggrieved. "I wouldn't have been any better than Seton."

General Hawkhurst frowned in the holo-vid. "He killed my son, Riley, your half-brother. We could have been avenged. But that damned metal beast beat us, saved Seton." His voice was cold.

"Sorry, sir," Matt Riley repeated. "I still want out. Seton won't have me back, I've put in for a transfer."

"Hnn," grunted Hawkhurst. "Probably best for now." He regarded Riley dispassionately, before saying, "Why not join me on Earth? We need new blood in Earth Command."

Riley thought about it. "Perhaps." But he wanted to be as far away from Command as possible.

"I'm travelling just before Christmas, so let me know in the new year, son."

Before Riley could register his surprise at being addressed with such intimate acknowledgment, Hawkhurst cut the holo-link.

He sat in stony silence contemplating his future.

Simon Exmoor frowned, closing his own link. He had never known Hawkhurst's secrets. Of course, trying to hack a holo-link was next to impossible so he had done the next best thing and bugged Riley's quarters. To say the conversation had surprised him was an understatement. But one worth knowing for what was to happen next.

Exmoor had read the clandestinely acquired official and personal logs of the officers onboard the *Falcon*, trying to discover more about the Starfighter Machine. But his efforts had actually led him to another course of action.

He already had the date and time. And he was already hacking into the north-western Europa weather net system. It would fail when required, necessitating repairs, and down time for the grid. Just as Hawkhurst was entering the zone during a storm.

Exmoor assessed his handiwork. In a few weeks, Xaul Relentus would be the new Commander Earth Forces. He knew in his heart it was murder.

But in his mind he told himself, *it's already history.*

Exmoor left his quarters walking the corridors of Consention base. Now all he had to do was plan his escape for the Christmas Day Massacre.

APPENDIX C

FAMILY LINES

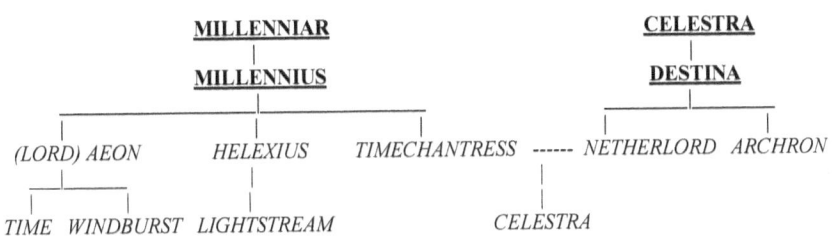

MILLENNIAR
|
MILLENNIUS

(LORD) AEON   HELEXIUS   TIMECHANTRESS ------ NETHERLORD ARCHRON

TIME WINDBURST LIGHTSTREAM   CELESTRA

CELESTRA
|
DESTINA

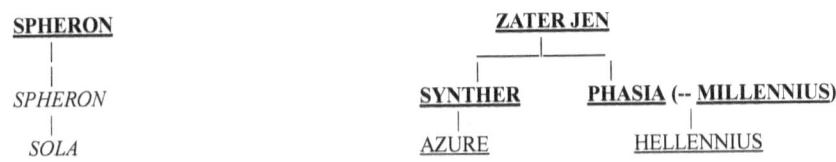

SPHERON
|
SPHERON

SOLA

ZATER JEN

SYNTHER   **PHASIA (-- MILLENNIUS)**

AZURE   HELLENNIUS

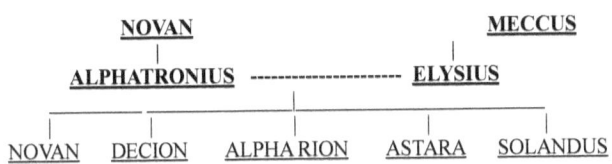

NOVAN
|
ALPHATRONIUS ---------------------- **ELYSIUS**

NOVAN   DECION   ALPHA RION   ASTARA   SOLANDUS

MECCUS

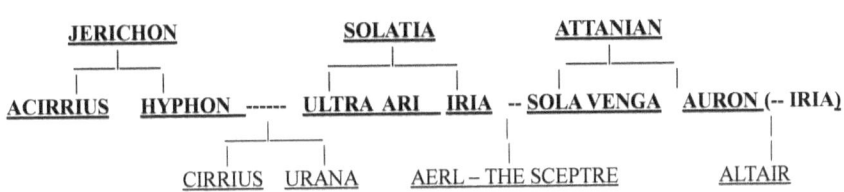

JERICHON   **SOLATIA**   **ATTANIAN**

ACIRRIUS   HYPHON ------ **ULTRA ARI   IRIA** -- **SOLA VENGA   AURON (-- IRIA)**

CIRRIUS   URANA   AERL – THE SCEPTRE   ALTAIR

CELESTIAN KNIGHT
STARGUARD
ASTRAL

Have you enjoyed this book?
If so, why not write a review on your favourite website?

THE STARGUARDS
OF HUMANS, HEROES, AND DEMIGODS

continues in

BOOK 3 – THE TERRA CHRONICLES

CHAPTER ONE

South France, AD 1197

"All I know, Decion, is that someone, somewhere, sometime is going to pay for this. I swear it!" Alpha Rion cursed again.

This was a wretched world. Cold, wet, muddy and getting dark; not that it affected him or Decion, but he wondered how anyone could live here. Wherever here was.

A few days ago, according to this world's rising and setting sun, Alpha Rion, Decion and Astara had been on Alphatron City-State listening in alarm as reports came in that other Starguards were disappearing.

And just as suddenly Decion started to disappear, but Alpha Rion had instinctively reached out to stop him promptly disappearing as well. The brothers could only suspect the Astrals for this despicable act of cosmic interference. Now they were both stuck somewhere, where people resembled them, but were not of superior breeding.

In fact, he and Decion hadn't believed that anywhere else in the universe had been inhabited by others like themselves. The people here may have looked like Celestians, but they weren't. They were inferior Fifths: primitive in being, barbaric in nature. Emphasising this, the region was at war, or at least a form of it, for armies rode around on magnificent beasts that Decion would have given his lancesword to ride, and the metal-clad warriors fought with metal swords that bloodied the fields. It made them both yearn for battle. But so far, the two had kept a low profile. They were alone, away from the other Starguards.

Alpha Rion felt incomplete without Astara and wondered how his twin sister was faring—no better than him, he suspected. He cursed again. Who knew for how long they were going to be here.

One thing which had kept them fascinated with this world was the forest they were in. It was greener and larger than anything on Halcyon or Placia, though not as magnificent as the treefields of the forest continent of Anturia on Galatia they had played in as younglings. They had revelled in the new environment at first, but now it was wearing thin quickly.

"Hold your tongue, brother," Decion cautioned in his usual growl through his thick black beard, from across the cooking fire they had started. "We will make those Astrals atone for what they have done to us. We may be the only ones left alive, so we need to conserve our thoughts and energy."

He tossed over a piece of roasted meat he had carved from the hide that lay spit-roasting over the fire. Alpha Rion caught it.

His beardless face was framed by his long black hair and chiselled cheeks, blues eyes accentuating his handsomenes. His demeanour and looks far less rougher and wilder than his older brother's.

"Are you . . . sure . . . it . . . was . . . the Astrals?" he asked between mouthfuls.

They had watched other people eat this animal while on nocturnal scouting patrols, a large grazing beast not built for battle. It was new food for them, not exactly intoxicating like Alphatron's food, but at least it was cooked, tasty, and filling.

Alpha Rion thought about Decion's words and though he wasn't an ardent admirer of his older brother, he had to grudgingly admit that he was right. And anything could happen at any moment so they needed to be ready. He was still thinking and chewing when both he and Decion heard the distinctive thundering foot-falls of the riding-beasts approaching.

They rose together and headed for their lookout point. They had camped at the edge of a forest, just enough to hide from prying eyes, yet still able to spy on the outside world with their enhanced vision or through their visor imagers. In the coming twilight, Decion saw twenty warriors riding purposefully toward their position. He turned to Alpha Rion, who kept on chewing while turning to douse the fire. No sense in their meal getting burned.

Decion donned his helmet and cape and was now his usual huge giant of a warrior in red and black armour. They had no set defences, they didn't need any, save for themselves and their weapons.

The riders grew closer, Alpha Rion seeing that one of them wore no armour. His curly, blond hair flowed freely in the brisk wind away from a handsome angular face. His loose-fitting purple garb was of a thin, shiny fabric, but Alpha Rion knew he was no less of a warrior than the rest of them, even though he was also unarmed. He could see it in the blond one's eyes, sense it. This one was dangerous.

262

The riders slowed as if they knew danger awaited them. Decion let them approach. He and Alpha Rion had left their formidable weapons stowed in their other-dimensional sheaths. The riders stopped at the edge of the tree line and dismounted, the big animals nervously grunting and stamping. Alpha Rion could smell the riding-beasts now as they were much closer and he could see how powerful they were.

Beautiful, he thought.

Alpha Rion and Decion watched as the mysterious warriors dismounted and approached cautiously, but purposefully, staring at him and Decion as if they were the strange beasts. They may have appeared strange to each other, but Alpha Rion knew they were all no strangers to battle and that they were about to renew their friendship with blood and death.

The blond leader signalled and his warriors marched forth to form an ominous semi-circle around the two brothers who stood still. Not a word was said, not a sound was to be heard in the forest, save for the sigh of impending death.

Without warning, half the warriors charged Decion. Alpha Rion didn't move and didn't have to look to see that Decion's left hand had shifted toward his right hip to activate the dimensional sheath. Before the warriors had gone five steps, Decion had forcibly drawn his lancesword which stretched out and in one back-handed swoop ten heads had fallen to the mossy ground. Decion continued the cutting arc in a figure-of-eight motion, until the end of the lancesword rested in his right hand, holding the weapon out in front of him before turning it ninety degrees and planting its tip into the now bloodied ground.

Alpha Rion hadn't even waited for the lancesword's tip to reach the ground before he launched himself at the other terrified warriors who had started to run away. He'd released his two energy swords from their sheaths and in half a dozen lethal swipes had felled the rest of them. His last strikes had landed him on the opposite side of the blond leader across from Decion. The last warrior was trapped.

But the blond warrior still wore his arrogant smile and remained unmoved. He regarded them, almost in kinship.

"Well done, Decion. I expected no less of you and I must say that I'm quite, quite impressed. I must admit, however, I only expected you to be here," he said (translated to the Starguards through their crystalators).

He turned his head to look behind him at Alpha Rion, who remained silent; the stranger remaining unperturbed.

"No matter," he dismissed the younger Starguard's presence. "I've never seen weapons quite like yours before. May I touch it?" He stepped forth toward Decion.

Decion hefted the sword two-handed upon his own shoulder. His demeanour needed no explanation.

The stranger halted and retreated a step, hands up in supplication. He laughed at their mutual predicament.

"I'm sorry," he apologised, before Decion grew angry at being laughed at. "My name is Marquis Edgar de La Valtare and I am your host here on Earth." He bowed to the brothers.

"Earth?" Decion harrumphed. "A fitting name for a mud ball of a place. And what is to stop us from killing you Marquis Edgar de La Valtare?" Decion hissed, his hands resting on the crystal pommel of his lancesword.

"Please, call me Valtare," he grinned. "And, well if you kill me, I guess you'll never know why my master wanted you here," Valtare answered back, confidently.

There was silence as Decion and Alpha Rion traded glances.

"Your master? You mean the Astrals?" Alpha Rion was suspicious, Decion's hand twitching on the pommel.

"The Astrals? I know them, but as for being my master, no, I detest them as much as you do. My master is no friend of the Astrals as you shall see. I take it that this means my life is to be spared?" Valtare inquired, seeing Decion and Alpha Rion visibly relax. He was clearly having fun at being in charge.

"For now"" barked Decion. They had no choice really.

"Good!" Valtare said, without a care that his life was in danger. "Good. Then follow me."

With a rueful glance at his dead men, he turned and walked back toward his horse at the edge of the forest. He mounted and trotted in the direction from which he had arrived. The two Starguards started towards the horses who reared and galloped away, much to Valtare's amusement. The brothers looked at each other, sheathed their weapons in a flash of dimensional energy, and followed on foot, Alpha Rion resisting the temptation to curse again. He had a feeling he would be using them later.

Along the way, Valtare explained patiently to them where and when they were.

"This world is called Earth, we people are called humans. Currently you are in a country called France ruled over by different Kings. The year is 1197, after the birth of a divine man called Jesus Christ, a so-called son of God, which is one of the reasons for the conflict. The country is afflicted by the Crusades, of which this is the fourth such war, affecting most of the northern landmass called Europe and a part of Asia," he pointed eastward.

"Although this is supposedly a religious affair, it is mostly political, greed-ridden, expensive, barbaric and unnecessary, all in all the usual human contradictory ingredients of war," he shook his head in pity.

Decion and Alpha Rion had already suspected this world was the one mentioned in Olesseus' tales of Adantus. It explained the humans' war-like Fifth nature. And Decion's curiosity was also sated:

"The riding-beasts are called horses."

They talked more as the sun went down.

Presently, they came across the settlement where Decion and Alpha Rion had watched the folk prepare their meal of cow meat called beef. They expected to be stared at, but Valtare had turned to them.

"Don't worry, we won't be bothered."

And to the brother's surprise, nobody had even seemed to take notice of them, as Valtare had watered his horse and picked up some supplies from a local merchant. Then they were on their way again.

But as they travelled, Alpha Rion became even more suspicious of Valtare. He didn't talk much about himself and was evasive in manner to the many questions about him. From the sideways looks Decion gave him, Alpha Rion could see he was thinking the same thing.

It was night when the three had arrived at Valtare's castle, on a rise above the village. Alpha Rion's crystalator-enhanced visor scanned the dark, solid-stone structure; men walking along the battlements. There was nothing there that could harm them, he decided. A drawbridge lowered across a half-swampy moat. Some servants came to attend Valtare and groom the horses, barely acknowledging the two Starguards, taking away their master's horse to the stables.

Valtare led the brothers through into the courtyard, various buildings of stone or wood cluttered together in the centre and other knights, as Valtare had called them, milled around or stood on duty. Before entering into the main halls, Valtare turned to the brothers.

"Forgive my ill manners, Decion, but who is your companion?"

Decion patted Alpha Rion on the shoulder, "This is my brother, Alpha Rion," he said, as if it was the most obvious thing.

Valtare nodded. "Of course, I should have seen the resemblance," he noted, the joke lost on the two black-haired, red and black-clad warriors.

On entering the main hall, there were two men waiting. Valtare introduced them.

"Sir Decion and Alpha Rion, this is Duke L'Coyle," Valtare spoke warmly, clapping the man on the shoulder.

The young, brown-haired man nodded a grim greeting. His predatory looks reminded Alpha Rion of Valtare. He was no doubt his protégé. And Valtare seemed fond of him, Alpha Rion noted.

"And this is Guillaume de Roth," Valtare said of the young-looking man with a shock of white hair. Guillaume also nodded hello, but his blue eyes flickered friendship.

"I wish my wife were here to greet you," Valtare indicated a large painted portrait on the wall above the fireplace, of a beautiful woman. "But the Lady Van Tager, is unavoidably away due to family matters. For now, L'Coyle and De Roth will be your guides and will tell you everything you want to know about our customs. I have a meal prepared for you . . ."

"We are not hungry," Decion answered for them both. "We ate in the forest."

"Well then. Your rooms are ready and in the morning we shall talk of things of interest to you."

"We are ready to talk of such things now," Decion said as politely as he could.

But Valtare declined, "The morning would be better. We need time to rest, for tomorrow will be a long day, believe me. Now, if you'll excuse me, I'll leave you in the capable hands of my two best knights."

He bowed to the two Starguards before turning and disappearing up some stone stairs, leaving the four men alone.

It was L'Coyle who spoke first. "You have travelled far, then?"

"Far enough," Decion replied with in humorous growl.

"We had hoped to meet some of our . . . other warriors here," said Alpha Rion, trying to drop a hint. L'Coyle nodded, as if he understood, but Alpha Rion knew that he didn't. So he asked, "Do you know why we're here?"

"Do any of us really know why we're here?" Guillaume replied, looking up at the skies above them. Decion also looked up and saw a rough-hewn ceiling of thick wooden beams. Nothing untoward, he scowled, the humour lost on the brothers. Guillaume rephrased his answer, more cautiously. "I mean, we're here for the same reason that you are, which will be explained to you tomorrow. We cannot tell you," he said, "Because we do not know either." He looked pointedly at Alpha Rion.

Alpha Rion, for his part, sensed that this was a man to be trusted. But there was something not right here. And if he and Decion didn't get their answers tomorrow, then they would go on their own crusade.

He wasn't going to get any answers now, so he decided to make his excuses and retire for the night. Decion looked displeased, but followed suit.

"This way, if you please, sirs," L'Coyle led them up the stone stairs and showed them to their rooms.

Somewhere else

Waiting. In another place, a solitary figure watched. He'd sacrificed lives, interfered here, manipulated there and now all his plans were coming together; the pieces in his grand scheme coming alive: Valtare, the Starguards, his army. The end of the universe was fast approaching.

!

www.ingramcontent.com/pod-product-compliance
Lightning Source LLC
Chambersburg PA
CBHW031229120726
47905CB00002B/524